For Mary Anne Hogue,

I love the light in your eyes and the sparks in your soul.
Thank you for teaching me about the human condition.
It's a privilege to be your daughter and a
blessing to be your friend.

XO

Chapter 1

Sitting in the kitchenette of the avocado-colored efficiency above Miss Delphine Walker's garage, I thumped the chrome table leg with the edge of my flip flop. It happened. *SexwithJack*. I mean, I had to own the fact that ultimately, I threw the match, but let's not ignore the fact that Jack was using all the lighter fluid this side of the Mississippi. And now, I basically had two options. A) Lose my marbles, or B) Revert to option A).

This was Jack's fault. He'd been pedaling his friends-to-lovers hokum since I came back to Marshall a week ago. I had my doubts, but in classic Jack Turner fashion, he meticulously built his case, brick by brick, with all that smelling-my-skin nonsense and Principle of Proximity bologna. In reality, any near-sighted nincompoop could have seen his theory was as solid as the mist coming off a chunk of dry ice at a Halloween party. Jack and I were no longer best-friends-since-kindergarten. Nope. Introducing sex had irrevocably altered the status quo, pushing me off the deep end in the process.

Cha-ching.

That was the fourth text message since he dropped me off fifteen minutes ago on his way to a shift at the firehouse. I hadn't looked at any of them so far, but I was keeping careful count. I knew I had maybe two more *cha-chings* before he drove back over here to assess (and by *assess* I meant *fix*...and by *fix* I meant *alter my perception of*) the damage in person. Too bad the firefighter/mechanic tract was such a perfect fit for him, otherwise he would've made a great politician. He was really good at manipulating the way an event is interpreted, which, if not the exact definition of spin-control, is pretty dang close.

The thought crossed my mind that while he might not be able to get away from work, that didn't necessarily mean I was safe. Over the years, Jack had constructed an impressive network of spies, loosely linked to his role as a first responder. It included representatives from the police department, the sheriff's office, every branch of the military, Coast Guard, Homeland Security, and Transit Authority. If I cared to delve deeper, I'm sure NASCAR and UNICEF were also involved. I was vaguely curious who he had pressed into service to keep me under surveillance while he was on duty today.

As that thought began to percolate, I stepped over to the window and moved the blue and white gingham curtain three inches so I could peer out. No black sedans in the drive, but the trees could be crawling with SWAT. An unexpected *thwack* from the air conditioner startled me, tipping off a sequence of events right out of a vaudeville routine. I jumped, lost my left flip flop and banged my hip on the low bookshelf under the window. My nerve endings were clanking like a cow bell at a hockey game, and in my mind's eye, I saw my hero, Stephanie Plum, shaking her head at this sad display.

To quiet myself, I paced between the table and the kitchen sink and finally grabbed the phone to check the four messages.

1) "Better than my wildest dreams, Lily."

2) "Don't overthink this."

3) "You okay?"

4) "Call me."

As I scanned them, message number five *cha-chinged*..."Lily."

I needed time to build my case, but in order to get that, I needed to put this guy on ice. What would settle him down? Tell him I was looking forward to round three? Or was it round four? What round was it exactly? Let's see. We did it down at the lake in the bed of his truck. Then we went back to his house on Wisteria Lane and did it in the master bedroom. Then we did it again this morning before he dropped me off. So the next round would be number four.

Rounds one through three were all about the sex, no talking, no analyzing, no second-guessing. Wild monkey sex as Mother Nature intended. Jack saw to it. He was a maestro in his element. By comparison, I was the person who runs her finger over the Braille letters in an elevator, knowing what the texture is for but incapable of discerning any real meaning. To his credit, Jack kept me squarely in the moment, not giving me a chance to hyperextend my natural ability to create resistance.

* * *

Flashing back to yesterday, I remembered driving from the lake to his house in a haze of afterglow having just had sex for the first time in our sixteen years of friendship. When we got to his place, he pulled me up the front steps of the porch. He could barely get the door closed before his arms were around me again. Lips near my ear, he breathed a question, "Will you come to the bedroom?"

It was an obvious place to land, since we were in the midst of this whole do-it-again-as-quickly-as-possible state of being. His question held slightly more significance, though, since he told me just a few days earlier that he had been fantasizing about the two of us having sex in the master bedroom. It was such a big deal to him that he hadn't brought any other women into this house since he moved in.

"Yes," I said it quietly. So quietly, in fact, I wouldn't have known the word came out if he hadn't started guiding me from the foyer toward the bedroom.

"Do you need to use the bathroom?" he asked, smiling. He knew that was my go-to play when things got intense. I shook my head no, and he drew me toward the bed. He was still wearing his swim trunks, but I was in shorts and t-shirt. I hadn't bothered to put my swim suit back on when we left the lake.

In the back of his truck, he had gotten me naked first. This time, he got himself naked while I remained fully clothed. Jack was fair-minded by nature, and I figured this was his way of being equitable. I stood there, half frozen from disbelief or trepidation, one, mesmerized by the sight of his body. He brought my palm up to his chest and when it stayed stuck, he nudged my hand downward until it started moving unassisted. As I grazed his chest and stomach, I felt him watching me, but before I could submerge myself in a mud puddle of self-doubt, he took hold of my wrist and moved backwards. Plopping onto the bed, he laid back and stretched out. The invitation was clear: he wanted me to explore his body the way he had explored mine earlier. Feeling a surge of confidence, I did just that. I touched and teased, kissed and licked, until he couldn't stand it. Then he ripped off my clothes, put on a condom, and pulled me on top of him.

* * *

Thinking about it now, I was breathing hard. Hercules himself would've had trouble breaking free of this daydream. No wonder my weak-ass effort wasn't getting me anywhere. I went to the sink and splashed water on my face, getting most of it on my shirt and some on the floor. Regardless, it helped me focus.

This was my first opportunity to step back and appraise the wreckage without Jack getting in the way, and I needed to make the most of it. He knew I'd have second thoughts, which is why he left me with that warning this morning.

Holding me in a hug, he said, "Lily Barlow, you think I've been all over you up 'til now, girl. But I swear to God, if you try to pull away…" The end of the sentence was lost in the chasm of a deep, dark kiss right here in this apartment. The message may have been incomplete, but, knowing his patterns as I did, the intent was clear—if I pulled away, he'd be on me like static cling on a hooker's tube top.

He also knew *my* patterns, unfortunately, and he wouldn't buy it if I texted that I was looking forward to round four. So, I sent a basic reply that was borderline honest and hoped for the best.

"I'm okay. See you tonight." I considered putting something in there about me not freaking out, but he'd see through that smoke screen.

His response was instantaneous. Clearly, he had been watching his phone. "See you tonight. Text me if you need me."

Text him if I needed him? Oh, for the love of a monarch on a milkweed. If I needed him to do what? Go back in time? Undo the last twenty-four hours? Yep. Okay, Jack. I sent him a cheeky thumbs-up emoji, and shoved my phone into the back pocket of my shorts. I had to clear my head.

Opening the door in search of some new scenery, I bumped into a slab of thick, humid air. That's summertime in Virginia for ya. So much for ventilating my brain; the day was already too hot to think, and it was still morning. Clomping down the steps, I noticed that gangster chicken, McNugget, and her cronies way over by the tree line behind the coop. They were doing the first reasonable activity I'd seen them do since I moved in—lounging in the shade. That was one small blessing; I didn't have to contend with a crazy bird right now.

As I continued down the stairs, my landlady, Miss Delphine, came around the corner wearing her gardening uniform—pink gloves, floral print blouse, big straw hat.

"Lily, child, you look a mess." She said matter-of-factly as I stepped off the bottom stair, producing a little puff of dust from the dry dirt.

"Didn't get much sleep last night," I said, intending to keep the whole *SexwithJack* thing on the down low. Then out of nowhere I blurted, "and I have a really big problem."

"From the looks of ya, I reckon so," she agreed, giving me a once over. "Is this a weed-pullin' problem or a porch-sittin' problem?"

I considered those two options. Pulling weeds could be therapeutic, but given my propensity to wilt in the late morning heat, I opted for the porch-sitting solution. She invited me to pick a rocker, while she went inside to wash her hands and get us some ice tea. Not wanting her to wait on me, I followed behind, wiping my feet on the mat. As she used a tiny brush to scrub the dirt from under her fingernails at the kitchen sink, I filled two glasses with cubes from the tray and grabbed the bumpy green glass pitcher of sweet tea from the fridge.

Back on the porch, in the leafy shade of a big oak tree, she said, "Tell me about this problem, girl."

Shaking my head, I said, "Miss Delphine, I don't even know where to start." Then, a rush of events tumbled out of my mouth like cars on a roller coaster coming down the big hill. "The only reason I came back in the first place was to get the bakery going again after Dad's heart attack. The good news is, my friend, Mercedes, has

agreed to take over as manager. The bad news is, Jack—
you know Jack—has decided he and I should stop being
friends and start dating. *Dating* of all things."

I paused for a drink of tea then held the cold glass
to my temple, as if I'd just finished tractoring the front
forty. Miss Delphine nodded, and it occurred to me that
she was already familiar with the biggest chunk of the
back story. Sucking in a deep breath, I added, "And I
slept with Jack yesterday."

Technically, I should have shared this juicy
development with Mercedes first. Even my inner
Stephanie Plum was uncharacteristically quiet, refusing
to back me up. The laws of friendship were, in fact, very
clear on this point—friends that date back to training
wheels supersede acquaintances from a week ago in the
hierarchy of who gets told first. I struggled briefly with
the internal conflict before mumbling the rest of the
news. "And this morning," I said.

Without giving so much as the tiniest judgmental
twitch, she nodded again, so I forged ahead. "As you
can see, it's getting really hard to hide behind my this-
is-a-bad-idea argument." Waiting a beat to be sure I was
finally finished, she gave me a sympathetic smile.

Ordinarily, sympathy was one of my favorite flavors,
ranking right up there with self-pity, but I didn't slow
down to savor it. "He's been blowing up my phone all
morning with text messages, making sure I'm not doing
anything…crazy." I rolled my eyes when I said the word.

"Crazy?" she asked.

"Oh, I don't know, like applying for the witness protection program," I explained. "I really don't know what to do. And did I tell you I thought a friend of mine had been murdered? Storie Sanders. Turns out she's fine, but I spent a lot of time looking for her the last few days." After it was out of my mouth, I realized I needed to be careful here.

The *friend* in question was a woman with whom I'd had a two-night stand at a music festival near Charlottesville last summer. First and only time for that. Swear it. It was buried so deep it would never have surfaced if Jack hadn't badgered me, trying to figure out why I suddenly, in his eyes, became sexier and more confident a year ago. It took a little digging before I made the connection myself, and when I did, he was…well…come on. What guy doesn't enjoy a lesbian daydream? Let's just say he was extremely supportive of my experimentation. Still, it wasn't information I deemed appropriate for public consumption in my quiet little hometown of Marshall, Virginia. Point being, I didn't need to share all these details with Miss Delphine. Granted, she was probably not all that far from the grave, but she was a spunky ol' bat, and I still wasn't quite sure where her loyalties stood.

"Murdered?" She said it with all the shock it deserved.

"Murdered."

"Why on God's green earth did you think she had been murdered?"

"I found a website that records all the dead bodies the police haven't been able to identify."

"The Doe Network," she said, stating it with a touch of authority on the matter and giving one of those little clucks with her tongue.

My mouth gaped. "Yes," I said, drawing it out slowly, aghast that she knew anything at all about the Doe Network. All the surreptitious little references to murder I remembered her making over the last week converged in my brain, and I wondered if the murders she had committed were included on the website. Suspected murders, that is, since I still didn't have what a prosecutor would consider irrefutable evidence, or even circumstantial evidence, for that matter.

Correctly interpreting the alarm scribbled across my face, she elaborated. "I will occasionally watch a program on the television about a murder," she explained, convincingly enough. "I like true crime stories."

I nodded, filing that goody away for a day when I had more time to overreact, and continued my summary. "Classes start in a couple weeks at UVA. I'm on my third year. I mean, I know I haven't declared a major yet, but I really don't need this kind of chaos right now. With Jack, I mean. You know? When it comes to crowding me, that boy gets a blue ribbon every time. But my family can come in a close second when they want to. I think they wish I would take over Poppy's, even though everybody in this blasted town knows how that would turn out."

"Burned baked goods?" She quipped, barely smiling at her assessment.

It was true, but it was also funny, so I smiled back.

"The best thing to happen since I got home last week was finding your garage efficiency so I didn't have to stay with Dad, Aunt Millie and Uncle Dave. It was lucky you had the apartment available, making it easy to get in and out quick like, without all the associated hullabaloo." She was basically letting me stay here for free, because she said she wanted a reliable person coming and going. My end of the bargain was to feed the chickens. Yes, I said chickens, but you could substitute what you wanted here—Domesticated Velociraptors, Voodoo Hellbirds, the Devil's Poultry, all came to mind. Let's just say, that part of the arrangement didn't seem to be working out too well for me or for the chickens.

Miss Delphine set her glass on the little wrought iron table near her rocker and rested her head on the back of the chair. "Lord, child, that's a problem with a lot of sharp edges."

"I know. I'm just kinda stuck."

"What's Jack sayin' about the recent turn of events?"

"You mean the sex part? We haven't really talked about it, but I can guess. The whole let's-date scenario… he's been gunning for that since I got home. I don't think you've seen this side of Jack, but if he gets his mind set on something, he can be a real oligarch."

"Oligarch?"

I nodded.

"You know, Lily, that *oligarch* loves you."

"Well, I love him too, in the good Christian way Jesus wants us to love everybody. I probably love him a little more than that, to tell the truth, because we've been such good friends all these years."

"I mean he loves you like a man loves a woman."

"Please don't say that, Miss Delphine. I cannot possibly manage any heightened level of affection just now."

"Well, what's the point of glossin' over it? That won't help y'all find any type of resolution, now will it?"

Noting that she had a valid point, I sighed softly. "Do you happen to have the number for the witness protection program?" I asked, just to break the tension, both in the air and that accumulating in my own shoulders.

She chuckled. "He called me earlier in the mornin', Jack did. Asked me to look out for you. Said you had a lot on your mind just now."

I shook my head slowly. "That sounds like something he would do."

"True love might be a scary thing, Lily, but it's not a bad thing."

We sat quietly, drinking our tea and rocking, and I tried to get my arms around the difference between true love and regular love. My eyes fell on the woods that bordered her back yard, and I caught myself glancing through the canopy, wondering if I'd see a SWAT guy up there after all. Then it occurred to me that Miss Delphine's trusty dog, Velcro, Cro for short, wasn't barking and hadn't barked all morning. So, nobody was hanging out on the perimeter.

Cha-ching.

The phone was still shoved in my back pocket. "That's him," I told her, but I didn't reach for it.

Miss Delphine smiled the smile of a wise person.

"Want to see what he said?" I asked her.

"Only if you have a mind to share it, honey."

I fished my phone out and pulled up his message.

"Thinking about you," I read. Then looking up I asked, "And what am I supposed to say to that?"

"Well, unless I'm mistaken, you are thinkin' about him."

"I can't tell *him* that."

"I see." She said it the way you would if you wanted to stay connected to a conversation yet didn't really follow the current line of reasoning.

"Can I?" I dug for clarification. "Can I tell him that? I mean, if I do, it'd be like pouring cement on a sand castle. Seems like a good idea as the tide rolls in, but it does nothing to preserve the castle and then you've got a big stupid lump to deal with later." I nodded at the appropriateness of that analogy. Jack Turner—big, stupid lump.

It dawned on me that she was right. I *was* thinking about him. He knew I was thinking about him. What was I standing on here? Obstinance? False bravado? Both of those, probably. And you might as well throw in a little hysteria to round it out.

My thumbs flew over the keys, and I read the resulting message aloud. "Thanks for thinking of me. I guess you want to talk later."

Cha-ching. "Damn right I do."

"Okay. Come on by when you're off."

Cha-ching. "See you at 7."

"Can we eat first?"

Cha-ching. "I'll bring food."

That last message was accompanied by an emoji of a chicken leg, but I didn't mention it to Miss Delphine, sure she didn't know what an emoji was or why you needed it in correspondence. Since he typically didn't do a lot in the realm of pictographs, I suspected the emoji was entirely for my benefit. That, in and of itself, proved he intended to use any subliminal sliver he could drum up in order to shimmy his way back into my good graces.

The rockers took away the urgency of my situation, and the rest of the conversation moved like Tom Sawyer's raft in the slow part of the river. When all the ice in our glasses had melted, she invited me inside, but

I declined. It was early afternoon, and Jack got off at seven. Factoring in travel time, he'd be here by seven o' five. I calculated that I could pack up the whole apartment, drive to Charlottesville, and be unpacked by the time he got off work. And I admitted to myself that I was only half joking.

Hugging Miss Delphine, I thanked her for the tea and the talk and headed back upstairs to grab my keys. Jumping in the Jeep I had named Sandi-with-an-i, I rolled down the windows and let the furnace air blast me as I drove up the quiet lane.

Chapter 2

No destination in mind, I must've been in one of those time travel modes, because the next thing I knew, I was pulling onto the dirt road of the Upperville graveyard where my mama was buried fifteen years ago. Dad picked this place because it was close but not on a route he normally traveled. He couldn't bear the heartache of driving by her grave every day if she was buried at the Presbyterian cemetery in town. And when people suggested he'd get used to it, and it wouldn't always hurt so much, well, that sounded to him like forgetting her, which made him even sadder. He probably visited here more than anyone knew. I came with him every so often, but this was the first time I'd ever come solo. Not a big fan of all the spirit energy that collected in and near graveyards, I never would've considered stepping foot in a cemetery without a body guard before now.

Yet here I was. Alone in a graveyard. I had no idea where this burst of backbone came from, but I got out of the Jeep and shut the door as quietly as possible. I borrowed a page from the survival guide of my friend, Mercedes, and crossed myself. It wasn't a gesture connected in any way to my Presbyterian upbringing, but I periodically used it as an extra layer of spiritual bubble wrap in certain extreme situations. Surveying the scene for ghosts, good or bad, I started picking my way to the far side.

Fortunately, the grounds had recently been mowed so I wasn't faced with tall grass harboring unseen spiders and their shifty little associates. It was an easy stroll, even in flip flops, and when I arrived, I used a broken twig with some leaves still attached to dust off a section of the stacked stone wall. Once it seemed free of hazards, to include pests, pest carcasses, and webs, I parked myself in the shade of a big old pine tree. From where I was sitting, I could see her marker about thirty yards away. I glanced skyward, then back toward the general area, letting my gaze soften. In a yoga class I tried once for a full forty-five minutes, I learned about this practice where you let your eyes fall on a point, a stationary object somewhere in your line of vision. It was supposed to help you stay balanced or focused, one. What was that called? Something with a D? Drowsy? Droopy? Drippy?

Still wracking my brain, my eyes landed on a point on top of the grave stone. My gazed steadied, and I sent some energy into the universe. I guess I was trying to contact mama. Growing up without her, I never had the luxury of her wisdom when it came to boy trouble, although Aunt Millie was a remarkably good stand-in for things like that. However, I found myself in the uncomfortable position of not wanting to go public with the Jack story yet, hence my current strategy of channeling the dead.

Drishti! The word came to me like the bright splat of a paint ball on a sweatshirt. Drishti. The point of focus is your drishti. It was such a relief to have the word that I lost my deep focus. Okay. Medium focus. Fake focus? Weighing the actual depth of my focus, I realized I had been staring at a bump on top of the grave stone. What was that? Why wasn't the stone smooth on top? Was it the cap from an acorn? Maybe something manmade?

People leave tokens on graves for different reasons; it's not uncommon. Soldiers leave coins as a way to pay their respects. In a Greek mythology course I took, I studied the story of the Ferryman who gets paid to take a person's soul across the River Styx. Some people leave coins to ensure safe passage. Those of the Jewish persuasion might leave stones. I think this originated from the idea that the stone pressing down would keep the spirit in the grave, but I could be making that up. These days the stones communicate to the loved ones that they are not forgotten. I could be making that up too though. Some famous baseball player had roses delivered to Marilyn Monroe's grave three times a week for decades. And didn't a mysterious visitor leave a bottle of booze on Edgar Allan Poe's grave every year for his birthday? Oh, and here's a good one—people leave pennies for John Wilkes Booth, heads side up. Get it? It's Lincoln's head on the penny. While I contemplated the rich tradition of gifts on graves, and marveled at my vast knowledge of the topic, I was drawn toward the item in question.

As I approached, I saw it was some kind of game piece; a six-sided checker came to mind. Once I got closer, it looked more like a tile, the kind you might see fitted together on the backsplash of a stove in a modern kitchen. This one was green with a splotch of white. Unsure of the protocol for moving or even touching tokens left for the dead, I analyzed the pros and cons of picking it up. While it didn't seem like appropriate etiquette, it was, after all, the grave of my own relative. Surely she wouldn't be mad at me, her only child. Right?

I was vaguely aware of asking permission in my head, but since I didn't get an answer, I picked up the tile. It had a stylized white V on the face. If you turned the V upside down, it looked like a tent with the flaps opened. My finger skimmed the smooth ceramic surface. What a weird thing to leave. And more importantly, what weirdo left it? The affection people had for Connie Barlow surged through the Commonwealth of Virginia, and if you believed the stories, which I did, even spilled into the neighboring states of Maryland, West Virginia,

Kentucky, Tennessee, and North Carolina. No telling who stopped by with this funny little rune.

I slipped it in my pocket. It was something my dead mama may have come in contact with, and I decided I could use a little contact with my dead mama just now even if it was through a third party. I stood there for a few more seconds and rubbed my thumb along the top of the granite marker before turning back.

Behind the wheel, I sighed and tried to figure out where to go from here. For any other problem, I'd go straight to Jack, but I couldn't talk *about* the problem *to* the problem. That'd be like…like asking a tobacco company for tips on cancer prevention. My other reliable go-to in a crisis was Mercedes, but I knew she was with Dad and Uncle Dave, going over bakery business so she could take over as manager. Aunt Millie divided her days into a hundred different pieces, mostly doing good deeds on her own or through nonprofit organizations. She'd make time for me if I asked, but my little ol' baby pool dilemma wasn't as serious as homelessness or hunger, so I probably shouldn't take her away from the real work of making the world a better place.

Then it hit me like a black jack dealer in Vegas. I grabbed my phone and shuffled through a few screens to bring up the contact info for Storie Sanders. Storie was the…um…woman…I slept with last year. The one who thankfully had not been murdered. In all likelihood, the victim I had discovered on the Doe Network, the one with the purple flower tattoo, was someone close to her though. As it turned out, she and five friends from high school all got the same flower tattooed on their ankles.

Was it only yesterday when Jack and I drove up to her family's farm, thinking I had to deliver the devastating news that she was both deceased and decapitated? When she appeared, unharmed, the profound shock was followed by a swell of relief, but we offered to help her track down which of her friends had gone missing so she could alert the authorities. She wanted to take some time to think it through herself, first, which was cool.

It was now barely twenty-four hours later, but I decided an appropriate amount of time had passed and I could give her a call. Checking on her well-being would get Jack off my mind, at least temporarily.

* * *

Culpepper wasn't that far from Marshall, but Storie offered to meet me halfway, at a gas station outside Warrenton where there was a soft serve ice cream shop called Sprinkles. I was standing beside Sandi-with-an-i when Storie pulled up in an old pickup with a "Farm Use" license plate. She wore cut-off coveralls and a tank top, no bra. Beat-up work boots hid the tattoo of the purple flower on her ankle. Blonde hair in braids tucked under a red bandana, she looked every bit the sexy farm girl she was. Without hesitation, we hugged, and it was as natural as fringe on a flapper.

We didn't say anything important while we placed our orders. I got a Bluster (the knock-off version of a Dairy Queen Blizzard) with vanilla ice-cream and M&Ms. She got a vanilla cone with, as the name of the shop urged, sprinkles. I wasn't at all surprised that she chose a classic. Everything she did charmed me.

On a late Monday afternoon touching the five o'clock hour, the place was crowded, but there were plenty of picnic tables and benches. Judging by the unequal number of dads doing the corralling, I guessed this was a popular drop off for parents sharing custody, and I wondered if the moms would be happy to get kids who were full from ice cream and hopped up on sugar. We walked to the other side of the gas station, which immediately eliminated a good seventy percent of the chaos created by kids and dads. Spying what was probably an employee break table for the gas station clerks, we took up residence.

Devoting her full attention to a drip running down the side of her cone, she said calmly, "I know who was murdered."

"Storie," I breathed out. "Who?"

"Luanne," she said quietly. "I got in touch with Dana myself, and I found another friend who had spoken with Pauline a few weeks back, so it has to be Luanne."

If I remembered right, Luanne was the one who left the group when her parents moved out of state. While it's not that hard to stay in touch with people these days, the teenage life has a way of completely redrawing itself when distance and a new cast of characters are introduced. I wondered how I would have been redrawn if my Dad had decided to move at some point in my growing-up years. I was startled by the idea that Jack and I might not have kept in touch. That would definitely eliminate the current problem, but the thought was disquieting, until I realized that he had just wormed his way back into my brain.

Blowing out a breath to dispel the uninvited figment, I took a big bite of Bluster and asked, "Do you know what you want to do?"

"I don't really know. I've been thinking about it. And I've been crying a lot. I even went on that creepy website of yours."

I wanted to point out that the Doe Network wasn't mine, per se, but decided it might not be relevant at this juncture.

She kept on going, "I thought about driving down to Florida to talk with the authorities in person. You know, for closure."

I did know the need for closure. Closure was the mysterious force that pushed me to track her down this past week, and that was some mighty fine sleuthing if I did say so myself.

"Wanna come?" she finished, and went back to her dripping cone.

"Yes," I said. The word rolled off my lips without so much as a two-second delay.

"Okay." She nodded then said it again. "Okay."

We surrendered the next two hours to the task of getting to know each other. Sitting at that table, we reconnected, and I was a little startled to sense the physical energy that had first brought us together a year ago was still simmering. Neither of us acknowledged it. Instead, we learned about each other's families. We talked about the glories of our lives—the defining moments, great dates, and perfect sunrises. And we talked about the dirty disappointments—the broken promises, flat tires, and tonsillectomies. We were both blessed to be reared in families who loved and respected us. Both worked with our hands in family businesses, her on the farm and me in the bakery. I shared the drama of how I found her through Ditch Miller, the bass player for Gravel in the Whiskey.

"I never slept with a guy named Ditch," she told me. "I never slept with a guy period. I thought you knew I was gay."

"To be honest, Storie, I didn't think too deeply about your previous encounters."

"And since our time…" she looked at me seriously but didn't finish whatever she was about to ask. "I see you're with Jack now." While I don't remember discussing Jack when we were together, she seemed to know who he was when we showed up at her farm yesterday. I must've mentioned him to her at some point last summer.

"In a way," I admitted, and for the second time in one day, I gave someone else the news about me and Jack before sharing it with Mercedes. This undoubtedly solidified my status as a terrible friend. "I recently had sex with him for the first time," I said, "so I'd bet money *he* thinks we're together." And I made a mental note to call Mercedes on the way home, before I shared this news with the next toll-booth attendant or assistant librarian I bumped into.

Cha-ching.

The noise made me jump. "Oh, shit!"

"What?" Storie asked.

"I was supposed to be somewhere at seven. What time is it?"

"Ten 'til," she said, checking her watch.

Oh no.

I pulled up the text message, but I already knew what it said. And the paraphrase in my head was pretty darn close, expletives and all.

"Goddammit Lily. Where the hell are you?"

Usually, I don't like to be tied down to an immediate need to reply to text messages, but I also didn't want Jack to get one of his boys in blue to do him the favor of putting out an all-points bulletin on me.

"Speaking of the very devil himself, it's Jack. Besides the fact that he thinks he should have some say in literally everything I do, he is particularly sensitive to my desire to disappear at the moment," I explained.

"Ahh," she empathized.

"Let me just text him real quick."

So I did. "I'm fine. Having ice cream with Storie."

Cha-ching. "Where?"

"Sprinkles"

Cha-ching. "Want to meet for a burger?"

Well, he knew how to play his cards. I'd overlook just about any amount of intrusiveness for a hamburger. And being in Warrenton, I had a few premium options available to me.

"Smokey's?"

Cha-ching. "Be there in 20."

Turning to Storie, I said, "Jack's meeting me at Smokey's over there by the courthouse. You wanna join us for dinner?"

"You're sweet," she said, smiling. "I have to get back home. I told Nana I wouldn't be gone too long. She's fine, but Dad left for Richmond this morning, and I'm keeping an eye on her."

Sharing her need to watch after an older generation, I nodded my understanding, even as I wondered absently about her granddad, Jimmy. I saw him mentioned when Jack and I did a little online searching for her farm. The fact that she didn't mention him now made me wonder if he was still alive.

"But I'll call you about Florida, if you're serious."

"I am. Call me."

It didn't occur to me to consider when this trip would take place, or the length of time required to complete it, or how that would impact the fall semester at UVA. I just figured the universe would help me out for something like this, something that was important to another human being.

After hugging good bye, I headed over to Sav-a-Ton, a quirky grocery store in line with the hometown minimart in Marshall called Cumquat's. Both wanted to be bigger commercial enterprises but probably never would. Sav-a-Ton had a wider selection of nail polish, and since I had time before Jack got to Smokey's, I ran in for a new color.

Chapter 3

Either he drove really fast, or I took a long freakin'
time picking out the pale pinkish beige polish called
Cinnamon Fluff, because he was leaning on the front
fender of his truck, looking at his phone, when I pulled
into the parking space directly behind his. It looked like
he identified Sandi from the sound of her engine alone.
I saw him turn in my direction, head still down as he
finished one last thing on his phone, before he stuffed
it in his pocket and looked up to confirm it was even
me. One of his weird mechanic skills at work, I guessed.

As his daddy had trained both him and his brother
to do from a young age, he opened my door. I wanted
to hear the end of a song I liked on the radio, and while
the Jeep was in park, it was still running. Instead of
waiting on me to exit, he popped the buckle on the seat
belt himself and drew me out.

"I have to turn it off," I protested.

"I have to give you a hug," he responded. He won strictly on the merits of strength, and he kept me there until I relaxed into it and gave a little hug back. I was keenly aware that there was no groping or monkey business of any kind. I suspected he realized I was not on solid ground with the shift in our relationship, and it seemed like he was acting on his best behavior. That went beyond physical restraint to include mannerisms and bossiness in general. Any other time, I could have predicted a lecture about something to do with personal safety but unrelated to anything that was going on in the present moment—like why I don't have the number for Poison Control programmed into my phone or how I'm supposed to lift with my legs, not my back. I noticed he had dialed all that way down, though. He was no dum-dum, this one.

He breathed into my hair and said, "I missed you."

"You saw me this morning," I pointed out, hoping to emphasize that the period apart wasn't nearly long enough for one person to start missing another.

"Feels like two days," he replied.

When he let me out of the hug, he stood close while I reached in to turn off the ignition. Then he shut the door and grabbed my hand, walking beside me toward the restaurant. Without drawing too much attention to it, I tried to slip my hand from his grip. He barely tightened his fingers, signaling that he was on to me, then released without looking.

After ordering (burger/fries/sweet tea for me and burger/onion rings/beer for him) it occurred to me that I should have had a beer instead of the tea. This past week, Jack made it clear that we wouldn't sleep together if I'd had anything to drink because of his need to make sure he wasn't taking advantage of me. Note to self: Chug a beer as soon as we get back to Miss Delphine's.

The tension I was creating between us eased a bit as I started to fill him in on Storie, the things I had learned about her, and how she identified which of her friends had been murdered. I intentionally left out the part about driving to Florida with her. I had to come up with a bulletproof way to deliver that little nugget.

Dinner was fine, the food was good, and he didn't broach anything about our situation. I let him get the check. I may occasionally triumph in other arguments where he attempts to pay for me, but I had long since given up on the restaurant check as a no-win. On the way out, he grabbed my wrist again, forcing me to turn toward him. I half expected a kiss, or at the very least another hug, but instead he simply said, "Follow me home?"

I nodded. Giving my hand a friendly squeeze, he said, "Drive careful." I nodded again as he opened my door. "You, too."

When I pulled in behind him at my place, he was already out of his truck, chatting with Miss Delphine who was rocking on the porch. The chickens were safely tucked into their little hut for the evening, and Cro was laying at her feet, slow thumping his tail. Jack opened my door, and I waved at my landlady. She and I shared a secret thought between us, having dissected the relationship thing this very morning on that very porch. Then Jack followed me up the stairs to my apartment and waited for me to unlock the door with the key on the orange starfish key ring. Once inside, I made good on the promise to myself and went for two beers in the fridge. He gladly accepted and opened them both, successfully bending the caps and snapping them into the garbage can. How did he do that every time?

Plopping onto the couch, I noticed that he took the chair opposite me instead of crowding in beside me, lovebird style. It appeared he was making every effort not to spook me. I appreciated it and decided this was a good time to take advantage.

"Will you show me how to shoot a gun?"

"No."

For the love of the last man standing. I expected some resistance, sure, but I didn't think the conversation would be over in one stinkin' syllable.

I repositioned to try again. "Why not?"

"You want a list?"

"Just the top three will do," I said, lowering my chin to drill him with a particularly intense glare.

"You're spectacularly uncoordinated, both in general terms and where the hand/eye connection is concerned. You jump at loud noises. And I don't trust your survival instinct."

In my head, I noted that I had survived his bullshit for sixteen years. And counting. "Listen," I eased into it. "What if I have to kill an enemy."

"You don't have any enemies."

"An intruder, then."

"I'll take care of any intruder."

"Jack," I could not possibly have breathed any more exasperation into his name. "It's unrealistic for you to think you can protect me every second of every day." The look on his face pleaded for me to make this a dare, and I realized I was dangerously close to being assigned a permanent, live-in body guard. Tippy-toeing around until I found what seemed like a decent line of reasoning, I said, "Like when I'm at school." Secretly victorious, I elaborated. "What about when I'm at school, and you're here?" As sound an argument as I knew that to be, it didn't alter the look on his face.

Taking a deep breath, I opted for a strategy just shy of surrender and recapped the conversation, "So, you won't show me how to shoot a gun."

"No," he said firmly. "If you're concerned about intruders, I can teach you some defensive moves that'll drop a guy to his knees."

The corners of my mouth lifted as I considered dropping one particular guy to his knees, but Jack was there ahead of me. "They won't work on me, if that's what you're thinking. It took me to our freshman year to figure this out, but at any given moment, I know your next move before you make it." He smiled a superior smile that I didn't like at all, then he grabbed a receipt off the coffee table and reached for a pen beside my computer.

"What are you doing?"

"I'm writing down your next move."

Not wanting to get drawn into his convoluted little challenge, I punted, "So, Storie asked if I'd go with her to Florida to talk to the investigators and identify the victim."

"Is that why you want to know how to shoot a gun?" he asked, reaching his arm across the coffee table to hand me the receipt. I glanced at it, *change the subject* was scrawled in thick letters. Damn it. But I didn't give him anything to work with. Instead, I wadded the paper into a tiny ball, turned around on the couch so I could see the garbage can in the kitchen, and took the shot. It landed roughly two feet to the left of the basket, conveniently underscoring his point about hand/eye coordination. But I chalked it up to the poor aerodynamics of the ball.

"Well, two hot women on a road trip to Florida... might make sense to have a gun in the glove box. Just in case."

"Do you know the regulations for transporting a weapon across state lines?" he asked.

"It hasn't come up before now, wing nut, so when I buy a gun, I'll learn the regulations."

"You're not buying a gun, Lily."

I looked at him dumbfounded. "I appreciate the fact that you want to be in charge of each and every teensy-weensy thing I do, Jack, but I'm not a minor. I don't need anyone's consent." Casting about for a way to prove that I was indeed of age, I said, "I can buy my own booze; I can buy my own porn; and I can buy my own gun."

"Mmm, girl, I'm so hot for you right now." His voice was heavy, and there was a good chance he was serious, but he kept talking. "I think most gun owners and enthusiasts would agree—you're the poster child for gun control. You're the exact person who should not add a weapon to a life-threatening situation, because when it comes time to pull the trigger, you'll second guess your ability or your desire, one, at which point you'll end up shooting yourself. And if that doesn't happen, the person you're trying to stop will grab the opportunity to disarm and probably shoot you."

I stared at him flatly, which he took as an invitation to continue. "Mace I could support. That's not to say you wouldn't accidentally mace yourself nine out of ten times, but no one has ever died from mace exposure. If you're worried about needing protection while y'all are in Florida—and don't think for a second that I missed what just happened here—then I'll come. I'll come to Florida. I'll be the protection."

I knew it. I knew he'd try to come.

"You can't come to Florida," I said. And I meant it.

"I know you don't *want* me to come, but that doesn't mean I *can't* come."

"Would it make you feel better if Miss Delphine came?"

"Not in any way," he said evenly. "Just out of curiosity, why would she go?"

"She seems to be interested in weird murder mysteries. I thought it might give her a kick to go."

"Sure," he said with a shrug, "there's room for four in the truck."

I sat there, shaking my head with purpose. "Jack, why do you insist on a battle of wills every time I tell you I plan to do something?"

"Lily, why do you insist on putting yourself in dangerous situations over and over?"

I squared my shoulders and prepared to defend my choices. "What is it about me being with Storie that you find dangerous? Is it that she and I might have sex again?" I really thought that would put a pin in it. If he answered yes, then he had already made this new situation between him and me exclusive, something we had not discussed much less agreed upon.

He got a dreamy look in his blue eyes. "I just wanna stay in the room next door," he smiled and gave me that trademark wink of his, "and bring y'all coffee in the morning."

Uh. So he wasn't at all disturbed that my wild naked thing with Storie might reignite and get in the way of my wild naked thing with him. Well, that backfired, huh, Stephanie? I imagined she was nodding in agreement.

He spent a few more seconds in his lesbian wonderland before gradually emerging. "The last time y'all were together," he started, "there was no beer or pot? No tequila?"

Oh, I got it now. "No, there was." I nodded yes. "There was beer, pot, *and* tequila," I confirmed, even though I knew he already knew that. "But we weren't *driving* anywhere."

"Okay. And what about skinny dippin'? There was none of that going on. Right?"

I found it distasteful that he used the term *skinny dippin'* instead of *swimming*; it was accurate, but distasteful all the same. He knew that tidbit was privileged information, and even though he brought it up in the privacy of this conversation with no eavesdroppers or onlookers present, I preferred he didn't bring it up at all. Regardless, I realized where he was going. It was dangerous to be in the water while under the influence just like it was dangerous to get behind the wheel. Leave it to Jack "The Lifeguard" Turner to hone in on that bone of contention.

"I don't really want to talk about this right now," I said in a way that I very much hoped would end it, at least for the time being.

"Good, I don't either. I'd rather talk about what happened yesterday, last night, and this morning."

Great. The *SexwithJack* conversation. Good job, Barlow. "I don't want to talk about that right now, either."

"Alright," he said, and I saw him start to whittle out a thought in that pea-sized brain of his. It was safe to assume that the thought would come with some kind of bargain attached, so I waited. "Even though we sort of agreed to talk about the events of the recent past when I got off work today, I know you well enough to know you're in freak-out mode."

That may have been the understatement of the decade, but I didn't point it out. He took my silence as a form of consent and kept motoring along. "I'd be willing to honor your request to...not talk about it right now...is that how you put it? As long as you understand something." Here he paused, I could only assume for emphasis.

I lifted my eyebrows to show I expected him to continue, because let's face it, Jack would say what Jack wanted to say, whether the other party was interested in hearing it or not. "As long as you understand that I will not let you 1) pretend it didn't happen, 2) act like it didn't mean anything, or 3) wait for it to fade from view so you can gloss over it. Okay?"

I wasn't precisely sure what I was agreeing to when I nodded. Turns out, he wasn't either, ...and he asked me, "You're nodding..." he started. "...does that mean you understand?"

"I understand that you are committed to talking about the thing that I don't want to talk about." Formulating meaningless confirmations was one of my specialties, and this one made me feel particularly smug.

He shook his head. "Girl, that's a mighty fine loophole you got working there."

"What loophole?" I asked, feigning ignorance.

"Acknowledging that I'm committed to having the conversation isn't the same as acknowledging that I won't let you out of having it."

Well, that was my intention, and in my head I referred to him as something along the lines of a great big boob. With nowhere else to go besides into the exact conversation I was working overtime to avoid, I said, "I promise to have this conversation with you, at a date and time I find more to my liking."

He let his lips slide into a slow motion smile and nodded. "That's fine. But if you're thinking you can delay indefinitely, I feel obliged to warn you that I figured out one or two things when we were making love, and I'm not afraid to resort to those tactics again." He let me hold that thought for a few seconds before adding,

"Strictly for the purpose of advancing the conversation, of course." To give weight to his sentence, he came over to the couch and sat down beside me so he could tuck a strand of hair behind my ear before pulling the back of his hand softly down the side of my face to my throat, where he toyed with a necklace I was wearing.

I stayed very still and said nothing for one extremely important reason—the hand on the cheek took my breath away, and I didn't want him to know it.

As if nothing had happened, he moved away to re-establish a reasonable amount of space between us on the couch. "So," he said, "since we're not talking about Florida, and we're not talking about us, what would you like to talk about?"

What I wanted to talk about was Florida and us, only I wanted to talk about it with Mercedes, not him. Unfortunately, it was doubtful I'd be able to shake him at this point. Just because he agreed not to force the conversation, didn't mean he'd be willing to leave me on my own so I could make preparations to begin the formal withdrawal process. Who was I fooling? That's what would happen, after all. I'd go on the Doe Network and get lost in a couple dozen depressing unsolved murder cases. Then, I'd sit in the dark until I eventually found myself in a deep, moldy, anti-Jack funk.

I looked up and shrugged which gave him the perfect opportunity to swoop in with a great idea. "Wanna talk about my dog?"

Jack's family dog, Lucy, recently had a litter of four puppies, and both he and his brother, Joe, were taking one. His mama, who loves me dearly, declared that I got to pick Jack's first, before anyone else could claim one. I *did* want to talk about the puppies. Even more than that, I wanted to *see* them. They were cute, and funny, and safe. No relationship crap. No murdered friend crap. Just fluffy balls of enthusiasm. Fluffy balls that were probably asleep at this hour.

My smile gave me away. He pulled out his phone, and I schootched so we were shoulder-to-shoulder in order to see the screen, which he probably loved but didn't seize on. I'd spent time with the dogs during the week, trying to decide which one had the personality to put up with Jack's shit, and I had a pretty good idea.

Lucy was a version of a border collie, black and white. The four puppies had absolutely nothing in common, and by looking at them, no one could have guessed the breed of the dad dog. These four were textbook examples of the Heinz 57 mutt. One pup looked almost exactly like Lucy, only with more curls. She had a shy disposition. The second one was khaki and white with speckles like a hound and a little black on his ears and muzzle. He was the only male and was also known to be the ornery one. There was a brindle grayish-brown one who loved to eat; her sleek fur and fat belly made her look like a seal pup more than a dog pup. The last one was a kaleidoscope of white, black, gray and two different shades of brown, and she was curious about everything.

We flipped through the pictures, going back and forth. I wanted to hear his thoughts before I gave him mine just in case he had already bonded with one of them. It didn't seem like he had, and when I told him to take the multi-colored one, he was sold.

"What should we name her?" He wanted to know.

"She's *your* dog," I pointed out, inwardly hoping that he would let me be in charge of the name.

"Yeah, but you're the one who assigns names to everything."

That was true. I gave names to everything; probably why I was so good at it. That troublesome chicken of Miss Delphine's was McNugget. My Jeep was Sandi-with-an-i. Whenever I was drinking, Jack morphed into Jack-a-lope.

"It's the beauty of having you around," he added. "I'll never have to worry about coming up with a name for anything. Ever."

I smiled because, while I knew he was giving me a hard time, I took my naming duties very seriously. "Can I get to know her a little better before I decide?"

"Sure."

"And while we're at it, I think Joe should take the tan and white one."

"I'll pass that along."

Jack texted someone, I'd say either his mama or his brother, and then brought up the picture of his dog again. We talked about what he would need in order to get set up for her arrival. There was a trip to the pet store in our future.

"We can go when we get up," he said. "I don't have to be at the garage first thing."

"You're staying here?" I asked, with a level of caution that had become the norm over the last few days but still felt unfamiliar given our long platonic history.

"I am," he said. "No funny business." Grabbing my knee in his hand, he squeezed and released to show me he could do it. I was too tired to complain about him inserting himself into my life. A few days ago, I wouldn't have registered any complaint about him staying over. I decided not to pursue it for now. The fact that I could probably get him to feed the chickens in the morning was a good trade off.

"What are the sleeping arrangements?" I asked.

"You have two options," he said very seriously. "You can be on top or on bottom. I'll go either way."

I had reached for my beer, and when he made the sexual innuendo, the bottle froze in midair.

His laugh boomed in the tiny apartment, effectively thawing my frozen beer bottle. "Jerk," I said, right before taking a swallow.

Still laughing, he said, "I'm sorry. I couldn't resist. I'll be good. I promise. I know you're wigged out about crossing a line we never expected to cross. I'll sleep on the couch."

I guessed that was the right decision. Although I still kind of wanted him closer than that. In spite of all the grief he constantly gave me, and the amped up grief attached to this particular turn of events between us, he was and always had been a source of comfort when stress was high. We had fallen asleep together like a million times throughout our sixteen years of being friends, many of those nights in the very same bed. It was never X-rated, or even PG13 for that matter. Thinking about it made me wish for the days when we were chums, before this crazy hybrid thing got started less than a week ago.

I knew I could trust *him*. He was very reliable once he gave you his word. I just didn't think I could trust myself. When he saw me waver, he moved his head so he could lock eyes with me, a trick I hated. "Lily," he said, "do you *want* me to sleep in the bed with you?"

In response, I looked away. He tried again. "Tell me what you want."

"I don't know what I want…in the grand scheme. I just miss having you in the bed, but I…" The rest of the sentence faded away. I was too embarrassed to admit I didn't trust myself not to have *SexwithJack*. He took my hand in his and laid his other hand on my forearm, squeezing lightly.

"I know it's confusing," he said. "The definition of our friendship was so clear before, and now it's not." I nodded, but I wasn't looking at him.

"I can promise you two things," he added. My curiosity piqued, I glanced up. "I won't let the physical thing damage our friendship. Period. And I won't take advantage of your uncertainty tonight. If you want me to sleep in the bed, I'll sleep in the bed. I won't initiate anything, and I won't let you either."

"How can you turn it off like that?" I realized I was edging closer to the topic of conversation I had intentionally banished earlier, but I couldn't fathom his level of control.

"Darlin'," he started, "I wanna be clear. I cannot possibly turn this off. But what I can do is hold it in reserve until we find a path forward." He didn't say it in a way that was threatening, or even challenging. And frankly, I was relieved that I wasn't the only one who couldn't seem to turn it off.

Gesturing toward my empty beer bottle, he said, "I know that beer was your insurance policy." He looked like he was seeking feedback, which I didn't provide, but it made me wonder if he really did know my next move before I made it.

"What?" I asked with a shrug. "I just wanted a beer." I lied, but I did it with conviction.

He nodded, but I'm not sure he believed me. So to further manifest the lie, I stood up and got us two more beers. Since he wasn't heading back to his house, I knew he'd take it. In my head, I saw a large crowd of people giving me a standing ovation for knowing his next move before he made it. I might only get it right like thirteen percent of the time, but he wasn't the only one of us who knew something about the other of us.

We finished our beers and fell into the bed. True to his word, he stayed on his side. It was all I could do to stay on mine, reinforcing the fact that we needed to get this relationship issue figured out before I latched onto the free love philosophy of the '60s and just did it at will, ignoring all consequences.

Chapter 4

I rolled out of bed sometime around eight, the chickens having never crossed my mind. Jack didn't wake me up to ask if I wanted another lesson on how to manage the human-chicken alliance, so I could only hope that he knew I didn't and took care of the feeding responsibilities himself. Not wanting to parade around in pajamas, I pulled on my shorts and t-shirt from yesterday and moseyed into the kitchen. Jack was fully engaged with something on his phone. I greeted him as I made my way to the coffee pot but noticed he was only half paying attention. Neither my greeting nor my presence in the room seemed to register.

Turns out I was wrong about that. He was behind me with silent cheetah-like speed, and he wrapped his arms around my middle as I stood at the counter facing the cabinets. It startled me, and I took a sharp breath in. He had been pulling these sneak attacks disguised as "hugs" for the past week, building up to *SexwithJack*, but I thought while we were still sorting through the aftermath, I'd be relatively safe.

I went rigid, kind of like those fainting goats whose startle reaction is so strong they fall over on their sides like little stone statues, legs sticking straight out. Only thankfully, I stayed upright. He didn't laugh, just squeezed a smidge tighter and said, "Mornin'."

Waiting him out, I stayed still. "I'm not gonna rip your clothes off," he assured me. "And I wouldn't've ripped your PJs off, either." I said nothing so he added, "Just saying good morning is all I'm doing." He unlocked his arms and let his hands rest low on my waist, fingers splayed out across the front of my hip bones, thumbs around the side. Then he started to knead, along the lines of a deep tissue massage, which, while technically not a sexual gesture, still felt like he was dipping a toe in that pool. Unaware or unconcerned with the message my silent rigidity was sending, he kept massaging my hips.

As his right hand moved across the pocket of my shorts, he grazed the tile from mama's grave, which I had forgotten was still in there. He fingered the piece through the fabric, learning everything he could before he slipped his hand in to touch the smooth surface.

"What is this?" he asked, caught up in the guessing game. The only thing that stood between him and a total invasion of my privacy was the fact that he didn't remove it from my pocket.

Still facing toward the counter with my back to him, I tugged his hand away and pulled the piece out. Extending my palm, I showed him the item, color-side up.

"Oh," he nodded his recognition. "You went to see your Pop yesterday." He said it as a statement, not a question, which was interesting.

"Dad? I didn't see Dad yesterday," I said, confused.

At this point he turned me around so we were face to face, doing me the courtesy of talking half a step backwards, but even then I still felt we were dangerously close. He flat-out ignored it, though.

"Really? You didn't go by?" The confusion was catching. "Your dad has a jar of these," he clarified.

"What do you mean he has a jar of these?" I asked, stymied. It felt like we were in some updated version of an Abbott and Costello routine about baseball players and bases, and it was becoming more ludicrous with each line.

"When he got out of the hospital after the heart attack, I helped him move some stuff over to Dave and Millie's," he explained. "One of the things he asked me to get from his closet was a jar of these things. I'd say there were probably a hundred of 'em." He plucked the tile I was still holding and showed it to me, as if I just needed a closer look to know what he was saying was true.

"I've never seen this thing before in my life," I insisted. "Why don't I know anything about this jar?"

"He didn't act like the jar was supposed to be a secret," Jack said. "It was at the back of the closet, but it wasn't hidden. Where'd you get this one if it didn't come from the jar?"

"I found it on my mama's gravestone yesterday."

This unexpected news took precedence over anything related to the jar, the closet, or my dad. "You went to the graveyard?" The surprise in his voice was authentic. And rightly so. It was a known fact that I don't do ghosts. Either kind—the spiteful ones or the playful ones. No creepy things like Halloween haunted houses, horror flicks, graveyards, ghost tours. One time in middle school, I was peer-pressured into joining a seance at a sleepover. While nothing provocatively supernatural occurred, I slept with the light on for months afterward. Even Jack's current residence, previously owned by a witch and still infused with her witchy presence, gave me the chills; visiting there was really asking a lot. So, nothing from beyond-the-grave for me, or frankly, beside-the-grave either.

"Yeah. I was driving around yesterday and stopped by the graveyard."

"Alone?"

"Shocking, isn't it?"

"Well," he pondered, "What brought that on?"

What brought it on was the fact that Jack had completely disrupted my life, and I fled to a cemetery seeking comfort from a dead person. How much of that should I share, though…?

He asked again, "Why'd you go to the graveyard by yourself?"

"I went to talk to my mama," I admitted.

He raised his eyebrows. "About?"

"About you." Trying to keep the wobble out of my voice, I added, "And us."

"You've never gone to the graveyard by yourself," he said. "Have you?"

"No. Not by myself," I confirmed. "Maybe a handful of times with Dad."

He kept staring at me, and the look in his eyes implied that he had just uncovered an exciting new cavern to explore, and he couldn't wait to go spelunking. I imagined it was the way I looked at Miss Delphine when she mentioned knowing about the Doe Network this morning.

"Did you find any clarification while you were there?" he asked, and there was a note of genuine sweetness in the way he said it. "Any comfort?"

"Not really. All I found was this weird green and white tile on her grave stone." I felt like that sentence drew us again toward the unexplained connection to my dad, but I also felt like Jack planned to circle back around to my mama at some point. If I had to guess, he'd be seeking more information on the fact that I was so unhinged because of him that I broke the cardinal rule of keeping a safe distance from spirits and took myself smack dab to the very place they congregate.

There was a softness in his blue eyes that was highly uncharacteristic of Jack. I was against him creating a tender moment so he could deepen the Jack-to-Lily connection. It's possible that he was showing honest concern, but I couldn't take that chance, and I nudged the conversation back to my dad. "So, you think Dad leaves these things for mama?"

"Seems like it," he said, still holding on to the tenderness.

"Why?"

"Don't know. Maybe it's something that had meaning to them before you were born, like those plastic hotel key rings from the old-timey hotels. My mom and dad have one of those from their honeymoon in Big Sur. Dad keeps the spare garage key on it. Must've been one helluva wild night is all I can think to hang onto it after all this time." He smiled the smile of a man who has himself enjoyed a helluva wild night (or forty). And the way he was leering at me, I couldn't tell if he was trying to remember one from the past or trying to place me in one for the future.

I tossed the tile toward the table, and it landed with a crash. The fact that it landed on the floor was irrelevant, because it generated just the right amount of noise to bring him back to the present.

"If you're curious about it, why don't you ask your pop?"

I nodded, absently. "Yeah. I will."

* * *

Before heading to the pet store, Jack and I made a pact that we would stick to a budget. The pet industry was known to be a billion-dollar business for a reason, and the reason was suckers like us. In the truck, I made a list on my phone to keep us on track. We agreed to the basic necessities—collar, leash, puppy food, treats, and two chew toys. I talked him out of using old Cool Whip containers for food and water and added bowls to the list. He would make a bed out of some boards he had at his house and stuff it with an old blanket. I approved of that for two reasons—he was good at building stuff out of old boards, and I would get to paint a design on it. He'd need to buy a crate at some point, but not knowing how big his puppy would get, it seemed prudent to wait on that.

I was proud of us for coming in under budget, especially since I had a ridiculously hard time limiting myself to the two toys. Really, the only thing that worked to move me along was when he invaded my personal space to smell my neck. Neck smelling had proven very erotic for him this past week. I tossed the two toys I was holding into the buggy and headed to the checkout.

On our way back to my place, Jack did not make any references about us or about our predicament. That lasted up until he opened my door and let me out. "I'm on tonight, but can I see you tomorrow? I want to talk."

"I guess that depends on what you want to talk about. Weatherstripping for under my door—yes. What happened between us when we took our clothes off—no."

"Lily, it'll just get awkward the longer it festers." He put his arm around my neck and pulled me to him. He might have been giving me a way to avoid the dreaded eye contact, and I was grateful for it. While I was pressed to his chest, I debated whether I should tell him it was already awkward, but he kept talking. "We don't have to make any big, life altering decisions, but let's just have a conversation. Okay?"

Oh, for the sake of a Hindu Gila monster. "Okay," I said, with lukewarm conviction, more to get him on his way than to actually buy into this conversation of his. I had texted Mercedes this morning when Jack was in the shower, telling her I needed to talk, so the faster I ditched him the faster I could get over to her.

"Great," he breathed it like a sigh of relief. "I'll come over tomorrow morning."

Yeah, yeah, yeah, I thought to myself as I tried to lure him back to the driver's side of the truck. I stopped short of opening his door, sure he'd catch on and do something to intentionally belabor the exit. Aware the belaboring could involve at least three of my five senses, I was being very careful not to provoke him.

Eventually he drove off. I waited before jumping in the Jeep, giving him just enough of a head start so he wouldn't see me leaving behind him. While I burned a few more minutes, I noticed Miss Delphine's car was not in the drive, and I automatically assumed she was off somewhere disturbing the peace by committing a crime of passion. I needed to find out what that ol' gal was up to. She dropped little thoughts and phrases about death and murder that would make anyone suspicious. Jack assured me she was harmless, but I had my doubts, so uncovering her killing spree was on my list of things to do.

When I pulled into the parking lot at Manny's, there were no cars even though it was getting close to lunchtime. I popped in through the delivery door, sure that Manny wouldn't fuss at me for breaking kitchen rules since I had my hair in a ponytail. On my way past, I gave him a quick side squeeze and then found Mercedes rolling silverware in napkins at the back corner booth everyone referred to as ours. I washed my hands and then sat down to help her.

Knowing I was coming, she had fixed us both a cup of coffee, hers sweet and black, mine sweet and blonde, just like Storie. Sweet and blonde. I had no idea why that connection surfaced. Probably she was on my mind with the Florida trip and all. As soon as I plunked into my side of the booth, I looked at Mercedes and her eyes got shiny. She demonstrated no self-control whatsoever, because before I could start blabbing one word of my sob story, she gushed, "You slept with Jack, didn't you?"

Our reactions were one hundred eighty degrees opposite each other, me nodding solemnly like I had just taken a vow of silence at a somber stone monastery on a hill and her squealing like she was coming down from the very top of a double Ferris wheel. "Listen," I warned her, "I know this news holds a certain tickle factor for you, but what I really need right now is a calm, logical approach."

"No, *Lilita*," she challenged, "what you really need right now is to get all wild and crazy with a man who is wild and crazy for you." She rolled her shoulders seductively in case I was unclear on what she meant.

We did the usual back-n-forth, each trying to convince the other to see it our way. Since she was resolute and I was on the fence, I'd have to say she won. After we talked through the pitfalls and came up with a plan that basically spelled out me keeping an open mind, I told myself the best thing I could do for the time being was acquiesce. Much the way I had agreed with Jack's request to talk in order to get him out of the driveway this morning, I agreed with Mercedes. It was the easiest way to move on, seeing as I still had to get her caught up on the Storie non-murder before heading over to grill my dad about the green and white tiles he was leaving on mama's gravestone.

"You know Jack and I went over to Sanders' Ridge Farm in Culpeper so I could let that family know about the tattoo I recognized on the murder victim from the Doe Network." I knew she knew this, because she helped me formulate phase one of the plan over a few shots of tequila at Miss Delphine's a couple nights back. In addition, she went with me to interrogate the bass player we thought might have had something to do with Storie's murder. What Mercedes didn't know was that I had a very brief carnal thing with this woman. I was sure she wouldn't care, but it was a complicated layer that would require more time and tequila than it was worth at the moment. Jack was the only one who knew about it, and that itself was proving risky.

Mercedes shook her head softly at the mention of the murdered woman, crossed herself, and muttered something that I think may have invoked Our Lady of Guadalupe. Either that or Our Baby with a Toupee. The first one made more sense, but the girl did reach out to a *lot* of representatives, so it could've gone either way.

"Hold on to your Hail Marys," I told her, "because Storie isn't dead!"

"What?"

"Alive," I reiterated.

"The woman whose head and hands were chopped off?"

I knew my friend could run with an idea even when it was a wrong one, and part of me wanted to follow this down the rabbit hole just for funsies, but I didn't have that much time.

"Well, not her, exactly. But as it turns out, the dead woman is not my friend, Storie Sanders."

"Oh, *Lilita*," she whispered. "Oh, thank you," she said looking up at the ceiling and crossing herself again.

I filled her in on the highlights, including the part about Storie asking me to go to Florida with her. "You have to go," she said firmly. "There's no other choice."

"I kinda felt that way, too. I told her I would, but we didn't get into when or how long. I'm a little worried it'll bump into the fall semester."

"There's time for y'all to go now," she pointed out, "before school starts."

We continued to process it as we finished the coffee in our cups. All the knives and forks in the bin were wrapped securely in the colorful cloth napkins, and I would defy anyone to pick out which ones I did and which ones Mercedes did. Manny had trained us both to do it when we were kids, and I'd been rocking it like the Queen of Napkins ever since.

When we got up to hug bye, she said, "This thing with Jack makes me happy. Give it a chance, and it'll make you happy, too." I squeezed her in lieu of a verbal response and headed out.

* * *

"Hey, Dad," I said strolling into the living room over at Aunt Millie and Uncle Dave's. He was stretched out on the couch, a book opened across his chest like he had put it down to close his eyes. He looked a whole lot better than when I'd seen him a few days ago. I knew getting Mercedes to manage the bakery was part of the reason he had perked up, emotionally. However, he seemed more tired, physically. Some of that was from the heart attack but I felt like some was from the busy-ness associated with showing Mercedes the ropes and getting things in place to open again. "What can I do to help y'all get ready for the grand reopening?"

"Not a thing in the world, Snickerdoodle," he smiled and started to get up but decided the effort required more energy than he was willing to devote to it.

I pulled the ottoman over to the couch, so I was more eye-to-eye with him, and I fished the green and white tile out of my pocket.

He took it, studied it for a second, then turned toward me. Sounding as if he just cracked the code in the Voynich Manuscript after years toiling as a full-time cryptographer, he said, "You."

"Me what?"

"You're the one's been leaving these on your mama's grave?"

"*Me*? No! I don't go to the *graveyard*. I thought you left it."

"Why would I leave it?" He asked, puzzled.

"I don't know…people leave things for loved ones sometimes. Jack says you have a whole jar of 'em. Why would you have a whole jar of these weird things if you weren't leaving them for mama?" Then it occurred to me to wonder, "If you thought I was the one doing it, why didn't you ask me?"

"Of course I didn't think you were doing it!" He said with the force of a strong feeling. "How would you be doing it? You never step foot in the graveyard!" Then it seemed like that fact made him wonder out loud, "You either got this outta the jar in my room over yonder, or you went to the graveyard…"

"Why do you have a jar of these?" I cut in.

"Why'd you go to the graveyard?" He cut back.

My head was spinning. Any conversation about these tiles seemed to break down in utter comic confusion. Trying to figure a way off this ridiculous merry-go-round, I said, "It's a long story, Dad, but I went yesterday, and I found this on mama's grave."

"Well, add it to the bucket," he suggested, pointing toward the office that Aunt Millie had converted to a temporary bedroom for him while he was convalescing.

I managed to hoist myself up off the low stool with less grace than I would've liked, but Dad was used to that so he didn't bat an eye. As I turned the corner into the tidy bedroom, the first thing I saw was a framed photograph of me as a little kid holding my mama's hand. I was maybe four years old, and she was horse healthy in the picture. No sign of the cancer that would drain her life's essence just a year or so later. We were by the edge of a pond, and I looked like I was about to lob half a loaf of bread at a wayward duck swimming up to the bank. You could tell from my stance even at that age I'd never be good at ball sports of any kind. Standing there in his room, I held her hand for a moment longer, not in grief, just in that way you do when you remember a time.

The second thing I saw in the room was a big jar of six-sided green and white tiles. Jack was right; there coulda been a hundred in there. Instead of depositing the single tile I was holding into the larger collection, I picked up the jar and toted it out to the living room. "How come I've never seen this before?" I asked, cradling it in the crook of my arm.

"Well. It started out as just a few. In the beginning, I tossed them in the drawer of the nightstand. Over time they added up. I eventually dumped them in this pickle jar and shoved it to the back of the closet. Not to hide it," he clarified, "just to get it outta the way."

"Why didn't you mention it?"

"Honey, you were always so squirrely when it came to the graveyard...worried about ghosts and zombies. I just let it be," he said, kindly. "And it doesn't really matter all that much. So many people loved your mama. Lots of friends go visit her there. I've found other stuff over the years."

"What kinds of other stuff?"

"Coins, pictures, a key, a pin with Greek letters, maybe from a fraternity, a tiny cross carved out of wood. There was a penny that looked like it was smashed on a railroad track. A purple river rock. There was a postcard from Ocean City, no writing on it. There was a ribbon once. Bright blue. A shark's tooth. A bottle cap. I saved all of it for the last fifteen years. It's all in a box in my dresser. You're welcome to look through it and take anything you want. This is the only item that repeats itself; whoever delivers it is the most frequent flyer by far."

"How often do you find these tiles?"

"Every other month or so. Sometimes more. I once found a new one four days after I collected the last one."

Four days later? In my mind I contemplated how often my dad had been visiting the graveyard all these years. No wonder he never had time to date anyone. Based on the number of items that were left, it sounded like it was a regular little disco down there. Too bad he didn't bump into one of the female mourners while she was leaving her token. That'd sure be a funny story to tell—clubbing at the graveyard.

* * *

Back at my little apartment, I took stock: Storie wasn't dead; there was a pending road trip to Florida; Mercedes was up to date; Poppy's Bakery was on track to reopen; Dad was good; the green and white tile, while a mystery, was at least a known mystery; I still had work to do where Miss Delphine was concerned, but I had a window of what was turning out to be free time before school started; and Jack was off my back for a night. It all made me smile, but that last point was particularly smile-worthy. A Jack-free night all to myself. Whew. Some peace and quiet.

I rummaged around the fridge for leftover Chinese food, which I threw in the microwave and ate standing at the sink. Then I grabbed a beer and pulled out my computer. This chunk of time on my hands was a decadent treat, and I intended to indulge in my new favorite past time—the Doe Network. The sun was off my porch, so even though it was still hot outside, I decided to do a little porch sittin' in my Adirondack chair. I saw the chickens down below, and I waved to McNugget as an olive branch between us. Not that I expected her to, but she did not wave back, and I felt a pinch of disappointment regardless. Cro ambled through the yard, sniffed the bird, then came to the bottom of the steps, waiting for an invitation.

"C'mon up, boy," I summoned, and he happily accepted.

Chapter 5

With Cro making himself comfortable by my feet, I pulled up the page titled "United States Unidentified Males Geographical Index," and, as I always did, I hit the "view females" link. Scrolling alphabetically from the top, it intrigued me that Alabama listed seven unidentified female victims, Alaska only two, but Arizona had almost a hundred. Out of curiosity, I did a quick audit. California had the most at two hundred twenty-three. Nebraska, both Dakotas, Puerto Rico, Rhode Island, and the Virgin Islands all came in at zero. Although any armchair detective, like yours truly, could tell you those locales may very well be hiding murdered women whose bodies had not yet been discovered. And just because there weren't any females didn't mean there weren't any males. Since the men were listed separately, on the other page, that required an additional keystroke to cross reference, which I wasn't inclined to make at the moment.

I went back to Arizona and counted. Sixty-eight of the profiles showed only a black silhouette with the words "No Image Available." Many of these files contained no images of any kind, but some had pictures that the nonprofit organization may not have had time to upload in order to create a defined profile picture.

I opened a tab for the first of the black silhouettes in Arizona—Case File 1202UFAZ— who was found on July 31, 1960. She was a child somewhere between two and seven years old. Despite the black silhouette, there were actually three images in her file. The first appeared to be a computer-generated reconstructed face, but the other two pictures were far more heart wrenching. One showed a pair of men's flip flops, cut down to the size of the child's feet. These were found near the body. The other was that of a grave marker the town had provided. On the marker, she was called "Little Miss Nobody," and there was a Bible verse from Matthew. The detail that moved me the most may have been the fact that her toenails and fingernails were painted red when she was found.

I couldn't remember when I first started painting my toes, but it was when my mama was still alive, I knew that much. Thinking back, there hadn't been a dozen days since then that my own toes had gone their natural unpolished color. Little Miss Nobody was a kindred spirit, but no one should be Nobody. I named her Cindy, short for Cinderella, another female identified by a shoe. Doing a rough calculation in my head, I figured she would have been about sixty now. In my mind, I ran through all the experiences she never had, all the colors of nail polish her toes never got to be. As a tribute to little Cindy, I went inside to grab my nail polish remover, a paper towel, and the new Cinnamon Fluff color I bought last night.

Painting my toes, I reflected on the fact that the people who had originally been assigned to Cindy's case would no longer be working on it and might not even be sucking oxygen at this point. I said a little prayer that someone would see this profile and maybe remember something that would help thaw the ice-cold case. When I was done, I looked at my pedicure but didn't get the bubble of joy it usually triggered.

Feeling forlorn, I arrowed down to Misty-Storie's profile in Florida. That tattoo originally belonged to a stranger who became my Jane Dough. The pun evolved when I combined alcohol with bad spelling during a google Google search of dough but accidentally typed doe. That's when I stumbled on the Doe Network. I called her Misty when I first read the profile. Then her name morphed to Misty-Storie when I thought it was Storie Sanders. I decided I should change the name again to Misty-Storie-Luanne. Or, better yet, give the girl her name back and call her Luanne.

"Luanne," I said softly, "we're coming, girl. We'll tell them who you are, and we'll get you back home." Cro thumped his tail once in agreement.

I swatted a skeeter, then another, and figured it was time to move this operation indoors. My route took me past the fridge to grab a second beer and then over to the couch. Thinking about Luanne, I googlemapped the route from Marshall to Key West where her body was found. Eighteen hours and five minutes. For a journey of that magnitude, Jack would definitely play his mechanics' card and force a tune-up, regardless of whose vehicle we planned to drive. I did a search for things to inspect before a big road trip to see if it was something I could manage on my own. Uncovering a series of check lists, the first item on the first page was "fluid levels." Hmmm. What was there besides the oil? Or did it mean one fluid had multiple levels?

Acknowledging that this might be a bigger pain in the ass than putting up with the mechanic himself, I did a little visualizing—me in a pair of coveralls, greasy Pep Boys ball cap on backwards, dirty rag jammed in my back pocket. Just as I was reminding myself that plenty of women maintain their own vehicles, my phone interrupted me with a text noise.

Cha-ching: "Hey"

Horseflies at a housewarming...of course...Jack. Since I'd been home this visit, he was exhibiting the annoying habit of texting whenever his aura entered the sphere of my awareness. At this point, it was pushing the boundaries of coincidence and approaching a conjuring situation. Not that I craved the responsibility of a superpower, but if I had to be burdened, conjuring didn't even make the top ten best powers that would be super to have. I didn't want to bring him *to* me. He was doing that plenty good on his own. What was the opposite of invoking? Repelling? Yes, that's what I needed to do. Repel. Note to self: Look up spells that repel.

But, since I had him here, may as well ask. I texted back:

"Hey. How many kinds of fluids are in an engine?"

Cha-ching: "Your engine has eight. What are you doing?"

"Eight??? Nothing."

Cha-ching: "Oil, coolant, power steering, transmission, brake, differential, transfer case, windshield washer."

As I wondered what the hell the differential was and if I could cope with checking its fluid, he sent a follow-up message.

Cha-ching: "Don't mess with the fluids. I'll check before we go to Fla."

I did not care for the *we* in that last sentence, and I cared even less for the winking emoji. So you could imagine how I felt about his next one.

Cha-ching: "PS I miss you."

Rolling my eyes and shaking my head, I typed: "I'm working on a spell to repel you."

Cha-ching: "Resurrecting your Wiccan phase?"

Ah, my Wiccan phase. That made me chuckle. I had forgotten all about it. The Moon Goddess and ritual practice of magic. I was in the fourth grade and for some still inexplicable reason, I was convinced the crows were laughing at me. I came up with a spell to reduce laughter in the crow population, which by today's standards could best be described as a bad interpretive dance accompanied by the lyrics of some crow-related folk song I may have made up. Jack steadfastly refused to participate, but he would hold my backpack after school and stand guard in case anybody tried to interfere. Lost in the memory, his next text jolted me.

Cha-ching: "Sexy college witch. Love it."

I thought it best to let this conversation die a natural death before the kissy face emoji made an appearance.

"Bye."

Cha-ching: "See you in the morning. (kissy face emoji)"

Damn it. That boy was beyond frustrating. Although, let's be honest, I sorta had it coming, stirring the pot with my question. Asking Jack about engines was like offering me a bag of Squirrel Nut Zippers, my all-time favorite candy. Uhhh, yes, please. I gave him the perfect opportunity there, and what was it Dad always said? Don't be mad at the zebra for having stripes? So that one was on me.

Time to regroup. First—don't respond to the emoji. Second—focus on the road trip. I could possibly handle maintaining one fluid level, two fluids at the very outside, but even that was a stretch given the breadth of my disinterest. I was in no way up to checking, let alone maintaining, *eight* fluid levels in either the Jeep or in Storie's car, whatever that might be. If it was that jalopy truck she drove to Sprinkles yesterday, it'd take a lot longer than eighteen hours to get to Key West. So we should probably take Sandi-with-an-i.

Planning for Florida seemed to involve two distinct steps: 1) getting Jack out of the way and 2) the logistics of the trip itself. Having no idea how to go about step one, I concentrated on step two. The drive would take two days down and two days back. One day to speak with the detectives in charge of the case and identify Luanne, and maybe one day to drink a beer on the beach and toss a purple flower into the ocean in her memory. So six days total. The budget needed to cover gas money, hotel for five nights, and food. I did a quick search for room rates. August was still part of the rainy season in the Keys, only a few weeks ahead of the hurricane season, so there were cheap rooms available. That'd help keep the cost down. I assumed we'd be sharing a room, and at that thought, I got a little lightheaded remembering the physical attraction from a year ago. It was still bubbling just under the surface when we saw each other yesterday based on the way my skin tingled after we hugged hello. What if this turned into a five night stand? I was intrigued, but that would pile another complication onto my newly complicated life.

As I weighed the ups and downs of complications, my phone *cha-chinged*.

"Damn it, Jack Turner! Can I please get three minutes peace?" I hissed as I snatched the phone that was resting on the coffee table. The picture in the circle confused me though. It wasn't Jack's smiling face, so unless he was texting me from a different number, it wasn't Jack. The circle was blank, and I didn't recognize the number underneath. I touched the line and the full message popped up.

"I found a fare sale for flights to key west. $79 roundtrip. But you gotta fly thursday and come home monday." Ah. It was Storie.

Storie's news about the cheap flight was less interesting than the fact that I was thinking about her the exact moment she texted. My power to conjure appeared to be getting stronger. Was anybody else weirded out about that? I glanced around the small, empty living room. And, as usually happened when I sought feedback, my go-to girl, imaginary Stephanie Plum, came to mind. The extent of her feedback was limited to a noncommittal shrug with a half-hearted head tilt. So, no, nobody but me. Electing to explore my powers later, I went back to the flights.

Today was Tuesday. If we left on Thursday, home on Monday, that would be plenty of time to conclude the purpose of the trip. Mental math wasn't my forte, but it seemed like it would work out about the same, cost-wise. One less night in a hotel and no gas money, but we'd need transportation when we got there, either a rental car or Uber, one.

I texted back: "Sounds good. Let's do it."

She sent me the carrier, flight number, and times. A few minutes later, I had a $79 ticket to Key West leaving Thursday morning. Pleased with myself for resolutely addressing step one of the planning process—getting Jack out of the way—I closed the computer, yawned, stretched and promptly fell asleep right there in the nest of macramé pillows I had arranged on the sofa.

Sometime later, I jumped at a loud bang. My startle response was strong, and my knee paid the price as I lurched off the couch with the grace of a giraffe on rollerblades. Off balance, I slammed into the coffee table. This same thing happened earlier in the week, so even though my knee hurt, I was slightly less panicky this time. From my side of the door, I hollered, "Who is it?" And I got the answer I was expecting.

"It's Jack." Bruised kneecap aside, it was good he was here, since I wanted to tell him about my trip. Although the hour of his arrival spoke to his mental instability.

"What time is it?" I asked, standing in the doorway.

He nudged his way past me with two cups of coffee which smelled wonderful. I glanced out across the yard, because the chickens were stirring. Time to bolster my resolve for the dreaded chicken duties.

"It's six thirty. And I did you a favor." He smiled like I might owe him something.

In my head, I chanted, *please say you fed the chickens please say you fed the chickens.*

"I fed the chickens."

Yes! I smiled. I didn't have to brew coffee *and* I didn't have to deal with the damn chickens. There were benefits to having him around. Few and far between, but they did exist.

"Are you tired?" I asked.

"Nah. No calls last night. I got good sleep. But you can lay back down if you want."

"What will you do?"

"Lay down beside you."

"Jack," I started to come up with reasons I didn't want to do that.

"Lily," he cut me off, "I'm just laying down beside you. I'm not grabbing your ass. I'm not taking your clothes off. I'm not jumping your bones."

The temptation to pick it apart was very real, but going for a shade of maturity that typically eluded me, I quietly agreed. We put the coffees on the table and headed to the bedroom. I had never changed out of my clothes from yesterday, and I didn't see the point this far into the morning, but I did swing by the bathroom to pee. While I was in there, I brushed my teeth and immediately regretted it. What the hell, Barlow? You can't play both sides.

Tamping down my guilty feelings about wanting to kiss him, I let the drowsy gradually overcome me and eventually fell back asleep. An hour or so later, I woke up to pee again. Jack got up and ambled toward the kitchen. As I came out of the bathroom, I decided it was go time.

"I need a favor."

"The first one was free," he said, referring to the chickens, "but the second one'll cost ya."

"What's the rate?"

"Depends on the favor."

"I need a ride."

"You're in luck. I just dropped the price for rides— one kiss only."

I leaned in and pecked his cheek, thinking I'd better seal the deal before he found out it was a ride to the airport. He put his hand on his cheek and said in a super sappy way, "Aw, that was sweet. Thank you." Then, in a much smokier way, he added, "But the cost of a ride is *me* kissing *you*, and it's not on the cheek."

The kisses had gotten very steamy since this whole thing started. I crossed my arms in an effort to look defiant. "If you say anywhere but on my lips, the deal is off." Hell, I'd get my recuperating dad to drive me to the airport before risking that.

"Lips'll do just fine." He put his arm around my waist and pulled me into his chest with a tinge more physicality than it required, anchoring me up against his body so that I could tell kissing wasn't the only thing on his mind. I was surprised and a little pleased when he didn't tighten his grip as I took a discrete step backward. He regained the exact same positioning by matching me with a small step forward. It took two more steps like this for me to figure out his game. I was backed up against the front door of the apartment.

All this transpired in the course of maybe a minute, and in those sixty seconds the blood rushed from my head, and I was half tipsy. In times of stress, I have been known to hyperventilate. And I wouldn't put it past me to faint, either. My words were too breathy when I said, "This is still only a kiss, right?"

"Mmhmm," he hummed. The vibration of the sound in his chest felt like the far away beats of an ancient native American drum circle echoing down a rocky canyon out west. Worse, it had the effect of a sedative. I drew a sharp intake of air to fight the reaction.

"You're okay, Lily," he whispered. "It's okay to ride this wave with me. I won't let you go under." And with that, my resolve was done. He grazed my cheek with his lips in a way that was softer than the tip of a kitten's ear. The next thing I realized, my lips were on his, and I couldn't be sure I didn't put 'em there myself. I heard the drum circle again; this time it was deeper, maybe a little closer. And the kiss went on and on.

When he took his mouth from mine, he moved his head back far enough to look at me. The eye contact at this close range was intensely uncomfortable. Since the right side of my face was wedged against the forearm he had planted on the door jamb, and the left side was held lightly in place by his other hand, I took the only option available to me and cast my eyes downward.

His response was the hated chin tilt. Technically, you could still keep your eyes pointing down, it just felt stupid to do it. So, I looked at him.

"I want you more than my next breath," he said with a very husky voice. "But...I believe I owe you a favor."

Frankly, I'd forgotten all about the favor. I had to regain a modicum of control in order to break the news that Storie and I were flying down to Key West tomorrow. And that wouldn't happen unless I could generate some space between our two bodies.

"There's a jar of jalapeños in the cupboard, and I can't get the lid off."

"That's the favor?" He dropped his hands and stepped back. I think he was mystified that it was an uncharacteristically simple task for all the built up.

"No," I said as I ducked around him and moved toward the coffee we had left on the kitchen table when he came in this morning. "That's an actual problem," I said, "but that's not the favor." Continuing to build a buffer zone, I went to the counter and made a big deal of transferring the contents from the paper cups into ceramic mugs and reheating the coffee in the microwave. When I turned back around, Jack was patiently waiting for me to get to the favor. There was a look of amusement in his blue eyes, but if you didn't know him well, you wouldn't know it was there.

I almost wanted to stay quiet, just to see how long it would take for him to ask about the favor, but I never had the chops for a standoff like that, so I caved.

"Storie and I need a ride to the airport tomorrow." I stated it as simply as I could. Then to be clear, I added, "That's the favor."

I watched him, coming as close to full-blown eye contact as I could stomach, but I didn't detect the level of surprise I expected. I didn't detect any level of surprise at all. In fact, I didn't see a change in his expression whatsoever.

"What time is your flight?" He asked evenly.

"Plane leaves at eleven, so we want to be there by nine." Then, to be as kind and graceful as I possibly could, I added, "You can drop us off early, though, if you have to get to work."

"Sure, I could drop y'all off," he agreed, nodding, "but it might be easier if we all ride together."

"What?"

"Joe and I are flying out tomorrow, too."

"Where are y'all going?" I was floored by this news.

"Key West." He said it like you'd say what you had for dinner last night—tuna casserole. Then he added, "Fishing trip." The way you'd add—and sweet tea.

I stood there, mouth agape, shaking my head no. "There's no way in hell you two blockheads just happen to be fishing in the Keys the same weekend we're going down to identify Luanne. No way." Historically, JT never bluffed about anything. He just didn't. But this was way outside what you could call a coincidence.

Jack pulled out his phone, hit speaker, and hit a contact. On the second ring, Joe answered, "Yo."

"Dude, are we fishing in the Keys this weekend?"

"Hell yes we are!" Joe answered emphatically.

"Are we flying out tomorrow before noon?"

"Damn straight!"

"You'll never believe this, but Lily and her friend, Storie, are flying out at the same time."

"What are the odds?" Joe asked. And if I hadn't been so outraged with the two of them at that moment, I'd'a spent more time analyzing the quality of Joe's voice to see if there was a drop of phoniness I could use as proof that this was all fabricated. But I was just so freakin' outraged. "Why don't they ride to the airport with us?" Joe asked.

"I'll see if they want a lift. Later."

"Out," Joe ended the call. Or fake call, as it were.

Still fired up over this ploy to highjack my trip, I demanded, "And what exactly are y'all fishing for this time of year?"

"Permit," he said flatly.

Damn it. I wished I knew if people fished for permit in August. Furthermore, I wished I knew if permit was a real fish.

"What time is your flight out?" I continued the interrogation.

"Don't know. Joe made the arrangements. Call him if you want." He held out his phone.

"You gave him enough information!" I was catching up to everything that just happened. "He knows we're leaving tomorrow. I bet he already found the fare sale and booked tickets on the same damn plane."

He smiled his lopsided grin, and without confirming my suspicions, he said, "I hope my seat's close to yours."

Chapter 6

"If you're finished intruding on my life for the next few hours, I need to go tell Dad I'm flying to Florida." I couldn't have bathed that sentence with any more testiness if I'd tried.

"Want me to come?" He sidled up, shoulder to shoulder, and gently knocked into me.

"I do not." High from his win, he was a big fat liability. Last thing I needed was him letting slip that I was going with Storie, that I had slept with Storie, or that our objective was to identify a murder victim. The dad generation was best kept in the dark where the details were concerned. The fact that Jack and Joe were going, albeit uninvited, would be an advantage here, although I'd take it to the grave. Dad trusted the Turner boys to be responsible. I would leverage that to advance my agenda.

Jack grabbed me up in a big hug that lifted me off my feet. "We're not gonna get in your way. I promise. We won't even be around. We'll be on the water all day."

"Fishing," I reaffirmed, sarcastically.

"Fishing," he smiled, setting me back on the floor.

"Get outta my house."

"Kiss good bye?"

"Kiss my ass," I said quietly.

"I plan to," he replied, just as quietly, before he slipped out the door.

I slid the curtain back and watched him tip his ball cap to Miss Delphine at the bottom of the steps. They chatted for a minute before he hopped in his truck. I still intended to invite her to Florida. If I could get her off the home turf and surround her with the macabre, she was bound to spill the pintos about some crime or other in which I knew she was involved. Don't get me wrong, I liked the old biddy well enough. It might have been her dark side that appealed to me. But she was covering something up, and I wanted to know what it was.

Once the truck was outta the driveway, I headed down the stairs. "Hey, Miss Delphine!" I gave the greeting an extra bit of brightness.

"Child," she greeted me back, a little less brightly.

"Whatcha working on today?"

She glanced at her garden gloves and over at a pile of wilting weeds before looking back at me and stating the obvious. "Weedin' the bed."

"Hmm." Not wanting to waste any more time on the niceties, I jumped in. "Ever been to Florida?"

"Lord, no. Don't care for all the sand."

"I know what you mean," I said, nodding. "I don't particularly care for all the sharks."

"Those neither," she agreed.

"I'm going down with my friend Storie tomorrow so we can ID the murder victim I found on that website. Wanna come?"

A look crossed her face for just a quick second, but it disappeared. "Now, that does sound interestin', Lily."

"I know it's short notice," I offered, trying to think of another way to entice her, "but it's a real cheap flight."

"Indeed it is short notice. Too bad I have a funeral of my own on Friday."

At that my head shot up. Funeral of her own? Was it for a victim she had murdered? Sweet Jesus. Now we were getting somewhere.

"My good friend's son, Nolan. The cancer took him. That blasted cancer has stolen so many people I love."

Oh. Cancer. She really couldn't be accused of murder by cancer now. "Yeah, me too."

"Your mama," Miss Delphine finished my thought.

"My mama," I confirmed.

"Connie Barlow fought a good fight, that girl did." Granted, it was common in a small town to know a little about everybody, and a lot about some people.

Miss Delphine seemed to know a lot about everybody, though, including my mama. I just hadn't figured out where their lives had intersected. It coulda been before I was even born. School teacher or something like that. I didn't know nearly enough about Miss Delphine's life before I moved in a week ago.

Trying to get out of my own loss and back to the loss down in the Keys, I said, "So, no to Florida this time?"

"No, honey child, but I do appreciate the invite."

"Happy to," I said.

"Y'all go and take care of things down Florida way, and don't worry about the chickens."

Humph. Having not given the chickens a passing thought, I felt it would be appropriate to acknowledge her grace on this point. "Thank you, Miss Delphine."

"You're welcome, girl."

"I guess I'd better head over to tell my Dad about the trip." Another thought occurred to me after I said it, since she possessed some, if not all, of the qualities of a busybody. "If you see him, don't mention anything about a murder."

She was already back to weeding, hunched over and head down. "Wouldn't think of it," she promised from under the brim of her big straw hat.

✳ ✳ ✳

One quick shower later and I was pulling up to Uncle Dave and Aunt Millie's. The house was quiet. Uncle Dave's car was gone, I assumed at Poppy's with Mercedes. Aunt Millie's car was gone, probably delivering meals to shut-ins. So, I entered in a way that was as close to quiet as a klutz like me could manage.

Dad was in his bedroom, stretched out on top of the Black Watch quilt. He loved that color plaid, and in cooler weather, even had a collection of several long-sleeve shirts out of it. I pushed his foot lightly, and his eyes fluttered opened. "Lily Bean."

"Hey Dad," I greeted him cheerfully.

"I'm happy to see you."

"Me, too. How you feeling?"

"If I was doing any better I couldn't stand it," he said with conviction.

In lieu of a hug, I leaned over and laid my cheek on his before I plopped down in the armchair in the corner. It was a good spot, because he could see me easily, but I wasn't crowding him by perching on the bed.

"What are you up to?" he asked.

"I'm taking a little trip down to Key West."

"Key West? What brought that on?"

"Jack and Joe are going on a fishing trip for the weekend, and I thought I'd tag along," I lied. Well hell, if they were gonna lie about their involvement in this trip, seemed only fair I should be allowed to steal the lie and use it for my own purposes. I felt pretty confident that I couldn't even be convicted of lying in a court of law, since the fishing trip was presented to me as "truth."

"You? Fishing?"

"Oh, for the love of matchsticks and matzo balls. Not *me*. The boys are fishing; I'll be relaxing in some shady hammock reading a book until they get off the water. We'll be together for dinner and breakfast." Okay. The jury might convict me of *that* lie, and to shimmy away from it as quickly as possible, I added, "They're fishing for permit. You ever hear of it?"

"Heck yeah. Some people call it a celebrity fish."

"Celebrity?"

"Yes, it's a big deal in the saltwater world."

"Bigger than the taffy?" I asked, laughing. When he didn't get it, I explained, "It's a joke. Saltwater taffy. Get it?"

"Good thing you're smart, 'cause you'd never make it as a comedian," he said, smiling. "You need money for the trip?"

"No. I've got some in savings."

"But you haven't been working this last week, and that's because of me. Let me give you some money."

"Dad, please," I signaled the end of the discussion by standing up to kiss him goodbye. Then I headed to the bathroom where I peed, washed up, and read his prescription bottles. When I came out, Dad was off the bed and nowhere to be seen. Probably in the other bathroom. His aging prostate sprung to action at the mere reference to a toilet. I stopped in the kitchen for one of Aunt Millie's cookies, and he surprised me coming in the front door.

"What are you doing?" I said in a semi-accusatory tone.

"Checking your oil."

"Jack checks the oil for me. And apparently seven other fluids. You don't need to worry about it. Besides, I'm not sure you're even supposed to be checking things until the doctor gives the all clear."

"Doctor my ass. I'm fine to check my daughter's oil whenever I damn well please. Be safe in Florida. Don't give those boys too much trouble." He wrapped me in a firm hug that felt almost back to his full strength.

Ha. Me give *them* trouble? He was clueless if he thought that was the dynamic. Back in the Jeep, I put the window down and waved as I pulled onto the street. Dad was standing on the porch, adhering to the Barlow tradition of sending the driver off. Hardly mattered how far you were going. I'd had as many as three people send me off from a front porch when I was running up to Cumquat's for a gallon of milk. The store is like two miles away, and I was back in literally fifteen minutes. What can I say? Barlows like to send people off with a dramatic wave.

Once Dad was out of the rearview, I checked my travel mug to see if there was one last sip of coffee left.

In the cup holder I spied money, and that wasn't a place I ever left money. When I reached for it, I counted five one-hundred dollar bills. Dad wasn't checking my oil; he was sneaking me money! Why did every man in my life have to be so cantankerous?

I parked Sandi around back at the bakery and texted Dad a thank you for the money. He texted me an I love you. Jamming my phone in my pocket, I headed inside to say hey to Mercedes and Uncle Dave. Since Uncle Dave was around, I didn't dare mention the Florida trip. The Turner boys may have a special seamless form of communication that allowed them to perpetrate an elaborate ruse like the big travel-plan charade from this morning, but Mercedes and I did not have that skill. Rather, Mercedes did not. While she could definitely keep a secret, she couldn't control her enthusiasm when receiving the secret, so if there was classified intelligence to be discussed, it had to be shared covertly. This visit was really just to see how things were coming along with her new job as bakery manager.

"*Lilita!*" She greeted me. "We are so close to opening Poppy's." I gave her a big happy hug, delighted to see she was genuinely loving the role. I never would've thought of this solution if her dad hadn't connected the dots for me. And it was a good thing, because the applicants I had rounded up all had starring roles in the Theater of the Absurd.

"Will you have a coffee?" She asked.

"Please."

She went around the case to fetch me a cup. It was so strange to be waited on in the bakery. Strange and wonderful. Now this is the kind of relationship I could have with the bakery. Handing me the cup, I went to the coffee cart and poured the steaming java. Funny that even though Poppy's was officially still closed to the public, she had brewed coffee and filled the black insulated self-serve dispenser. I'm sure it was for Uncle Dave, but you had to appreciate the girl's attention to detail.

I saw she had fresh daisies on the tables, too. As Uncle Dave and Dad trained Mercedes on their systems—and that word should go in air quotes, by the way—I'm sure it was Dad who told her she had one choice and one choice only for the little bud vases on the tables. Daisies. It was a floral tribute to my late mama, and it was very important to Dad.

"How's it going?" I asked as she fixed her own coffee.

"Oh, it's so exciting!"

"Where's Uncle Dave?"

"*Tio* is at the grocery picking up a few things to get us by until the deliveries resume."

"Are y'all lighting the ovens?"

"Only for a few small quantities of popular items to re-establish some of the orders from local businesses. We probably won't be opened for people until Saturday a week."

"That's great!" I beamed. "And so fast!"

"I wanted to open this Saturday, but not all of the systems were in place." She smiled and we shared a laugh about the ways of dads and uncles.

"If Uncle Dave isn't here right now, I have news," I said, building in a few seconds to let the anticipation brew. "Storie and I are going to Key West tomorrow to talk with the detectives about the murder victim."

Mercedes crossed herself and muttered something that sounded like "the Father, Son, and the Holy Ghost," but could have been "Don't bother, hon, I'm having toast." She grabbed my hand and squeezed as she squealed, "That poor girl can go home! Finally!"

"Yes," I agreed, knowing she was talking about Luanne. "Finally." The weight of what Storie and I were about to do settled on me. We were embarking on the serious business of giving a murdered woman her identity back. It was an assignment most people thankfully never encountered, but if you did, I imagined it was something that would be part of your fiber forever after.

"The bad news is, Jack and Joe have wormed their way into the trip."

She shook her head slowly, "You were kidding yourself if you thought he wasn't going, *Lilita*. He's got you this close; you think he's letting you out of his sight now?"

"Really? What about school? I'm starting school in a few weeks. What's he expect to do then?"

"I wouldn't ask him that if I were you," she said and made a funny expression with her eyes. "Don't ask a question when you don't really want the answer."

Our hush-hush conversation was interrupted when Uncle Dave burst through the back door with a booming, "Lilybug!"

"Place looks great, Uncle Dave," I said, standing to hug him, "like you could open tomorrow."

"Soon," he agreed. "Mercedes is doing a bang-up job." He moved over to give her a side squeeze.

The three of us chatted for a minute more as I finished the coffee in my cup then said goodbye. I knew they were busy, and I had a few things to do as well. I was very proud of my ability to pack quick and light. Not everyone could pull that off. But besides packing for the trip, I needed to do a few other things, one of which was possibly declaring a major at UVA. Not formally, of course. I was going on year three and was still undecided. So, I didn't plan to rush into anything, that was sure as Sugar Pops.

However, all this business with the Doe Network and the mysteries surrounding those unidentified bodies had my attention. I was drawn to it. I wasn't any good at it, as evidenced by my inability to figure out whatever Miss Delphine was up to, but I had to assume that's what the degree would do, give me the skills and training necessary.

I couldn't see myself as a beat cop, so that ruled out detective since I was fairly certain you had to start with the one to get to the other. There were different fields though. What about forensic science? Pathologist, odontologist, toxicologist? Maybe a little heavy on science. Blood spatter analyst? Still, a lot with the science. What about a crime scene photographer? I snap pictures on my phone all the time. What about the person who reconstructs the faces from skeletal remains like on the Doe Network? I wondered if there were any jobs with similar non-profits—media specialist or something. What about private investigator? Bounty hunter? Hello, Stephanie Plum…I could go into business for myself. Maybe get a degree in criminal justice, just as the fall back.

Once I got to the apartment, I threw some clothes and toiletries in a carry-on suitcase, then I sat down to cull career options in the criminal science arena. I found out that UVA offered a summer certificate program, but they didn't have a Bachelor's. I sorta felt compelled to finish what I had started at a four-year institution. I don't know why the degree was so important to me. Many, many people I knew and respected did not have a college education and were still managing good jobs with growth potential—Jack, Joe, and Mercedes to name three.

My dad didn't go to college, but my mama had. Is that why I picked UVA? Because she graduated there? I mean, I didn't go down knowing I wanted to major in a program they were known for. True, I loved Charlottesville, but maybe that was because it was two hours away from Marshall. As I sifted through it, I reached for the green and white tile and rubbed my thumb back and forth across the slippery side. I concentrated on the white *V* shape and thought hard about why I was drawn to the University of Virginia. Abstractly, I wondered if the *V* on the tile was connected in any way to the *V* in UVA.

The *cha-ching* from my phone made me jump wildly. Not because the noise startled me, but because I was acutely aware of my new ability to conjure people. I was stricken by the possibility that I had just summoned my dead mama who was now texting me. I stayed paralyzed there on the couch until the reminder *cha-ching* sounded a few seconds later, letting me know that there was an unchecked message. Holding my breath, I grabbed the phone. It was Jack. Thank the Boogyman of Barcelona. I read his message: "Can Storie meet us at Miss Delphine's or do we need to pick her up in Culpeper."

"Probably here is fine, but I'll check."

Cha-ching: "Thanks babe."

I didn't even register any true upsetment over the term of endearment, because I was so relieved that I wasn't being contacted by a dead person. But I still felt like I needed to set him straight.

"Don't call me babe."

Cha-ching: "Ok sugar."

I responded with an emoji of a skull and crossbones then texted Storie.

The final plan was that she would come here on Thursday morning, and the boys would pick us up at half past eight. After that detour, I peed, got comfortable, and went back to the catch-22 of college. That's what it was, wasn't it? Unsure, I googled catch-22 on dictionary.com and read *a frustrating situation in which one is trapped by contradictory regulations or conditions.* Not satisfied, I read on—*Figuratively, a "catch-22" is any absurd arrangement that puts a person in a double bind: for example, a person can't get a job without experience, but can't get experience without a job.* That fit. I couldn't earn a degree without a program, and the program wasn't available where the degree was being sought. Alright, maybe not a full-blown 22, but a 21…or 20 at the very least. Two things became clear. First, I needed to read the book *Catch-22,* and second, I needed to look at other schools, ones that offered a degree in something like criminal justice. I imagined I would be able to transfer most of my credits; I had taken a lot of the basic courses to cover things like English and math. Oh, and I had gotten through an intermediate level geology course, not because I was an especially talented scientist, but because Rocks for Jocks was so easy, even the football team could pass.

Tucking this intriguing new idea away for the time being, I decided to get ready for bed. The twisting, turning online searches had chewed up the remainder of the late afternoon and gotten me well into the evening. While it was unusually early for bed, I decided to call it a day. I had a feeling Jack would bang on my door way before the appointed time, so I tried to mentally prepare myself for being jarred awake yet again.

I had no problem dozing off in the beginning. However, it was with the vigor of an insomniac that I barreled through the wee hours wide awake, rolling from my right side over to my left and back again. When you can't sleep, I read you're supposed to get out of bed and do a physical task, like folding laundry, until you get drowsy. I laughed at the thought of Miss Delphine finding me down in her laundry room at stupid-thirty in the morning. I could see her standing there in her granny robe, hair set in a mangle of those antique pink curlers, the ones with the bristles, holding a frying pan or a shot gun, one.

As I debated the chore of getting out of bed to test the theory of the physical task, I heard the unmistakable sound of gravel being disturbed in the driveway. *Jack*. A little surge of enthusiasm surprised me, and I bounded right out of the bed. It was still more dark than light outside when I peeled the curtain back. That was definitely his truck. I stepped onto my little porch and watched him walk toward the chicken community with a scoop of scratch. He looked oddly at ease surrounded by the few who gathered around his feet. It made me wonder if there were chickens in his future.

Once he had delivered the meal, he turned back toward the garage but stopped walking when he noticed me. We were stuck in a frozen moment until I raised my hand in greeting and he smiled and returned the gesture. When he resumed his route to drop off the scooper, he kept his eyes on me until I disappeared from his line of sight. Thank the Lord for dim light and distance, because otherwise I would have been on eye-contact overload right about now.

I waited for him on the porch, and he took the stairs two at a time. Putting his arms around me, he said, "You know, if we were a couple, we'd have time for a quickie before you had to get ready," he paused, then added mischievously, "maybe two."

"It amuses me what you're using as a selling point," I said, trying (although not very hard) to push him away.

"I go with my strengths, girl," he teased, squashing my half-hearted effort to be in control and folding his arms more securely.

"Too bad your strength wasn't bringing me coffee." I shook my head sadly and added, "then you might've had something to bargain with."

He tightened his squeeze a fraction, and before releasing he whispered, "Be right back."

I realized then that the coffee was still in the truck. Of course he wouldn't have brought it out, not before he fed the chickens.

When he got back to the porch, he set the cups on the wide arm of an Adirondack chair   and   resumed his hug. "You were saying?"

I stayed silent because, well, I had already lost. He kept going, though. "That's right," he said, drawing it out like something important was slowly coming back to him. "You were saying it's too bad I didn't have a bargaining chip, like…coffee…was it? So, here's your coffee. Now where do we stand on that quickie?"

"You know, Jack, you can't be goofing around like this on the trip."

"Sure I can," he said solemnly. "You told Storie I was your boyfriend, remember?"

Unfortunately, I did remember. We had gone to talk with her family, and when she appeared, basically back from the dead, I was so flustered I introduced Jack as my boyfriend. I regretted it, but it was done, and I doubted I'd be able to erase it from the fireproof lockbox that was his memory. I changed direction, "Well, Joe doesn't need to know."

"Oh, he already knows."

I was uncomfortable with the way he said it. "He knows what exactly?"

"He knows I'm falling for you."

At that declaration, I Houdinied my way out of his arms. Too bad he was standing between me and the stairs, otherwise I could have made a break for it. However, the only avenue opened to me was the door into the apartment, which I took.

Inside I threw my energy into pacing with a purpose. Jack put the coffees on the table, then quietly closed the door behind us. Leaning against it, tracking my movements, he didn't try to impede me in any way, which was smart. He probably sensed the pending eruption, although, strangely, he didn't take cover.

I pulled up just as I rounded the kitchen table. Was he tricking me into having a conversation I told him I didn't want to have until, um, never? He was trying to *trick* me into talking about it. Well, if he *thought* he could get his way by bulldozing me into a corner, he had another *think* coming.

"I told you, Jack Turner, I will have this conversation at a time I find more to my liking, and for your information, this," I swept my left arm out for emphasis, "is not it."

He made one small nod of his head, acknowledging that he was busted. "I thought I had ya." He chuckled. "Just don't want you to forget that we still need to talk about it."

"I'm taking a shower," I said by way of ending it on my terms. As I turned my back on him, I added loudly, "No, I don't need any help. And no, you cannot watch."

Then I banged the bathroom door closed to take back a few ounces of authority.

When I came out, I was a little more relaxed. He was on the couch scrolling through something on his phone and drinking coffee from a mug. There was a second steaming mug on the low table in front of him. He had put it close to him, so I'd have to invade his personal space to get to it. When I did, he wrapped his large hand around my wrist, careful not to tip the cup, and looked at me with his lopsided grin. "Still friends?" he asked.

"Yes. But at the rate you're going, that's all we'll ever be."

"Well, technically, we've blown past *friends*. Now we're friends who slept together three times."

I looked at him flatly. "You're doing it again," I pointed out.

"I know," he said. Using his other hand, he gently took the coffee and put it back down. Without releasing my wrist, he stood and kissed the side of my head. Call it the surge of emotion from before the shower, call it pheromones, call it being a wackadoodle, but for whatever reason, I turned my lips toward his lips and kissed him full on the mouth.

Just then someone banged on the door loud enough to scare the crisscrosses off a peanut butter cookie, which was weird, since the one who typically did the banging was standing in front of me.

"Joe," Jack said softly.

"Don't you think we should let him in?"

"He can stand out there 'til Friday a week for all I care."

The next bang was accompanied by the words, "Y'all decent in there?" And it was shouted in a manner that seemed louder than necessary.

Oh, for the love of the lunar landing. To Jack I said, "Will you get that, please?"

Before he went to the door, he said, "I'm not gonna rock your boat in Florida, but when we get back, I'd like to pick up where we just left off."

"The door," I said, using my head to indicate the one I wanted him to open. He just smiled and let his brother in.

"What were y'all doing in here?" Joe asked Jack as he came in. The two of them pretty well filled the small space. Joe was maybe one inch taller, and Jack's shoulders were maybe one inch wider, but the differences were so subtle that some people even mistook them for twins. Dropping a bag of food on the table, Joe came over to greet me with the traditional hug. Then to be an even bigger pain in the ass, he whispered a racy comment for which I had no response.

"Joe, can you please not draw attention to anything on this trip?"

"What would I draw attention to?"

"Anything. Any single thing at all." My voice was heavy with exasperation. "Just don't."

"I won't have time to draw attention, not with all the fishin'." He smiled.

Right. The fishing. If I could just get them to confess to their real involvement…carefully I laid out a tripwire as I asked innocently, "What are y'all fishin' for again?"

"We're fishin' for permit," he said, not looking up, "and maybe a bonefish. Although that's better in the spring."

Bonefish? Now I was convinced they were making stuff up.

Reading my mind, Jack said, "It's a real fish. A lot like you, matter of fact—easy to spook but fights like hell when you get it hooked." Joe laughed. I did not.

Picking up the previous thread, Joe said, "Girl, I won't take it too far in front of strangers. I reserve this just for family." And in that moment, I realized where Jack got his trademark wink. Joe did it, too. How could I have missed that all these years?

I took a brief time out for a bite of breakfast and pulled a burrito out of the sack Joe brought. Deciding to steer the conversation to a less sensitive area, I asked Joe, "Which puppy did you decide on?"

"The brown and white one," he said, peeling back the tinfoil so he could get to the second half of his burrito. "I was told I didn't have a choice." He glanced at Jack.

I smiled because I liked that he accepted my recommendation. "Have you given him a name yet?"

"Waitin' on you, Sunshine."

Another smile. "I've got a list."

"I'd be devastated if you didn't. Let's hear 'em."

"Bumper, Bungee, Boomer, and Dodge."

"Do these names have any significance?" he wanted to know.

Duh, I wanted to say, but I dressed it up a bit. "Yes."

"Care to elaborate?"

"Bumper because you always liked the bumper cars at the county fair. Bungee because y'all did that crazy bungee jump off that really tall bridge. Boomer because you run a boom truck at Republic Building Supply. And Dodge because you drive a pickup."

He absorbed these four ideas as he chewed then swallowed. Finally, he pointed out, "I drive a Ford, not a Dodge."

"I know that," I said, although in reality I did not know that. "But *Ford*...is a stupid name for a dog." I gave a little huff, just enough to help him understand I thought he was borderline hopeless *and* give credence to my claim that I knew the make of his truck.

Joe looked at me hard like he was trying to figure something out. Finally, he asked, "Did you eat a lot of lead paint as a kid?"

"No. Were you dropped on your head as a kid?"

"Plenty of times," he said with a big laugh. "Probably why I'm able to tune you out." He gave me a playful jab in the shoulder and said, "I like Boomer. Boomer it is."

I respected both the Turner boys for their ability to make a quick decision, no agonizing over outcomes the way I did. Most of the time they never had to walk it back either, because they generally made the right choice first time around. But if they ever had to do something over, it was just the natural high-tide-low-tide cycle of the planet. They definitely were not plagued by the woulda-coulda-shoulda syndrome.

Just then, there was a light rap on the door, "Lily? It's Storie."

I looked at Jack and Joe who were grinning like two donkeys celebrating Eat Your Weight In Hay Day, realized any more instructions or reminders would be pointless, and turned to open the door.

"Storie," I greeted her with a big smile. I really was happy to see her, in part because she would help dilute the testosterone buildup in the room. Joe reached his hand out and introduced himself. Jack, who had formally met her the other day, came over and gave her a quick hug. Then for the first time that morning we pulled out chairs and sat down at the kitchen table. There were three burritos left in the bag, and Joe explained that one was veggie while the other two had breakfast meat. I thought it was nice he considered the possibility that she might be a vegetarian when he placed the order, and I was curious to find out if she was.

She thanked him and took the veggie, which in itself didn't prove she was vegetarian, maybe she just didn't like ham or sausage. There were four cups of coffee in a cardboard tray, and I passed one to her. The coffees were all black, so I got up to get cream and a handful of sugar packets which she accepted.

As she tore the paper packets she said, "It's so funny that our trip to the Keys lines up with y'all's fishing trip." She smiled at Joe and Jack.

Feeling compelled to provide full disclosure, I shook my head no. "Storie, don't buy into their nonsense. These two dim wits commandeered our trip, probably because they're so backwards they don't realize that two independent adults can take care of themselves. They were not planning a fishing trip this weekend. That's just a cover story they fabricated to follow us. And by follow, I mean annoy the shit out of." Even though I was talking to her, I was looking at the two racketeers in question.

Storie seemed shocked that there would be any deception involved. Jack and Joe looked at each other and shrugged. "I don't know what she's talking about," Joe said, shaking his head. "We've been planning this trip all summer," Jack added. He was an exceptionally smooth liar, an odd skill for a truthful person to possess.

I rolled my eyes and got up to get my coffee from the living room. I collected Jack's cup as well, and when I came back around the couch, he caught my attention and seared me with a stare that would have shaken the bolts out of a barn door. Afraid someone would notice, I moved directly over to the microwave and busied myself warming the coffee.

When I returned to the table, I didn't know if the moment had passed or not, because I refused to look at him. Instead, I laughed at something Joe said and played on that to ask Storie a follow-up question. Thankfully, breakfast was finished in short order, and we started to gather ourselves to head to the airport. That was a relief because I didn't know how much more maneuvering I could manage in order to steer clear of ol' blue eyes who was sitting directly across from me.

We took Joe's truck because the backseat was bigger than Jack's. We put the luggage in the bed, where Joe used a board to wall it off. It looked as if any one of the bags could easily fling out once we hit fifty-five miles per hour, but I decided not to obsess over it. In the big picture, losing my luggage on the highway was less of a problem than figuring out how to proceed with Jack or IDing a murder victim. Besides, this didn't seem like the first time Joe transported items using the board method, so he probably knew whether or not the bags were secure.

In the back seat, I took a second to breathe and get my head right. Maybe it didn't unfold exactly as I expected, but it was still an adventure. I'd never been to Key West, but I'd always heard it was a one-of-a kind town with an eclectic vibe. Plus, the weather looked good for a long weekend. I reminded myself that Storie came first. I needed to make sure she felt supported during this sad process. Once I committed to that, I was opened to whatever else awaited.

Chapter 7

Traveling with the Turner brothers was like traveling with the Coyote and the Roadrunner. There was a constant flow of needless commotion and cartoonish jokes. I knew this, having tagged along on a good many of their family vacations. Jack's parents always let the boys take a friend when they were little, and Jack always picked me. To reciprocate, Dad let Jack come with us on our trips. Then, as we got older, Jack and I traveled with groups of friends which periodically included Joe. Once, in high school, a bunch of us made a road trip to one of Jack's really big baseball games in Norfolk. He pitched a no-hitter. That was a fun weekend. Like I said, plenty of experience traveling with these two. So, as this particular comedy began to unfold, Storie was way more enamored than me.

First, the seats Joe had booked were toward the front of the plane, and Storie and I were more in the middle. Jack convinced Joe they were too far away and, in order to effectively entertain us, the two had to switch their front-of-the-plane seats for middle-of-the-plane seats. They artfully accomplished this switcheroo by flirting their way through three flight attendants (two females and a male) and the senior couple sitting across the aisle from us. Joe took the window seat in their new row so Jack could lean across the aisle and insert himself in our conversation. It was a small blessing that the plane was only four seats across, otherwise he would've worked his way smack dab in between us.

Discount carriers weren't known for leg room and seeing the boys squished into their seats, sweet Storie benevolently offered to trade places with Jack.

"Storie," he said with deep affection, "I liked you before, but you just became my favorite human being."

Storie squeezed my arm and gave me a knowing look. She seemed to notice my resignation which must have filled the air like honeysuckle in summer. "It's just for the flight down. We'll be on our own again when we get to the Keys," she said, referring to the fishing trip she still believed to be legit. Then she gave me a devious smile which appealed to me on several levels.

After making herself comfortable in the new seat, Joe's gift of gab kicked in, and the two struck up a conversation that had the potential to last the remainder of the flight. Over on my side of the aisle, with the frosty look I gave JT, it was somewhat surprising that the pilot didn't need to make an emergency landing in order to de-ice the plane.

"What?" he asked innocently. "It's just for the leg room."

"If you didn't like the leg room on this plane, maybe you should have taken a different flight," I said, articulating my words for emphasis. "Better yet, maybe y'all should've stayed home. There's plenty of leg room in your truck." I finished with less articulation but more snark.

"Plenty of leg room" he nodded his agreement, "but no Lily this weekend." Smiling sadly, he played the role of the martyr to perfection and added, "Don't worry about me. I'll be okay." He drew attention to his long legs as he angled them toward me in order to sneak a few more inches of space. Picking up my hand, he kissed my fingers and smiled a sugary grin.

I threw him a salty glare as I freed my hand and dug for my earbuds. My plan was to ignore the albatross sitting in the seat next to mine. As soon as I found a good playlist, I leaned back and shut my eyes. Approximately ten notes into the first song, the albatross lightly tugged the cord, and the right earbud popped out.

"What do you want?" There was a measured amount of frustration in my tone, but my eyes stayed closed.

"What are you taking this semester?"

I opened my eyes and turned my head. "What?"

"Your classes. You haven't told me what you're taking."

It came out of left field, that was true. However, it wasn't about our relationship, or the thing that I specifically didn't want to talk about—*SexwithJack*. Oh, what the hell. Shrugging, I threw the albatross a herring and proceeded to rattle off my schedule. He already knew about the psych class, since we picked that text book up when we went to Charlottesville last week. I walked him through the rest of my courses, adding interesting details and answering his questions along the way. At the end, I figured it couldn't hurt to get some feedback on my brilliant new idea, and I tossed it out. "I think I might major in criminal justice."

Jack, witness to the long parade of majors I had considered and rejected, raised an eyebrow at this one. "Criminal justice. You *are* weirdly interested in crime scenes. Does UVA have a program?"

"That's the problem. They don't offer an undergraduate degree. There's a certificate program I could take, but it's over the summer, and…"

Jack finished my sentence, "And it's not a degree."

"Right."

"Tech has a criminal justice program. Emmitt Hayden got his degree there. So did Crystal Jones for that matter."

Both of those people graduated a few years ahead of us. Crystal grew up using a double name, Crystal Bethany. Over time it was abbreviated to Crystal Beth, which, as it turned out, was unfortunately similar to crystal meth. Her parents probably never saw that coming. I think she picked Tech because it was three and a half hours from home, and she could effectively drop the Beth and rename herself plain Crystal. In another odd drug-related twist, if I wasn't mistaken, she now worked for the DEA.

"You know where else has a criminal justice degree?"

Jack's eyes showed a pleasant amount of curiosity. "Shenandoah," I said.

"Shenandoah University," he repeated, nodding. He looked over at me. "Isn't Winchester a little close to home for you?"

"Possibly." I heard jail cells slamming closed just thinking about the campus that was no more than a forty-five-minute drive, and that was if you were stuck behind a school bus on a back road. "But with Dad not a hundred percent, maybe I should be a little closer."

Jack considered it, probably trying to sort out how much he could say here without alienating me.

"I think your dad's outta the woods, Lily," he said, reassuringly. "But, if this is one of those things that's gonna drive you half nuts because you can't let go of it, you could always stay living at Miss Delphine's and commute to Shenandoah."

Part of me wanted to jump to the accusation that he was supporting a move back to Marshall to advance his own cause, but, for the love of fast food drive-thrus, I couldn't make it stick. It was written all over his face. We were not talking about me and Jack right now; we were talking about my dad and my future.

As he watched me, I observed in him the authenticity of an innocent man whose gesture was pure. Finally, I asked, "You think Miss Delphine would extend my lease?"

"Don't see why not. I mean, she's getting such quality chicken care out of the arrangement," he poked me with his elbow. I smiled at his smirk and offered him one ear bud which he accepted before commandeering the phone to pick a country-themed play list. We listened in silence, and I liked the way it felt to have our upper arms smashed together. But of course that was between me and my own mixed-up self.

* * *

A smaller plane puddle-jumped us from Miami to Key West with what a flight attendant assured me was a modest amount of turbulence. Come to find out, a modest amount was all it took to get me fully rattled. Between bumps, I watched my travel companions. Storie seemed to have retreated into some metaphysical state of bliss, while Jack and Joe remained completely unaware of any disturbance.

This plane was so small, there was only one seat on each side of the aisle. Jack was across from me, and although he was catty corner to Joe, the two of them ran their mouths nonstop. I think they were talking about motorcycles. No…masonry. Mashed potatoes? I really wasn't paying attention, and I can't say I was all that enthralled with the conversation to begin with. At the next big jolt, I plastered myself to my seat and held on, trying hard to borrow some of Storie's serenity. Bracing for another round of bounces, I felt Jack pry my death grip off the clunky armrest so I could squeeze his hand instead. While I accepted the offer, I did not look at him. At the moment I didn't have the capacity for any cutesy save-the-day rescue flirtation he might have in mind.

We finally landed, got our bags plane side, and headed through the muggy outside air into the freezing inside air. Storie and I had this spontaneous approach to Key West which involved grabbing an Uber and driving around until we saw a hotel we liked. Jack and Joe were one hundred eighty degrees opposite that. They had the idea of picking up the rental car they had pre-arranged and going to the hotel where they had already made a reservation for two rooms, one for me and Storie, and the other for them.

"So much for spontaneity," I mused, as we threw our bags in the hatchback. Then it occurred to me that

I might have them on a technicality. "And by the way, if y'all are fishing, where are your fishing poles."

"Rods," Jack said.

"Who the hell is Rod?" I asked.

"Fishing rods," he said, "not fishing poles."

Storie laughed as I gazed at Jack and slowly shook my head.

"Where are the things with which you will be fishing? Seems like you'd bring your fishing *rods* on a fishing *trip*."

"Nah," Joe chimed in, "the guide'll have 'em."

This was the first I'd heard about a guide, and I privately acknowledged that these two birdbrains may actually be fishing. Although I steadfastly refused to believe this trip was planned more than twenty-four hours ago.

"What guide?" I asked, piling into the backseat as Joe held the door.

"We arranged to fish with a guide," Joe explained. "Sometimes it makes sense to get with someone who knows more about a certain thing than you do."

Jack nodded from the front passenger side, then said in my direction, "You should try it sometime."

"Fishing?" I was slightly dismayed. If he thought I should try fishing, he clearly hadn't been paying attention for the last sixteen years of our friendship.

"It applies to fishing," he said, "but it's a good strategy for life in general."

I had the sneaking feeling we were nearing a conversation about his involvement in something I was doing, and not liking the inference, I hopscotched right on outta there.

"So where are y'all meeting up with this guide?" I asked.

Jack chuckled to himself before answering my question. "At the pier. Y'all can drop us in the morning, then use the car to do your running around."

Joe added, "If you're caught up in something and can't get back when the boat comes in, we'll catch a ride to the hotel and meet up later."

Before Storie could get concerned about taking advantage of the two who so generously rented the vehicle, I blurted, "Okay. We'll text at the end of the day if it looks like we can't get by the docks. What time does the boat come back?"

"Around six I'd say," Joe answered. "Send her the info," he directed Jack.

Jack made a few taps and swipes on his phone.

Cha-ching. I glanced at my screen and saw the address of the pier and name of the boat.

"*Touching Bottoms*? Are you serious?"

"It's a flats boat. They push a pole along the bottom to make it move," Joe explained. When that pithy explanation didn't change the look on my face, he said, "Darlin', I didn't name the boat, but I gotta say, I do like the name." I could see him smiling in the rear view mirror.

"I've got a good name…how 'bout *Damn Inappropriate?*" I leaned up from my spot in the back seat and gave his head a little push forward. Not hard, just enough to make my point.

* * *

After googling cheap accommodations the other day, the picture in my mind was of a long, low, faded, rusting hotel constructed of a pinkish building material made from some type of shell-composite. I knew a hotel like this wouldn't win any awards for the best place I ever stayed, but my tolerance for shabby was overshadowed by my desire for cheap.

In sharp contrast, the building I was facing as we pulled into the small lot didn't match up at all. Two levels, and the walkway along the second story was framed by an intricate wrought iron railing. I could practically see Earnest Hemingway standing there, one hand in his pocket the other on the rail, looking down into a hidden courtyard that was tucked behind palms and decorated with a collage of bright hibiscus blossoms. The whole place was steeped in charm and obviously well cared for. And it looked expensive. It also looked haunted. But the haunted part could have surfaced based on my awareness that locals of the Florida Keys boasted a rich history of resident spirits. To avoid making an outright declaration that I did not want to bunk with a ghost,

I said, "This place looks pricey. Y'all know we're on a budget back here, right?"

Jack fielded that one, and, in my opinion, did it a little too energetically. "It's off season. The rate is $79 a night. Same as what you'd pay for a roach motel on the water." Not giving me time to refute it, he added another layer, "Besides, Joe's reclaiming this place."

"Reclaiming?" Storie asked. "What does that mean?"

Joe twisted the mirror so he could see her. "I brought the love of my life here once."

I remembered the love of Joe's life. Paige Dorsey. It was the kind of situation where you wanted to hate her for breaking his heart, but you couldn't. She was a good person whose only crime was being true to herself, and I believed she loved Joe, just not as much as she loved France.

All through high school, Paige wanted desperately to move to France and make cheese. For real. Cheese. When she graduated, she offered to take a year before she did anything drastic, like jumping continents. She called it a test period; she wanted to see if the calling would fade into oblivion. Six months later, Joe realized Paige's desire was only getting stronger, so he gallantly bowed out. When she was awarded that hoity-toity apprenticeship opportunity, Joe even flew over to help get her settled as a newly installed ex-pat. I heard she has gone on to do some stunning things in the world of cheese. Who could

blame the girl for following her heart? Regardless, it was all very sad. I wondered if the scar left from Paige was the reason Joe hadn't been with one girlfriend for longer than a couple months at a stretch.

Storie gently laid a hand on Joe's arm. "I'm so sorry," she said softly.

"Thank you, Storie," he patted her hand. "I survived, and I'm a better man for it."

My comment was slightly less sympathetic. "We're staying at an inn where you brought Paige...*why*?" I wanted to know.

"So he can let go," Jack explained as he slapped his brother on the top of the shoulder, grabbing hold for an extra dose of brotherly love. "When a memory blocks you from ever enjoying a place again, you have to reclaim it. Take back the place. Plaster a new memory over top the old one."

I raised my eyebrows as I digested that. I was honored to be included in the making of Joe's powerful new memory, but the emotional pinnings of this trip just kept getting more intense—Storie's murdered friend... Joe's lost love...what was next? Jack losing an eye in a fish hook accident? Or maybe me getting myself tossed off the second story balcony by the resident ghost?

Joe turned off the ignition, signaling to everyone that we were getting out of the car. Thinking it might behoove me to check into any ghostly goings-on at this particular establishment, I mentally committed to an online search once we got settled. For now, I drummed up some fake courage as I waited for Joe to open my door. Working my way out of the vehicle, my own loud gasp caught me off guard, and I stumbled backwards, landing on the seat I had just vacated. I hadn't seen a ghost, mind you, but a chicken—a chicken who looked an awful lot like McNugget.

"What the hell is that chicken doing here?"

"Oh, right," Jack nodded. He had gotten out, but leaned back in to add, "There's a chicken culture down here."

"You are freakin' kidding me," I panted. Ghosts. Chickens. *Come on!* The little sliver of enjoyment I was prepared to shave off this adventure for my own personal gratification was quickly disintegrating.

I thought my farm girl was about to bust a gut laughing over on her side of the back seat. "You don't…" she started, paused to laugh, and tried again. "You don't like chickens?" she asked, catching her breath.

"Sure. If they're the primary ingredient in a recipe. Otherwise, no." I gave the sentence some finality with a sharp shake of my head. Then, with a semi-apologetic tone, I said, "Sorry, everybody. I'm fine, just wasn't expecting her, that's all." I'm not sure if I actually thought it was my nemesis or not. Getting myself together, I exited the car a second time, pushed my foot toward the offender in the hopes she would back off, and quickly walked around to the rear of the car. Joe and Jack exchanged a thought via their private line of communication but to their credit said nothing.

We passed three more birds on our way into the quaint lobby. Apparently, I had no choice but to make my peace with the presence of chickens in this town. They were almost everywhere—strolling across the street, lounging under cars, pecking casually as they meandered through shady patches of grass. There were even magnets and postcards on display at the front desk featuring what else but the town's mascot. The alarm bells roused my inner Stephanie Plum, who shook her head no, making me wonder if I needed to dump her for a more supportive figment.

While Jack checked in, Joe ushered me and Storie to a set of French doors at the far end of the lobby. This foiled my plan to overhear the price of the rooms and verify my suspicion that Jack was charging us the family rate and not the true off-season rate. I dropped the thought when I saw what Joe was pointing at—a gorgeous swimming pool straight out of *The Great Gatsby*.

"Now that's a pool," I said with admiration, the mermaid in me coming alive with anticipation. I'd be lying if I said the thought of me and Storie skinny dipping last year didn't cross my mind.

"It's gorgeous," she said and walked, or rather, floated through the doors, leaving her suitcase where it stood. Through the glass, Joe and I watched her lift her long skirt, sink gracefully down on the edge, and let her feet dangle in the water. I stood, transfixed by the beauty of her lithesome movements, until she looked up with a serene smile and motioned for us to join her. Her magic drew me through the door the way a stream draws a petal through a little rapid, and I left my bag beside hers, at Joe's feet. Kicking off my flip flops, I dropped down, minus her elegance, and put my feet in the water with a splash. We slipped into a conversation about nothing special that took me very far away, and I had forgotten all about the boys, until they appeared with four beers in plastic cups and no luggage.

"I need to get my suitcase," I said, jumping up.

"Relax," Jack said, handing me, then Storie, a beer. "We put the bags in the rooms."

I touched my cup to his, then Joe's, then when I sat down again and put my feet back in the water, Storie's. Jack and Joe took seats on comfortable-looking chaise lounges with heavy cushions in a tropical print, and they put their beers on a little table in between.

The four of us sat quietly, enjoying the peace of the place, and I realized I was in the process of blending two groups of people who knew me in different capacities. It didn't always work. Over the past couple years at

UVA, I'd brought home a few friends or an occasional boyfriend for a long weekend, and I gave them what I referred to as the chocolate milk test. There were two classifications—the powdered stuff or the syrup. Most of the time, no matter how much I stirred, the powdered mixture never completely dissolved. Dusty clumps clung to the sides of the glass, and a residue of undissolved product collected at the bottom. Once in a blue moon, however, the two parts came together easily, the way chocolate syrup blends in milk. Sure, you still had to stir like crazy, but if you put in a little effort, you almost couldn't tell.

As I reflected, I realized I wasn't working to bring this group together. They had taken to each other without me stirring. I had a brand-new category on my hands—store bought chocolate milk. No work to mix it, and it was the highest level of satisfaction where flavor was concerned.

Looking around at the group who had achieved this new high standard of chocolate milk-ness, I saw that Storie was hypnotized by the water. Joe's head was back and his eyes were closed, but I could tell he wasn't sleeping. When I glanced over at Jack, I was immediately tangled in his web of eye contact. The corners of his mouth curved in the tiniest fraction of a smile, and I got the feeling he had been watching me for more than a few seconds. Oh, for the love of mowed grass patterns in the outfield. I gave him a glare, like he was in danger of breaking some unwritten yet mutually agreed upon rule. He raised his eyebrows, like he'd be willing to discuss my complaint right here, right now. Knowing I wouldn't win this challenge, I aborted by asking Storie if she was hungry.

"Starving," she admitted. "You?"

"I am," I said. "Joe?"

"If you're waitin' on me, you're killin' time," he said, eyes still closed.

Although I already knew Jack's answer, I asked anyway, "You hungry, Jack?"

"Yes ma'am," he said, smiling.

Storie added, "After we eat, would y'all mind driving over to the spot where Luanne's body was found?"

Joe opened his eyes. "We can go there now if you want," he told her.

She thought about it but said, "No. I think I'd like another beer first."

I totally got that. I could use another beer myself.

"We'll do whatever, Storie," Jack added, "it's up to you."

"Thanks." She smiled, but it wasn't the happiest smile I had ever seen. "Let's eat."

Chapter 8

Joe got up and gathered the cups. There was a little stand tucked behind a row of lush elephant ears, and he put the cups in what appeared to be a recycle receptacle. On his way out, he kicked what looked like a tennis ball and it rolled under a fern. There weren't any tennis courts around, so I thought that was odd. Then I spotted another. It took me a second to figure it out. They weren't tennis balls at all, but juvenile coconuts that had fallen from a palm tree. Great. How long before I turned an ankle on one of those booby traps?

No one needed anything from the rooms, so we walked through the lobby together toward the car. Jack stood by the driver's side and held his hand up while Joe fished the keys out of his pocket and tossed them over. Jack snagged the key ring with zero effort. Both boys had played ball at a prestigious level through high school, for a while on the same team, and I always admired how easily they threw and caught things between themselves. It was a mystery to someone like me, who had no ball awareness whatsoever.

"I know what these two like," Jack said, referring to me and Joe, "but what do you eat, Storie?"

"I'm not that picky. I can find something I'd be happy with on any menu."

I just wanted to bless her heart for being so easy going. "Do you eat meat?" I asked, still needing resolution on the vegetarian question from this morning.

"I do," she said. "And I love seafood."

Joe seemed delighted with that answer. "You're in luck, girl. I got just the place." He gave Jack directions as we made our way through the town. I enjoyed the scenery along the drive. Even though it wasn't the busy season, there were people milling around; most looked like they lived here. I based that on the fact I didn't see a single tourist tattoo—sunburn lines. Dead giveaway you're from out of town.

The restaurant Joe picked was nondescript on the outside and could have easily been mistaken for an industrial warehouse or maybe a bowling alley if you didn't know. The sign, procured from some discount sign depot, stated plainly in block letters, Ollie's Fish Camp. To underscore the most important word, a kitschy purple neon fish blinked on and off in the window by the door. Cars lined the front of the building, always a good indication.

If I thought the owners were saving the decorations for inside, I was wrong. Plank floors, simple wooden tables and benches, butcher paper table clothes. No fish nets hanging from the ceiling. No thatch to impersonate a tiki bar. No big taxidermied fish on the wall. No fun Christmas lights haphazardly strung about. Out back there was a screened-in deck section, where the crowd thinned because of the heat. Since none of us minded, that's where we landed. You could smell salt in the air, something my freshwater nostrils were not accustomed to.

We ordered a pitcher of beer, which was delivered alongside a heaping basket of hushpuppies. When the waitress dropped it off, we gave her our dinner orders. Assuming the role of designated driver, Joe poured one for everybody but himself. I imagined those two would alternate while we were down here, letting me and Storie do the drinking for the most part. There was a benefit to them crashing our trip after all, if you wanted to look at it that way.

When the beers were poured, Joe lifted his sweet tea in a toast, and said simply, "To Luanne."

With varying degrees of softness, we each murmured her name and touched the heavy glasses together. Storie was sitting beside me, so I couldn't see her face directly. I suspected there was a pained expression, and I reached my arm around her shoulder and gave a tender squeeze.

"Where was she found?" Joe asked, quietly.

"She was tangled up in a mangrove…" she paused, looking for a word, "thicket? Forest?"

"I've heard 'em called mangrove *islands,*" Joe offered. She nodded.

"Best I can tell, they're all over the place. This section was near something known as the salt ponds. On a map, it might be called The Mangroves. I guess there are some abandoned buildings around, you know, before you get into the swampy part…"

She trailed off, and I wondered if she was picturing the murder, or trying not to. I was moved that she had done all that digging. From the profile on the Doe Network, I remembered the body being found near a swamp, but I hadn't looked into it further than that.

I watched Jack watching her. He was trained to deal with people in crisis, although training didn't account for all of it. His mama was an emergency room nurse before she quit to start her family. Both boys seemed to inherit her grace under fire. Across the table I saw in Joe a reflection of what I was watching in Jack. They were alert and attentive, their movements were controlled, as if designed to bring about a sense of well-being. There was a reassuring quality in their voices. On the flip side, I didn't bring a lot to the table—excitable, impulsive, hasty. I wondered abstractly if I'd be able to comfort Storie on my own tomorrow, when Jack and Joe were fishing.

She looked up as if something had just occurred to her. "I don't know how to get there."

"Not a problem," Jack offered. "We'll plug it into GPS. This place is big on ecotourism, I'm sure it'll come right up."

"If not," Joe added, "we'll ask around."

She started to nod acceptance, but before her chin dropped down for the second time, a waitress popped out with a tray piled high, passing plates and complimenting us on our incredible choices. The timing gods were on our side tonight. In another thirty seconds, we would've been sucked into the crime that had been committed. Instead, we were sucked into a feeding frenzy that any shiver of sharks could respect.

Storie and I gorged ourselves on boiled shrimp. The cocktail sauce was easily the best I'd ever tasted. Not too sweet and just enough bite. I could've eaten it straight from the bowl with a spoon. Joe had grouper. And Jack attacked the fisherman's sampler—a platter filled with two of everything the ocean had to offer.

The food and beer blunted the sharp line of why we were here. Coach Clevenger, my wood shop teacher in seventh grade, would have called that *breaking the edge*. Why Coach Clevenger made an invisible appearance now was hard to explain. Although…I did choose the wooden fish that year for my semester project. Fish decoration… seafood restaurant in need of some decorations.

"…Lily?"

That was an easy jump. And did I remember right? Did Coach Clevenger ding me on that project because I didn't *break the edge*. There ya go. Here we were breaking the edge with the beer and the food. That's how it fit together. *Hmph.* I bet ol' Ollie of Ollie's Fish Camp would proudly display my wooden fish, sharp edge and all. Hell. My dad hung the damn thing in the bakery for years, and it was far harder to justify a wooden fish as an accessory in a flower-themed bakery.

"Lily?"

I looked up to see the three of them waiting expectantly, and I wasn't one hundred percent certain which one had called my name. Wow. How long had I been swirling around in that daydream? A little while, if you based it on the fact that a new pitcher of beer had been delivered and glasses filled.

"What?" I said, as Coach Clevenger disappeared through the screen door and down the steps toward the inlet.

"We're talking about most embarrassing, slash, awkward moments," Joe filled me in. "You want to kick it off?"

"Yeah," Jack added, rooting around in his platter, "but the wait staff wants to turn this table before midnight, so you'll need to limit yourself to like your top fifty or sixty." He smiled and popped a fried oyster in his mouth.

"Are you implying that my embarrassing moments outnumber yours?" I asked, layering in a note of disbelief as I said it.

"I'm sorry," he said. "I didn't mean to imply that. I meant to state it outright."

"Oh, damn," Joe said, shaking his head. "Here we go."

Storie just ate and snickered.

"I have an idea," Joe offered. "Y'all each get to tell one story on the other. Make it good, and keep it clean."

Jack didn't need one short minute to scroll through his database. No. He laid it down like you'd lay down a royal flush at the high rollers' table in Atlantic City. "When we were in middle school, our two families went to the beach together," he said, looking at Storie while he rocked his thumb back and forth between him and me to illustrate which two families he meant. He had indeed picked a moment with a high embarrassment quotient, and I predicted he would embellish it for maximum effect.

"There were nine of us—me and Joe, mom and dad, Lily and her dad, Aunt Millie, Uncle Dave, and Lily's close friend, Mercedes. Everyone had scattered during the day, but in the evening we all came back together. With that many people, we booked a reservation for dinner, but even then, they couldn't seat us right away, so Dad, George, and Dave went over for a beer at the bar while we waited. When the waitress came to escort us to the table, Millie sent Lily to go get those three." Jack paused, took a big swallow of beer and then marched on, "Lily sidled up to her dad, put an arm around him, and said, 'Come on, big man, let's go.' Only, it wasn't her dad…" Jack couldn't keep it together any longer. He started laughing, and it took him a few seconds to collect himself in order to finish narrating the events. "It was a complete stranger who was there with his wife. The wife thought our Lily of the Valley was the dude's mistress. We tried to straighten it out, but that woman wasn't having it." He paused to laugh long and deep. "I'm pretty sure Home Wrecker over here single-handedly destroyed that marriage."

Joe howled as he relived the tale, and Storie laughed until a tear ran down her cheek.

I had to admit, Jack told a funny anecdote; I laughed along with them. "In my defense," I started to explain, "that guy was wearing a bright green sweater the exact same color as Dad's." It appeared no one was interested in the ramifications of the Kelly green coincidence, and the laughter rolled on.

Joe finally slowed to a quiet chuckle and gestured toward me. "Your go, Lily," he said, smiling.

I had a really good one to tell on Jack, but it involved a sneeze followed by a fart during the Lord's Prayer at a funeral. I shied away from introducing anything relating to funerals, ergo death, ergo decapitated friends from high school, because I didn't want to let go of the silliness we were all enjoying, so I fell back on another embarrassing moment of JT's. It was funny, but to truly appreciate it, you had to have witnessed it in person.

"Jack was helping me move into the dorm on campus my freshman year," I paused, giving him time to pull up the memory in question. He smiled and tipped his head, acknowledging that he knew what was coming. "The floor had recently been mopped, and there was a sign warning people to be careful because it was slippery. Jack, in his typical smart ass approach to everything, pretended to slip on the floor, skating around and bobbling the box he was carrying. In the process, he accidentally knocked into the sign and sent it skidding across the polished concrete. But that's not the truly embarrassing part."

Storie, laughing, asked, "No?"

"She's right," Jack said as Joe started laughing. He already knew the rest of it.

"No," I confirmed. "The embarrassing part was when the sign crashed into the fire alarm at a weird angle with just enough force to set it off." Jack nodded, big stupid grin on his face, almost like he was proud of it.

To my delight, Storie's laugh rang out.

I continued to lay it on thick. "The entire dorm was evacuated, and Jack, the aspiring fire fighter, had to own up to his involvement when campus security came tearing in, followed by the Charlottesville fire department." Now even he was laughing.

"Everyone was locked out of the dorm for a good hour and a half," he bragged.

Joe, still enjoying my rendition, rationed out the last of the beer from the second pitcher. "I don't know," he said, shaking his head. "I think we may have a tie on our hands. Storie, you wanna call it?

"Let's see…destroying a marriage or disrupting college move-in day. They're both epic. I think it's a draw" she said, siding with Joe.

In spite of my competitive nature and burning need to one-up Jack, I was happy with a tie. Maybe that was because I knew the accolades would have been mine if I had whipped out the award-winning funeral fart story.

Carrying out the theme, Joe prodded Storie to take a turn. She jumped right in, feeling enough at ease to share her own stupidity with us. Her embarrassing moment was vehicle related. Before she understood the ins and outs of four-wheel drive, she kept a pickup in four low for miles, on a regular road, going much faster than you're supposed to go. The two mechanics at the table had a ball with that one. Me, I didn't see the big whoop, but then again, I'd never even used the four-wheel drive function in Sandi-with-an-i, so what would you expect?

"It's a funny story," Joe explained patiently, "because you can cook the engine that way."

"I didn't…thankfully," Storie interjected, smiling. "But my dad doesn't let me forget that I could've."

After they finished ribbing her, Jack said, "You're up, Joe."

Joe laced his fingers and pushed his arms forward, palms out, preparing to deliver a story-telling display that would have dazzled the Bard himself. "It was the summer before my senior year in high school," he started.

"I thought you'd go with driver's ed," Jack interrupted, referring to another admirable moment, "but this one is way better!"

"Dude, you can't top this one," he said to Jack. Then to us, he clarified, "This really falls more on the side of awkward versus embarrassing, but I'll admit to a degree of embarrassment. I worked for a little ol' rental company in Warrenton that summer. Buckingham Rentals. On the truck there was a picture of two knights jousting, and the line read *Everything but the lance.* You could get chairs, tables, dance floors, event-related items, stuff like that. They weren't huge, but they had steady work for a kid with a strong back, and the money was good, so I supplemented my hours at the garage by driving deliveries. After a while, the jobs all started to look the same. Lugging folding chairs in, lugging folding chairs out."

Jack tipped his head forward, chin to chest, showing how he felt about it. He had some experience, having been recruited by Joe periodically when the crew was short on labor that summer.

"This Friday was looking good, though. It was an easy job, so I was by myself, nice day, nice drive, all that. Plus, it was way out, so I wouldn't have time for a second run, which meant I'd get to knock off a little early. I should've known something was up when the dispatcher smirked as she handed me the ticket, but I was busy thinking about how I'd spend that free time at the end of the day. I had a little trouble finding the place, which was in an area I didn't know well. It had some generic-sounding name, and no one was really familiar with it, so I figured it was brand spankin' new. Oh, wait…I mean nude. Brand spankin' *nude*."

"What?" Storie asked.

"Nude," Joe said loudly. "As in naked. It was a freakin' nudist colony."

The laughter from our table caught the attention of a few other guests and the wait staff, who were soon hooting at his Oscar-worthy performance as if they themselves had been along on the delivery.

"As I pulled into the drive, a woman came out to take receipt of the delivery. I'd say late forties, early fifties. She was carrying a clip board and wearing nothing but tube socks and sneakers." His expression was priceless, and it took us all a moment before we could catch a breath.

"Tube socks?" I asked, wondering at her motive. "If you're a nudist, and I'm not against it by any means, why wouldn't you eliminate the socks altogether? That would give you the option of wearing flip flops, which have to be far more nudist friendly."

"You know," said Joe, "that's exactly what I was thinking as I discussed the logistics of where she wanted the chairs and tables…that the tube socks really detract from the fact that a naked middle-aged woman was standing in a field conducting a business transaction." He laughed.

"What did you say?" Storie wondered.

"As little as possible." He smiled and repeated, "As little as possible."

During the frivolity, Jack had discreetly handed the waitress a credit card before she brought the check, squashing the part of the meal where me and Storie would try to pay. Storie was uncomfortable and continued to root around in her bag for cash, which he refused. I knew where she was coming from, and I felt for her, but there was nothing I could do to change this outcome. The Turner boys paid for their dates. Period. And in that blink, I, too, became uncomfortable. Jack always paid when he and I ate anywhere, but my phrase *paid for their dates* brought the dilemma of dating squarely back to my frontal lobe.

I looked over at him to find he was looking over at me. Smiling. Could he have guessed what I was thinking? Impossible. But the look in his eye warned me off, and I fell back on my go to.

"Wanna come to the bathroom, Storie?"

"Great idea."

"Back in a sec, boys," I said as we headed indoors.

When we came out of the restroom marked "Mermaids," we practically ran into the guys who were chewing on toothpicks and waiting on us near the entrance. I assumed the men's room was labeled "Mermen" but I didn't have time to verify that. Joe had already opened the door and was holding it for us, so I exited, thanking him as I passed. Outside I turned and thanked Jack for dinner.

"My pleasure," he said, then whispered, "mermaid." He dropped a heavy arm around my shoulder as we walked to the car. I debated how much energy I should put into extracting myself. I might prove a point but end up drawing unwanted attention in the process. While I noodled it, he fished the keys from his pocket and flung them, without looking, over his head toward the two people walking behind, accompanied by a single word. "Yo."

Fearing for Storie, I yelled, "Duck!" and wiggled myself free in time to see Joe snatch the keys mid-air while keeping his eyes on me the whole time.

"Don't duck, Storie," he told her, calmly, and to me he said, "Who do you think you're dealing with? Amateurs?"

I took the opportunity to engage with Joe, less because I wanted to engage and more because I wanted to increase the distance between me and Jack. "Amateurs, no," I said. "Idiots, yes."

Chapter 9

It was pretty easy to get to The Mangroves. We took a road which might have been the closest thing to a backroad that Key West had to offer. Leaning forward so I could see the map on GPS, I noticed we were parallel to the airport for a bit. Glancing out the window, I saw runway lights, but no planes and no other cars. It was definitely sparsely traveled, making it feel desolate this time of night.

As the idea of an actual murder scene closed in on me, Joe eased our rental up to a chain link gate that blocked the road. The road continued, but we couldn't see to the end, even though the headlights were still on and pointing that direction. We all got out.

"If they lock the gate in the evening," Storie mused, running her fingers over the padlock on the fence "the, um…crime…couldn't have taken place at night, then. Could it?"

"Well," Joe was choosing his words the way you'd pick those little brown hitch-hikers off your pant legs if you went through a patch of tall weeds, patiently and one at a time. "I believe there are ways to get back there that don't involve this road." I assumed that was his way of gently saying that the murder could have happened at night. For clarity, he added, "I think there's a neighborhood that butts up to these woods."

I wanted to ask him how he knew about this neighborhood, but I was trying to stay tethered to the moment. This was about Luanne, not about my own dumb curiosity regarding Joe's bizarre knowledge of places he'd been to once before. I did what I could to offer additional insight, being careful not to go too far. "Do you think they could've walked in, after the gate was locked?"

"Could've," Joe nodded.

"Where do you pick up the path?" Jack asked his brother.

"If we circle around over yonder," he said, pointing vaguely with his chin toward the expanse of twisting trees, "I imagine we'd see it." I guessed he was implying that the houses were on the other side of the dense mangrove forest.

"Storie," Jack said as he approached the front fender where she was leaning, "you wanna swing over and see where the path starts?"

She didn't falter even a hair; her answer was plain and steady. "Yes," she said. I was impressed with her definitive approach.

"Okay." Jack moved to open my door, while Joe got hers.

In the vehicle, I noticed Joe was no longer operating from GPS. He made a curt three-point turn, drove back down the road, and wound us over to a nice community. The neighborhood didn't have blocks but streets that pointed in the same direction all ending at a canal. Alternating between the streets were miniature canals, like fingers reaching back to the main waterway, I guessed so people living in the houses could park their boats out back. I repeated the pattern to myself as we cruised past—street, houses, canal, houses, street, houses, canal, houses, street, houses, can-...nope... mangroves. That was the end of the pattern; we were at the back side of the neighborhood. The final row of houses ran adjacent to the tree line. Unless you turned left, onto the last street in the neighborhood, the road we were on dead-ended in a little spur where Joe parked us. We were tucked just out of sight of the closest homes, although you could see us if you were coming straight down the main road.

When we got out, I noticed some beer cans and incidental litter, indicating someone may have partied down here and apparently did not practice the Leave No

Trace philosophy. Gauging the likelihood that this was a drinking and/or drugging destination that saw steady traffic, I began searching for clues as to how recently the spot had been used. Were those old beer cans, or had they been discarded last night? Meanwhile, Jack and Joe were walking along the edge of the trees, checking for an entry point.

"It's over here," Jack said, once he found what he was looking for.

Oh for the love of a business plan at a lemonade stand. We weren't going in there. Not now. Not at night. Were we?

I weighed my arguments—1) hard to walk with all the roots, 2) looked spooky in the dark, 3) could be an alligator habitat—and decided to go with the most life threatening of the three. Alligators.

"I don't think we should go in there now. I saw a picture on the internet of a swamp at night, and there were like 40 sets of eyeballs glowing in the dark." To clear up any misunderstanding, I added, "Alligators."

"There aren't any gators down here," Joe told me. "Too salty." He looked back over his shoulder so he could see my face before he continued, "Maybe an occasional saltwater croc, but no gators." He smiled, knowing he had just stirred the pot, and turned back around.

Before I could initiate the launch sequence for a nervous breakdown, Jack said, "Relax. You're not going in." Looking more at me than at Storie, he added, "Neither of y'all has the right shoes on."

Thank you, Jesus, for flip flops, I whispered in my head, and by the look on her face, Storie had just whispered the same sentiment regarding the kicky sandals she was wearing.

Jack went back to the car, opened the hatch, and dug around in the handy dandy backpack he always kept at arm's length. It only took a second for him to find a headlamp. He tossed his ball cap beside the pack and pulled the elastic strap over his messy black hair. So as not to shine it directly in anyone's eyes, he waited before clicking on the beam. He was thoughtful that way.

Turning toward the woods, he hit the switch, and like a couple of coal miners heading into a dark tunnel, he and Joe walked back to the place in the trees where people had obviously entered. The foliage was so dense, it wasn't long before the light nearly disappeared. Storie looked nervously at me, almost as if she was expecting the news that they discovered yet another dead body, so I took her hand and squeezed it. "Don't worry," I assured her. Or maybe I was trying to assure myself. Hard to say.

Fixated on the entry point through which fifty percent of our group had disappeared, we didn't notice the bicycles roll up behind us.

"Hey, hey, pretty ladies," one guy blurted. In addition to being unexpected, the greeting was a cross between cheery and husky, lending a distinct creepiness to his tone.

I jumped. Storie squeaked. We both jerked around to find ourselves face-to-bicycle-tire with two people our age. The people were shaggy; the bikes were beat up.

"We got company, Jimbo" the creepster said to his buddy. They were odd, and the oddness made them borderline threatening.

Before Jimbo could answer, I *sensed* more than *saw* the presence of two tall Turner boys behind us.

"Y'all come to party?" Joe asked, as if he had, in fact, come to party.

The one called Jimbo, who kind of sounded like maybe he had already started partying, said, "Yeah, buddy! Y'all in? You got any weed?"

"Nah. We're lookin' for some, but we kinda have a private party goin' on," Jack said, staking his territory by putting his hands on my shoulders, "if ya know what I mean." He said this part softly, as he put his mouth to my hair, and I wasn't sure if he meant it for me or for them. I suspected he winked at our two new friends. I played along, leaning back into Jack, in an oozy, wanna-get-naked way, which would cause problems for me later, but I did appreciate the construction of a good cover story.

"Oh, hell yes!" The one who was not Jimbo said, smiling and nodding at the suggestion that sex was to be had. "Landy'll be here any minute."

Landy? What kind of name was *Landy?* I wondered if Landy was a male or a female, and if that was a first name, last name, or code name. But what had my attention more than the nomenclature was the introduction of pot into the equation. Neither Joe nor Jack smoked, having jobs that drug tested, but last summer when we first met, Storie and I both enjoyed a little communal marijuana, so I knew she smoked. I used to partake more regularly than I did now. Back in the day, Mercedes and I probably smoked once a week. Now our high of choice was hard work and achievement. I laughed in my head. *That* was funny! Hard work and achievement, my ass. It was tequila. Smiling outwardly at my own private joke, I wondered briefly why my funniest material always surfaced at the most inopportune times. Hard to get credit for a funny line when you couldn't share it with the public at large.

Standing around, shooting the breeze with Jimbo and Not Jimbo as if we had nothing better to do than wait on Landy so we could make a drug deal, I perceived Storie's growing angst. Were these two people somehow involved in what happened here last February? Did they know anything?

Wanting to be of assistance, I took over. "These mangrove swamps are crazy," I said, plying my Virginia-girl innocence where the native ecology was concerned. "Anybody ever get lost in there and never come out?"

Not Jimbo perked right up. He might have been my kindred spirit where the dark and dismal was concerned. "Plenty a times," he nodded. "Remember when those kids got lost in there?" he asked Jimbo.

"Nah," Jimbo said. "Cops found those kids. They were just goofin' around. How 'bout the suicides, though?"

Not Jimbo nodded his head solemnly. "Yeah, it was looking like that suicide forest in Japan there for a while. You know the one?"

I did know the one. The Aokigahara.

Not Jimbo added, "There are like a thousand suicides a year out there in Japan."

Closer to a hundred, although I didn't correct him. Maybe he was using hyperbole to express that it was a big number that carried a lot of misery. While I knew that most of the deaths were the result of hangings or drug overdoses, I didn't know how many lives had been lost, total, in that forest. It was my understanding that the authorities no longer made numbers public in an attempt to discourage people who might be considering it. It was still way too big a number for suicides at a given location. Kind of like the Golden Gate Bridge, which had claimed the lives of around sixteen hundred people.

Unusual that I knew that. I owed my collection of suicide facts to a sorrowful time when a friend from school took his life. I found myself reading about places that drew those who were hurting and lost. Another friend from that time who was even closer to the classmate that died, actually tattooed the number for the Suicide Prevention Lifeline on her wrist as a tribute to him and a permanent outreach to others.

Using the platform I just built, Storie chimed in with a very nice segue leading us from suicide to murder, "What about murders? Anybody ever find a dead body out there?"

"Absolutely," Jimbo affirmed. "There was a guy who got shot in the head. Kayakers found him."

Not Jimbo said, "Oh, yeah, yeah." Looking over at his friend, he went on. "I forgot all about him. I was thinking 'bout that chick." He turned back toward us and finished. "We called her Valentine Girl, because she was discovered day before Valentine's. Girl's head was cut clean off. Hands too. Never found 'em either. The head or the hands."

I knew without looking that Storie had clenched. From the corner of my eye, I saw Jack adjust his position ever so slightly. It was barely an inch but more than enough to remind her we were all here for her and we could leave at any time. We waited to see what she wanted to do.

"Who found her?" She asked, soldiering on.

"Some guy." Not Jimbo shook his head slowly.

Jimbo said, "For a while they thought he was the guy who did it. Couldn't make anything stick, though."

Not Jimbo seized on the opportunity to reveal even more dirt. "Jimbo here got pulled in for questioning, too."

Jimbo nodded sagely. "I did. I know the Keys, and I am, let's say, on a frequent flier list of sorts, maintained by the Po-Po. Those two things together make me a prime suspect when shit goes sideways."

"That blows," Joe declared, in defense of his new friend. "They should be using a guy like you to help, not falsely accusing you of murder." I could practically see the confidante relationship sprouting from where I was standing.

Jimbo reached a fist out which Joe casually bumped. "Truth, man," Jimbo said. "Truth."

"So, who do you think did it?" Storie asked.

"I got some theories," he said, leading us away from any involvement he may or may not have had. "Tourist. Trucker. Drifter. There was even a group of gypsies came through 'bout that time."

"Yeah, yeah, those gypsies were wankers. Showed up right before the body was found. Disappeared not long after. Never saw 'em again." Not Jimbo thought for a bit, then added, "Always seemed funny to me about that guy living out there in the woods, though. The guy who *found* her. Kind of a crackpot." He gave the word *found* a special treatment so that it implied *murdered* and I hoped Storie didn't pick up on it.

"Crackpot?" Jack repeated.

"Yeah, yeah. Supposed to be real smart. Keeps to himself. Moves around. Weirdo."

I wondered to myself what about being smart, minding your business, or moving made you weird, but before I took it too far, another bike rolled up. As soon as the person on it realized we were not known to him, he turned around and lit out of there quick-like.

Jimbo yelled, "Landy, they're cool."

Landy yelled back, "I smell bacon!" Then he was gone.

"You cops?" Not Jimbo asked, growing suspicious.

"Nah, man," Joe said, "just some folks from Virginia down for the fishin'."

Jimbo nodded. "Thought so. I can spot a cop fifty miles in any direction."

I stopped myself from pointing out that fifty miles in three of the four directions would be smack in the middle of the deep blue ocean. I guessed it was possible for a cop to be running around out there in a boat or maybe a catamaran. Instead of worrying about how the police force established itself at sea, I shifted gears and privately lamented the loss of the joint we could have procured from Scardey Landy.

"Where was the girl found," Joe asked, pulling me back to the case. "Out yonder?" He motioned his head toward the woods behind us.

"Nah," Jimbo said. "Other side of the salt pond. You can get there from here, but it'd be a helluva lotta trouble and a long way on foot."

"How'd that guy find her?" I asked.

"Said he was *camping* back there." And again, he made the word he emphasized sound as if it was a poor replacement for *murdering*.

"But he's the one that took it to the cops, right?" Joe asked.

"Yeah, yeah."

Feeling like Storie might be getting saturated, I nudged Jack, signaling for him to find a way to wrap it up. He received the message. "Dudes, we're gonna roll," he said, wringing every drop of enjoyment out of the cover story as he put his arms around my middle and crushed my backside to his frontside, daring me to wiggle out. Joe chuckled at my predicament, offered no help, but took Storie's hand in a show of true friendship. I figured he was counting on the fact that Jimbo and Not Jimbo were operating under some kind of chemical influence and would misread the gesture, which they did. Hooting their approval, they turned their bikes around and sped off to find the wayward Landy.

"Y'all wanna head back?" Storie asked.

"If you're ready," I said, "sure." I knew the boys would do whatever.

"I think I'm ready." To me she said, "We'll get more information when we talk to the police tomorrow."

* * *

Back at the hotel, Storie pulled out her swim suit. I asked if she wanted company, but she politely declined. "Maybe in a few minutes," she said, and slipped into the bathroom to change.

I'd probably want to be alone with my thoughts, too, if I just dredged up details about the murder of one of my friends. Wait. Who was I kidding? I'd seek out the one person I always sought out in times of stress. Jack. And with Storie in the bathroom, I proceeded to do just that.

Exiting the room, I looked to the right. The breezeway made a ninety-degree turn, following the building, and where the railing came together to make the corner there was a little nook with a couple of rocking chairs and a low table. Joe was sitting by himself, looking down at the garden below. I wondered if he was watching a figment of Paige.

"Hey girl," he said when he saw me.

"Hey boy," I greeted him back. "Jack inside?"

"He is."

When I knocked lightly, the door swung opened. I stepped into the arms of my old and good friend who wrapped me in a hug with no funny business.

"Y'all gonna be okay tomorrow?" He asked when I finally moved away and plopped down on the closest bed.

"I suppose so," I replied. "Not gonna be much fun, though."

"Oh, I guarantee it won't be any fun."

"Storie's washing her blues away in the pool," I added.

"Joe's wrestling with his ghosts, too," he said.

"Kinda makes me sad, all this sadness."

"That's your tender heart talking," he pointed out, smiling.

"What? Your he-man heart doesn't have room for melancholy?"

"Oh, it has room," he admitted, "I just try not to give it voice." He walked over to the bed and sat down beside me, conscious not to crowd, and continued. "I worked an accident once where we pulled a family of three out of a mangled car. The family dog didn't make it. It hit me hard for some reason, but I had to put that aside so I could work on saving the parents and the kid. We did. We saved all three. When I got home, though, I cried like a fat kid who dropped his Ho-Ho in the baby pool." He waited a beat, then concluded, "So my heart has room for sadness, when I'm alone."

"You cried for the dog?" I asked, touched by this revelation.

"Yeah. The dog. And for the people, for what they'd go through when they found out their dog died. But the dog for sure. His name was Goalie."

"Goldie," I repeated.

"Goalie," he said, a little louder. "Like hockey."

"Oh. Goalie. How did you find out his name?"

"I read his tag."

"Maybe you should name your puppy Goalie," I said. True, I was relinquishing my appointed position as the giver of names, but this felt important.

"No," Jack said. "I want you to name the puppy." He reached over and tucked a loose strand of hair behind my ear.

Ok. Not fair plunking my heartstrings like that and then making a hair-tuck gesture. I leaned in, hovering near his lips for the longest time. He didn't make the move I thought he would, so I ended up doing it. The kiss was delicate, like the trail a hermit crab leaves in the sand, and gone before I really even knew it was there. Caught up in his heat, I laid my hand on his cheek. "I don't think we should do this now," I said.

"I agree," he breathed, before leaning in for another delicate kiss, which made a swirl of sparks rise through me as though a log had been tossed on a campfire.

"I can't seem to stop," I whispered, mesmerized by the sparks but completely oblivious to the flames consuming the log.

"Me either," he confessed, stealing another one.

There was a knock on the door, and for the second time that day, Joe interrupted what had the potential of turning into *SexwithJack*.

"Come in," Jack grunted. Joe opened the door, big smile on his face, enjoying his role as The Interrupter. I envisioned him wearing a cape, with a heavy zigzagging line down the center, which is how I thought a graphic designer would represent an interruption. The cape was dark gray. The zigzag, for some reason, was hot pink.

"Come on, y'all," he snorted. "Let's go dunk Storie in the pool."

Liking that idea a lot, I went next door to change and didn't wait for those two before heading downstairs. The garden area was lit with a shimmering purple haze. I searched the ground for the source of the light, but all I saw were some of those miniature coconuts scattered haphazardly around the edge of the patio, taunting me and all the other klutzy people who might be tricked into turning an ankle.

The area was completely empty save for Storie. I sat down on the edge of the pool, flashing back to the last time I went swimming. It was a few days ago at the lake, with Jack. He had convinced me to jump off the dock instead of sitting and schootching the way I always went in. Shortly thereafter, he and I were naked in the back of his pickup. After recollecting that steamy little memory, I found it hard to catch my breath. I really needed to get some composure before Jack came down and saw me on the struggle bus, which would only serve to reinforce the fact that he had some kind of hold on me.

Plunking into the pool, I had high hopes the transition from air to water would pull me out of that daydreamy slush. Unfortunately, the water merely acted as a conduit, transporting me from one daydream to another. I slipped below the surface to wet my hair and reemerged into the magical memory of the skinny-dipping incident last summer with Storie. Unfortunately, it wasn't the right time for reliving that, just like it wasn't the right time for those sweet little kisses upstairs in Jack's room. If only there was a way to divert.

The universe acknowledged my plea and sent two yahoos who bounded into the peaceful garden and threw themselves, cannonball style, into the pool. The resulting tsunami swamped us and soaked the deck on the far side. Thank you, Universe.

Chapter 10

I woke to a light but persistent knocking on the door and realized it might have been going on for a while. I may even have been hearing it in my subconscious before I came into full awareness. Glancing at my phone for the time, a text from Jack greeted me, and I put two and two together. Storie was still asleep, but she jerked under the sheet and made a snuffle noise at the sound of me cracking the door.

"Let's go for a drive," Jack said by way of a good morning.

I probably would've declined had the invitation come from anyone else, but I rubbed my eyes and sleepily agreed. "Okay. Let me brush my teeth first." Dragon breath was such a downer when the possibility of a kiss existed. Wait a minute! Wait a stinkin' minute! I warned myself to stop playing with matches until I

163

figured out whether I wanted to burn something down. I knew he thought it would all work out, and this was unfolding the way it was supposed to, but I wasn't so sure. I puzzled over that, staring at my reflection in the mirror while simultaneously trying to avoid making eye contact with myself. Not only was it difficult, it may have been physically impossible, but I worked at it for a while as I stood there brushing my teeth. Then I actually tried to convince myself it was a matter of good oral hygiene and that brushing my teeth had nothing to do with kissing Jack Turner. Being fairly good at deceit, both in deceiving and being deceived, I accepted the oral hygiene alibi and moved on with my life.

Jamming the usual stuff into the pockets of my shorts, I headed out the door. Jack was waiting in the rocking chair, looking at his phone.

He glanced up when he heard the door click closed. "I hear this town has some kickass Cuban coffee. Let's go find it."

If I knew Jack, we were not headed to a reputable commercial chain. Nope. He prided himself on bucking the establishment to uncover those crazy hole-in-the-wall kinds of places hidden down three side streets. The ones that don't have wi-fi and look closed even when they're open. You know the ones. Places where the servers eye-ball you funny when you come in because you're not one of the regulars from that block. And, if

I knew Jack, we were in for one helluva good cup of coffee.

Prepping me for this expedition, he shared the research he dug up online. "They call it *café con leche*. It's espresso with steamed milk."

"You?" I asked, shaking my head in disbelief. We had made it to the parking lot, and he opened my door. "Mr. Drink It Black For A Week And You'll Never Go Back?"

"I know," he conceded, bowing his head, "it's heresy. But when in Rome…" He paused.

"…drink coffee like a Cuban?" I filled in the blank.

"Yeah, baby. Drink the coffee and eat the bread."

"There's bread?" If the coffee topic hadn't done it, now he had every ounce of my carb-loving attention.

Smiling as he reeled me in, "It's called *pan Cubano*, Cuban bread. Toasted. With butter. And get this, you dunk it in the coffee."

"Do the Cubans put sugar in their coffee?" Because here's where I'd have to break with my newfound love of Cuban culture.

"Traditionally, not much," he said. "Not the way *you* put sugar in coffee, anyway. I think because it was rationed heavily back in the day, just like the coffee, which is why they used the tiny cups. That's also why it has a distinct bitterness. They added toasted chickpeas to stretch it."

"You got all this online while I brushed my teeth?"

"Yeah. It took you forever." He cut his eyes at me from behind the wheel like he was onto something, and I had a hunch it was only a short hop from there to some lecherous lesbian fantasy about me and Storie. I could barely believe I was thinking it, but an imagined lesbian fantasy was better than him knowing I had been standing in front of a mirror, talking myself out of kissing him. Needing to push us past those two equally tricky speculations, I found a way to move around it.

"What's this coffee shop called?" I asked. That was the secret with Jack. Gently lob a food-related idea in his direction. Bake sale for the band boosters. Roadside vendor in Aruba selling tamarind-flavored snow cones. Nutritional benefits of venison. Parking problems for the food trucks in Washington, DC. Didn't matter the content of the idea or even if he cared for a particular food item. You could draw him in like a purple Crayon to a clean white wall. He couldn't resist. The man enjoyed him some food.

"And," I continued down this road, "you'll be satisfied with toast and coffee for breakfast? That'll last you 'til lunch?"

"Oh, hell no," he said. "Consider this a post bedtime snack, or breakfast hors d'oeuvres, if you will. The joint is called Nine-O."

"The numbers nine and zero? Ninety? Is that the address?"

"No." Jack shook his head. "They say it's the last good cup of coffee for ninety miles."

"I don't get it," I confessed.

"That's how far it is to Cuba." He waited then added, "Ninety miles."

We drove in a checkerboard pattern for a few minutes as he advanced on the Nine-O. The streets were mostly quiet, indicating that it was too early to be roaming around. The place, tucked on a corner, was way underwhelming. In a town that boasted some of the most spectacular color combinations ever conceived, the owners of Nine-O landed on a bland dirty beige. As an afterthought, the name was painted on the plate glass window in bright green letters. Through the window we could see it was dark inside. He checked his phone and reported, "They'll be open any minute." Then, interpreting the signs of a parked car and a closed coffee shop as his opportunity to hold my hand, he picked it up and applied enough pressure to show me he didn't intend to let go. What a surprise.

I rolled my head to the side, raised my eyebrows at him, and gave a friendly little glare. He didn't pick up the message I was laying down, but before I could spell it out for him, he beat me to the podium. "I didn't just want coffee," he said, rubbing a thumb over my knuckles.

"If you wanted sex, I'm not sure you thought it through," I said and gestured to the guy in the shop unlocking the front door feet away from where we had parked.

"You're right." He made like he was about to start the car again but stopped when he got the overreaction from me he was hoping for, a combination of wild hand flapping and an uncontrolled lunge toward the ignition. Laughing deeply, he grabbed my hand again.

"Just so there's no misunderstanding, I do want sex." I refused to let him look me in the eye, and I didn't even have to be that evasive since we were sitting side by side. I just stayed straight, looking out the windshield.

With a history of saying too much at times like this, I clammed up. Non-participation was definitely the way to go here. Seeing my tactic, he prodded a little, "What about you?"

"Me? I'm just here for the *café con leche*," I said, giving a subtle little test pull to see if I could get my hand back. I could not.

"Splashing around in the pool last night had me thinking about the lake. I want to talk about it, Lily."

"I thought we agreed to table it until we got back home."

"I thought we agreed to talk about it before we left."

"So," I mused, "we appear to have what is known as a breakdown in communication."

"No," he disagreed. "That would suggest that some line of communication currently exists."

"We're talking about it. Hell, we're talking about it right now," I said, with a little more nervousness than I wanted to reveal.

"No, we're not," again with the disagreement. "We're talking about two people *not* talking about something."

"Well, Jack," I searched around for some kind of pitch fork or flaming torch I could push in his direction to make him take a step back. However, there was nothing readily available, or else I was too flustered to see it. The rest of my sentence shriveled and dropped to the ground like a dried-up palm frond.

"Okay. Okay. If I can't talk to you, can I at least kiss you?"

I swallowed hard, only vaguely vindicated that I had taken the steps necessary to practice good oral hygiene back at the hotel. "If I said no, would you do it anyway?"

"If you say no, I won't do it. I promise you, Lily, you have the power."

"I don't think I do."

"Is that because maybe you *want* to kiss me?"

I stayed quiet as long as I could, but when I lost complete control to the jitters, I said, "I'd like to plead the fifth here."

"That's your right as an American citizen. You don't have to answer that question. I'm gonna ask question number one again, though. Can *I* kiss *you*?"

Our heads were closer together now. Turning toward him, whether it was to answer yes or no would put my lips in kissing territory. I knew this, and I turned anyway. Willing myself not to make the first move, I tested the validity of his promise that I was in the driver's seat. I don't know how long we stayed suspended like that. In my imagination, the car was some futuristic sound enhancement chamber, and his voice ricocheted off every surface, repeating the question over and over. I lost count of how many times I heard him ask if he could kiss me? Thirty? Forty?

He hadn't moved not a millimeter closer to my lips. His control was admirable. In answer to the question, I finally whispered, "Yes." That answer became the new word bouncing around the sound chamber, racking up well over a dozen repetitions before he moved his mouth to mine.

The kiss landed with an unexpected urgency. I was convinced both parties felt it. And it lasted a good long time.

When we broke apart, he made a low muffled whir sound, like a blender under a blanket. I thought he'd make that same sound when he tasted his first sip of the *café con leche*. I would've made it too, expect I was breathing too hard to generate any type of noise other than a pathetic pant.

By now the shop was serving and two people were inside. One guy, having seen our exhibition on his way in, glanced back as he waited at the register. He smiled, and without turning around, gave us a pleasant little standing ovation over his left shoulder. I surmised that he belonged to the LGBTQ community of Key West. My assessment was based on the fact that his shorts were too white and too short. It was on the verge of a stereotype, and I wasn't necessarily proud of it, but the backup documentation was the rainbow flag in the shape of a heart sewn over the back pocket on his left butt cheek. I smiled, did a little curtsey, and blew him a kiss. He responded with another round of adulation, collected his food, and blew my kiss back to me as he strolled away. Jack smiled at the man and tipped his head as he passed.

When he stepped aside, we placed our order. In addition to our coffee and toast, which we were planning to eat here, Jack also got four more cups to go. The coffee was spectacularly dark, to the point my non-Cuban taste buds needed an additional splash of cream and two more sugars. When I had it right, it was in my top ten best cups of coffee ever. Maybe top five. Still vibrating from the kiss, the coffee stamped itself on my brain. The next time I smelled or tasted Cuban coffee, that kiss would come crashing back. I glanced at Jack, wondering if he was making the same association, but I would never ask.

We didn't rush but we didn't linger, either. We ate our toast at a sticky little table outside and watched chickens peck their way down the sidewalk. As one boldly hopped off the curb and ambled into the street, it came to me that I might be living a parable, the chicken representing me—a person afraid of something—and the road representing the fear itself. At some point, I'd have to answer the age-old question 'Why did I cross the road?' And there were only two viable responses, it was either to get away from Jack or to get over to him, one. I sat with that thought for a minute, then, realizing we were done, I gathered the plates and cups while Jack took charge of the cardboard to-go tray. I did not have a satisfactory answer about crossing the road, but I let it go for the time being.

Back at the hotel, we swung through the lobby to collect some sugar and half-and-half for those of us who needed it. To my surprise, Joe and Storie were at the breakfast buffet filling their plates. I surveyed the choices and would've been happy with cereal, my usual morning fare, but I never met a waffle I couldn't be friends with. They had both poured themselves a cup of coffee, but I convinced them to start with the ones we brought from Nine-O.

"Gimme here," Joe said, reaching for a cup. "Let's see what the fuss is about." By then it was plenty cool enough for him to take a big swallow, and he said, "Alright, alright, y'all are in charge of the morning coffee for the rest of the trip."

Great. More time with Jack not talking about the thing that I was too chicken to talk about.

Jack, who had tested the limit of what a plate could actually hold, set his food down so he could go back. This time he returned with two big glasses of water, one for him and one for Joe. I, on the other hand, didn't plan on doing anything that would dehydrate me, like reeling in an eighty-pound fish. So I stuck with coffee and in a nod to vitamin C, a small OJ.

The plan was simple. Eat and drop the guys. They were basically ready. If I was making my living as a bookie, I'd take bets on whether either needed to return to the room before heading out to spend the entire day on the water, secretly knowing neither would.

"So, around six we swing back by the marina to pick y'all up?" I asked.

"Yepper dawg," Jack answered, before shoveling another forkful of eggs into his mouth. *Yepper dawg* was a folksy little phrase Jack's dad used when responding in the affirmative. It sounded perfectly normal when Mr. Turner said it, but it always made me laugh coming from Jack.

"If you can," Joe added. "Let us know what's going on. We can always get a ride back to the hotel; it's not a big deal."

"What will y'all eat for lunch?" I asked. "Want to take a banana for later?" To show I cared about their well-being, I offered the banana off my plate that I was too full to eat.

"Whoa!"

"Hey!"

In a bizarre show of anti-banana sentiment, they both threw their hands up as if to ward off something disgusting. Joe even pushed his chair away from the table so as not to get any banana energy on him.

Holding the fruit pistol-style, I swung my wrist, pointing it at Jack, who then pushed his chair away from the table.

"Don't like bananas?" Storie inquired, both confused and amused.

"Not on fishing day," Joe said.

"What?" I asked.

"Bad luck," Jack explained.

I brought the banana in for a closer look, mystified by its power. "Bananas? Bananas are bad luck? Where in the hell did you get that from?" I reached around in my brain for the craziest person I could think of, then offered, "Miss Delphine?"

"This superstition pre-dates Miss Delphine by hundreds of years," Jack told us, keeping his eye on the banana. Sailors and fishermen believe bananas are bad juju. Most captains won't let you bring 'em on the boat."

"Hell," Joe chimed in again, "I've seen it painted on the transom 'No Bananas'."

"Is it bad luck if *I* eat this banana?"

"No," Jack said. "Eat your banana. We just don't want anything to do with it."

"Not today," Joe confirmed.

"Or tomorrow," Jack threw in.

Finding this whole thing a bit of a reach, I said, "How come I've never heard you talk about the banana curse before?"

"Because you didn't bring a banana either of the two times you came fishing with me."

"If I'd'a known all it took was a banana," I said this with gusto, "I wouldn't have come those two times. And now that I know, my fishing days are over for good."

Having resolved the issue of how not to curse the fishing trip or the fishermen, we loaded up and headed to the boat. They did not, by the way, go back to the room. So, if you took that bet, you owe me money.

Even though it was like a five-minute drive to get where we were going, Jack and Joe insisted on the front seats, with Jack diving. The Turner boys needed to be behind the wheel; it was a genetic mutation that presented as a dominant trait. They were born with it, like they were born with blue eyes, and until science found a way to manipulate the genes, they would drive.

Touching Bottoms was docked at the other end of a long row of boats. Storie and I got out to assume our positions in the front seats. Joe went around to pull their back packs from the hatch area. During the commotion, Jack invaded my personal space.

"I'll miss you today." He said it purely to antagonize me as he gave an unsolicited hug.

"Don't make me banana you," I responded, trying to free myself with no luck.

Laughing, he changed direction. "Seriously," he said, "y'all be careful."

Deciding one bad tease deserved another, I said, "Nah. I think we're gonna take chances and make bad decisions."

"It's not too late for me to bag the fishing trip and come with y'all instead," he threatened, smiling an edgy kind of grin.

Knowing his habit of not bluffing, I became slightly more cautious and decided I'd better throw him a bone. "We'll be careful." I made it sound convincing, then added in a peppy, go-get-'em way, "Catch a big fish!"

He squeezed before letting go, gave me the keys, and grabbed his pack from Joe. We waited 'til they boarded the boat, waved, and got in the car.

"Whew," I blew it out in a big breath.

"I like 'em both," Storie admitted, "but, Lord, they're a lot."

"Oh," I said, shaking my head, "you've only had a taste, girl, a little dab of Cheez Whiz on a Triscuit, if you will. I've been enduring their shenanigans for most of my life."

Cha-ching.

"How much you wanna bet that's Jack. Probably forgot his fish hooks or something."

I glanced at my phone. Yep. When I pulled up the text, there was a photo. I laughed out loud and handed the phone to Storie who immediately started laughing. It was a picture of a sign on the boat. The hand-lettered message read *No bananas on this boat* accompanied by a depiction of a dancing banana. "We gotta work this banana thing tonight." I said and pulled out of our parking spot.

As we left the marina, she asked, "You met Jack when y'all were kids?"

"Kindergarten. I pushed him in a mud puddle at recess on the first day of school. He stood up, big silly smile on his face, reached out a hand to me, and brought me into the puddle with him. Next thing I knew, we were jumping up and down, laughing our fool heads off. By the time the teacher got to us, we were covered head to toe. From that point forward, Jack and I were inseparable."

Storie was laughing, "I bet y'all were so cute, all muddied up like that."

"There's a picture somewhere. I think Dad has it."

"I'd like to see that sometime."

"The next year we were in the same classroom. First grade. That was the year my mama died." Storie, attuned to death at this point in her life, put her hand on my shoulder, and I kept fleshing out the details for her. "He was in my class in second grade, too, and every year after that all through elementary school. When I got older, I wondered if the administrators did that on purpose because he was such a vital support for me during that time, or if it was totally random. It would have been rough if I hadn't had Jack."

"Maybe it wasn't the school team," she said softly, "maybe it was your mama, or some other force at work." I felt like she was implying God but didn't want to be tied down to that one specific force. "You know what Shakespeare said."

No, I did not know what Shakespeare said on this particular subject, so I waited, and she didn't disappoint me.

"He said—*There are more things in heaven and earth than are dreamt of in your philosophy.*"

"*Macbeth?*" I asked.

"*Hamlet.*"

"Same thing." I laughed. She joined in.

Picking up the thread, I kept talking, "I'm not necessarily against it, the thought of mama orchestrating my class assignment so I'd be with Jack for so many years running. I haven't spent a ton of time connecting with her, probably because I was so young when she died. Also, being involved with the spirits of dead people in general gave me the heebie-jeebies growing up. And still does to this day."

"Spirits give you the heebie-jeebies?"

I nodded. "Ghosts creep me out. Chickens creep me out. Sharks creep me out," I paused and glanced over. "The list is long."

I didn't add this part out loud, but I thought it was interesting that I had recently reached out to mama the other day at the graveyard. I didn't feel as if she had really checked in with me on that visit, but maybe I just needed to work on my approach.

* * *

We had decided to drive back to the hotel. Besides the fact that it was still a little early to go bouncing into the police station, I hadn't taken a shower yet. When we parked, Storie opened her door to a chicken on her side. "Hey chicky-chick," she greeted it enthusiastically. I supposed all farmer folk interacted with chickens the same easy way. The bird ignored her, but the exchange was warning enough for me to look out the window before opening my door. All clear.

She sat in the rocker outside while I went inside to get cleaned up. Wondering what a person wore to talk to a police officer about a dead body, I decided it didn't matter because I only brought shorts and t-shirts. The fragrance of my orange oil soap filled the shower stall as I sudsed up the wash cloth. The memory of how the smell had completely captivated Jack over the last few days made me smile. I took a deep breath and got a little light headed, less from the soap than from flashing back to his reaction to the soap.

Dressing was awkward. Storie and I had seen each other naked, you know, when we were romantically involved at the music festival last summer. But now, given that we weren't together, and I wasn't a lesbian, the idea of her walking in on me getting dressed made me feel self-conscious, same way I would have felt if Jack suddenly walked in on me. We had seen each other naked, but…you know.

The towel wasn't nearly long enough to drape myself in a terry dress, so I left it on the hook and dashed out to grab my clothes off the bed. She was still outside, but I popped back in the bathroom just in case she decided to come in. Imaginary crisis averted, I continued with my after-shower routine. Even though we weren't going for a day on the beach, I slathered up with sunscreen all the same, brushed my teeth again, and glanced at my toenail polish. It was in perfectly good shape, but I was already bored with the color. I had remover in my bag. Maybe later in the day, I'd run by the drug store to pick out a new shade. For now, Cinnamon Fluff would have to do.

* * *

The police department was barely within the constraints of what I would consider walking distance from the hotel. However, Storie, hiker of the whole Appalachian Trail, delivered a convincing sales pitch— we were in the Keys, local color, blah, blah, blah. I caved, and we set out on foot, me in my shorts and flip flops, her in a breezy braless sundress.

It was already hot, and the blue sky above was bleached to a shade so pale you could argue it wasn't blue at all. The humidity glossed us over with a sheen of sweat in a matter of minutes, but that was not the biggest thing on our minds. Before I spoke, I solicited the input of my mentor in all-things-detective, Stephanie Plum, who was apparently on a coffee break, as she did not give me any advice on how to go forward.

"Come on, Plum," I said, shocking myself when I realized that the thought had not stayed between Stephanie and me as intended.

"What'd you say?" Storied looked over.

"I said—want some gum?"

"That'd be great!"

"Me to.' I nodded wistfully.

"What, you don't have any?"

"No. Want to stop?" I pointed to a corner markct.

It was a rather complex save, but a save, nonetheless. We exited the store, gum in hand, and resumed our route.

"Do you know the name of the agent working on the case?" I asked.

"No. There was a phone number to contact on the website, but I didn't call it."

"We'll just talk to the receptionist," I offered. "Can't be that many people on the force. This whole island's not all that big." If Jack was here, I bet he'd google the size of the island, down to the square foot, and the size of the police department, broken down into patrol cars vs. bicycle cops. And he'd get the name of the detective in charge of Luanne's murder investigation.

Cha-ching.

Did I just conjure him? Again? How in the name of leprechauns with light sabers did that keep happening?

I pulled my phone out and saw the text from Jack, swallowing hard at the notion that my knack for conjuring was still active. After tapping the screen to enlarge the photo, I saw it was a picture of Jack, holding a big fish. I nudged Storie with my elbow and tipped the phone so she could see.

"I was just thinking about them!" She squealed. "That's so funny."

From where I stood, not nearly as funny as it was a big fat relief. *She* was thinking of them; maybe *she* had conjured him instead of me. I gave myself an imaginary cheerleader jump, the kind where my feet came up behind me to meet the pompoms that I flipped backward over my head.

We walked on with a surprising lack of fervor, given the emotionally charged job ahead. The lane we were currently on was lined with trees and houses. Every house had a porch, and every porch had a blue ceiling.

"What's with the blue ceilings?" I wondered out loud.

"They do it to…" Storie stopped short. "It's a tradition, from the Gullah Geechee descendants of West African slaves."

"Why?"

"It's supposed to…"

I could tell she was tiptoeing around the subject. "It's supposed to what?" I asked.

She gave a soft shrug, like she was about to forfeit, and finally said, "They believed it would keep the… haints…from entering the house."

"Haints?"

"Now don't get excited," she warned me.

"Why would I get excited? What are haints?"

"Haints are restless spirits that haven't moved on."

"Ghosts?"

"Yes."

"Holy crap!"

"See, I knew that would wig you out."

"I'm not wigged out. On high alert for all the roaming spirits that can't get into these houses, maybe, but not wigged out."

"For a long time, it was culturally significant along the coast of South Carolina and Georgia and eventually all the way down to Florida. Wherever the Gullah settled. Families have done it for generations."

It sounded like she was trying to verbally save me from the haints now that she knew my haint history. I let her ramble on.

"Some people don't buy the spirit explanation. Instead, they say folks do it to keep the wasps from building nests on the porch. The wasps are supposedly so stupid, they're fooled into thinking the ceiling is the sky, so not a good place to build. Nowadays it's downright trendy in the interior design sector so you can find blue ceilings clear across the country. There's not one specific color, either, it's just any version of light blue. I think one or another of the big paint companies mixed a color they called Haint Blue at one point, which seemed like they just wanted to capitalize on the lore." As an afterthought, she shook her head and added with quiet contempt, "Commercialism."

First of all, I was impressed with her knowledge on the subject. "How do you know so much about it?" I asked, holding my ghost roll long enough to admire all her little factoids relating to blue ceilings.

"My mama's into Gullah Geechee traditions. She painted my bedroom ceiling blue when I was little. And she added puffy white clouds."

It occurred to me that I didn't know nearly enough about the life and times of Storie Sanders. It simultaneously occurred to me that we were across the street from the Police headquarters.

Chapter 11

Standing there in silence, facing our destination, we glanced at each other. I could have been mistaken, but the look on her face did not imply an earnestness to cross the street and enter the building. Unsure of the best tactic, I opted to wait it out.

Those who suffer the fate of a God-given propensity to fidget know it's not an easy thing to squelch. My foot inched forward and with the toe of my flip flop I rolled a pebble back and forth. In the heat of the sun, I was especially aware of the honey-scented homemade sunscreen she always wore and wondered if it was as effective as the extreme, chemically enhanced, dry-to-the-touch, water-proof SPF forty-five spackle I used. After we baked for another full minute, I pulled out the one go-to trick that worked in almost every situation. I turned to her and asked, "Wanna get a drink first?"

"Yes!" The relief washed over her like water down a log flume. "Let's get a drink first," she enthusiastically agreed.

Granted, it was this side of lunchtime, but we were on vacation. Sort of. Okay, that didn't sound exactly right. But we were in a vacation utopia, which meant the same rules applied—you could drink early and often. Plus, we had the brilliant idea to be pedestrians in this ninety-eight-degree heat so we weren't driving. When you put it like that, a drink was a logical reward for hoofing it. Win.

I pointed to a bar we had passed half a block back, Mookie's, and we retraced our steps. It was cool inside. The AC had a lot to do with that, but in addition, the use of wicker and the color green combined to give the illusion of shade. Large ceiling fans pushed air around in their own sweet time. Rattan blinds let in the light but kept out the glare. I liked it. A big man with a distinct Earnest Hemingway vibe stopped by the table.

"Welcome. I'm Mookie. What can I gettcha?"

"There's a Mookie?" I asked, delighted to meet the bar's namesake.

"Unless my heart gives out from beholding the two prettiest people south of Miami," he said it like a grandfather to his granddaughters.

"Or I push you in front of a bus," a middle-aged woman hollered from behind the bar.

"My wife of thirty-two years, ladies and gentlemen," Mookie said with mock disdain. "And the woman who stands to inherit this bar if someone were to push me in front of a bus, June Holiday." He swept his arm dramatically toward the bar and added, "She'll be here all week."

Applause erupted from the scattered patrons who all seemed to know and appreciate June. I leaned over toward Storie and whispered, "Great name. June Holiday."

She nodded and murmured back approvingly, "A summer month tied to a celebration. Love it."

"You girls here for a little vaycay?" June asked as she rounded the bar with a tray in her hands. She was one of those vibrant souls and her energy matched her fun name. Wearing the colors of a birthday party, heavy on the pinks and oranges, she looked like she enjoyed funnel cake and fruit pie. Bleached hair, long nails, loud voice, big earrings. June.

"No," Storie didn't mince words. "We're here to talk with the police about an unidentified body."

A man at another table looked up suddenly. He struck me as odd, but that could have been because he was wearing a baseball cap indoors. I was used to Jack always taking his off when he came inside. The ball cap was dark, maybe navy, maybe brown, and I couldn't decipher the insignia in the shadows where he was sitting. He and I made eye contact briefly before he looked back at whatever he was working on. I watched him for a second more, waiting for Mookie and June to digest the morsel about the murder.

"Is it that woman?" Mookie asked in a conspiratorial tone.

"What do you know about it?" I prodded him gently. I didn't feel too ill at ease pursuing the line of questioning since Storie had already opened the can of worms. It made sense in a town this size that everyone would have heard about it. Seemed like good investigating to gather information as we went. Jimbo, Not Jimbo, Mookie, June. Who really knew where it would lead?

"Well, her head and hands were hacked off," June volunteered. It was, after all, the most gruesome detail, so it would naturally be the thing any busybody worth her salt would lead with. Still, I tried to transmit some tranquility to Storie's side of the table. No one else would have noticed her flinch at the part about the head and hands; it was so subtle.

June delivered bottles to thirsty customers and made her way back to us. She passed the table where Ball Cap had been sitting, and I was startled to see he was gone. Not in the process of leaving. Not getting up to go. Not heading out the door. He was gone the way the flavor in a piece of bubble gum goes. No explanation. No going-going. Just plain gone.

Pulling up beside us, she said, "The guy who was sitting over there found her. He's the one you should ask." She waved a hand toward the spot that had been occupied by Ball Cap. "Doesn't really talk to anybody, though. Kind've a nut job."

"His name," Mookie interjected with authority, "is Simon." As if correcting a false accusation, he continued somberly, "He's off-the-chart smart and socially awkward. People think that makes him odd because they're confused by the antisocial piece and vexed by the brains. He doesn't know how to talk to regular folk, and regular folk are afraid to talk to him."

Quietly, I asked Storie, "Is that the guy Jimbo and Not Jimbo were telling us about? The guy who was camping in the mangrove swamp?"

"Maybe…" Storie said, working to see if those two pieces fit together.

June stopped wiping a table in mid-swipe and turned around. "Did you say Jimbo?" She asked.

I detected a note of dread in her voice.

"Did you talk to Jimbo?" She asked again.

"Jimbo and some other guy. We didn't get his name," Storie told her.

"Lord have mercy," June said, now fully alarmed. "James Bowen and his sidekick, Steven Mackey, are bad news. Capital B. Capital N. Nice young couple like you. Don't you two go gettin' tangled up with the likes of them."

"She's not wrong about Jimbo and Stevie," Mookie said. "Those boys are hateful, dumb, and lazy. I wouldn't be surprised to see they were involved in the murder when it all shakes out. Stay clear of 'em while you're down here." Then, changing the subject to lighten the mood he asked, "Where ya from?"

"We live in Virginia." I didn't try to clear up June's assumption that Storie and I were a gay couple. I wasn't intentionally misrepresenting us, mind you. Well. Not until I reached over and squeezed Storie's forearm in a way that was a smidge too intimate for a pair of regular BFFs having a beer together in a bar. The arm squeeze did look like something a partner might do. What? I defended myself to myself. I wasn't lying. Not with words anyway, and I was sure any law school professor would say the same thing in a lecture on what is and isn't considered a lie.

Not lying, simply painting a picture. It was good to have a couple choices available should the need arise. It wasn't lost on me that I was referring to fake choices in the relationship arena. While I meant that it was smart to have choices available when manufacturing a misleading identification to gain entrance or to escape a murderous clique, it could also have applied to my real life. I liked to have choices available there, too, hence Jack and Storie.

Cha-ching.

There he was, the conjured Jack. It barely even surprised me at this point. I pulled up the text to see a picture of him holding another fish. Could've been the same kind as the first fish, could've been a different kind. There was no way to measure how little I cared about the fish. It simply fell into a category of things I didn't care about. This category included, but was not limited to, microfiber, sperm banks, ball-peen hammers, car tires, energy drinks, and the art of crochet.

I contemplated responding to Jack's text with a banana emoji, but after this morning's Down with Bananas docu-drama, it was just mean-spirited to send that while he was on a fishing boat. Instead, I scrolled through the pictures, rejecting the giant squid and the lightning bolt for fear of generating a self-fulfilling prophesy. The trophy emoji was a way better option—it let him know I was alive without conveying anything too serious on this end, like the little detail that we may have brushed shoulders with the murderers last night.

Cha-ching.

Jack followed up with the fencing emoji. I didn't know how to take that. *Touché*, like the trophy pic was well received, or *en garde*, like, you know, get ready because he would soon be all up in my business again.

Mookie brought us two beers, which was odd, because while he had asked when we sat down, I didn't remember ordering anything. I was happy with the cold beer, even though what I really wanted was a shot of tequila. Slamming a shot then rolling into the police station with their surplus of breathalyzers laying around was a questionable move, even for me. The beer would do for now, but I'd make up for it when we were clear of the police and on our own again.

We thanked him and clinked our bottles. "Cheers," I said, out of habit. The word fell flat, though, I assumed because of the gravity of what was unfolding.

Mookie chatted with us for a minute longer, then headed back behind the bar. Alone to stew over our new discoveries, I said, "Wow, I did not see that coming. Did you?"

"No." Amazement tinged her voice. "Could you imagine what might have happened last night if Joe and Jack hadn't been with us?"

"Yes. I could imagine that," I said, "mainly because I have a fairly robust imagination. But I can assure you we never would've found ourselves on the outskirts of the airport, poking around any kind of wooded area in the near dark if they weren't with us. So, we don't have to worry about what could have happened."

She nodded but I don't think she had a full appreciation of how firm I would've been on that point. Nature and I had never been on the best of terms. Sure, I liked being outside, but spiders, bugs, snakes, alligators, salt water crocodiles for God's sake, were all way outside my comfort zone even with a capable person like Jack along. I knew Storie was woodsy in her own right, but there's no way she could've convinced me to go poking around the mangroves when we couldn't see what we were about to step on. Although, I could make an argument for checking out the crime scene in broad daylight, if she was up for it.

Storie looked up. "It makes me want to talk to Jimbo and Stevie again," she said with a touch of urgency, "knowing what we know now."

"Me too," I agreed. "Knowing they could've been involved, could be the murderers for that matter…we would have conducted the interrogation differently."

She nodded. We chewed on the idea a while longer as we finished our beers. Then we collected ourselves, paid the tab, used the restroom, waved bye to June, and headed on our way. Exiting the bar was like encountering a new atmosphere altogether. We stepped from the cool, dim, dry air of Mookie's into the kind of heat that glassblowers use to melt their globs of glass. It required a physical effort to push our way into the blazing sunlight since the outside air was thick with humidity. I had put my sunglasses on before we left the bar, but it was so bright, I squinted while adjusting to the light.

From the corner of my eye, I saw a beat-up beach bike leaning against a palm tree. I turned to study it and decided it looked remarkably similar to the ones Jimbo and Stevie were riding last night. A shiver of excitement ran down my arms as I thought about the possibility of bumping into one of them again, but neither of the two suspects presented himself, and I grudgingly acknowledged the possibility that the bike didn't belong to Stevie or Jimbo. As an eye witness, I had a questionable memory of the color or exact condition of the bicycles from last night. And how many beach bikes were there in a beach town? I guessed in the thousands.

Deciding it was irrelevant, at least at this juncture, I didn't bother pointing it out to Storie. Instead, we took a left out of the bar. Shored up by the alcohol, our fortitude was energized. We walked up the block and nearly charged across the street this time. In the crosswalk, of course. When we got the signal, obviously. Was that because we were in front of the police station? Hell, yes, it was. You don't break the law on your way to talk to the cops, just like you don't stop at a tanning booth on your way to an appointment with the dermatologist.

Inside, we approached the reception desk. There were a few uniformed cops milling around, which proved to be nerve wracking. I found myself scrolling through recent events to make sure I hadn't committed any crimes. I was used to bending the law where it suited me, if you knew what I meant. Underaged drinking. Recreational marijuana. Speeding. Were we trespassing last night over by the airport? I didn't see any signs, but I know for a fact that ignorance is not a defense.

"How can I help you ladies?" A gentleman behind the desk waited expectantly. He gave off a pleasantness that filled the lobby the way the smell of fudge fills a candy shop.

"We, um," Storie started. She didn't seem to know how to string the words together. Having suffered from mumble mouth myself on multiple occasions, daily, I felt pity and stepped in.

"We'd like to talk with someone about an unidentified murder victim we saw online."

"Oh my. Certainly," he said with a note of respect that made me like him even more. He was wearing civilian clothes, casual but hip, and his hair was cut short. He called someone on the telephone and conveyed the message without the tiniest hint of scuttlebutt, making it clear to me I could never do his job.

"Someone will be with you directly," he said reassuringly. "Would you like to take a seat? Can I get you some water? Diet Coke? Coffee?"

He was so well suited to his position of managing information and providing comfort, that I wanted to relax in his presence. We smiled and agreed to the water. An almost imperceptible gesture from his hand directed us toward a group of chairs. As if pulled along by the energy he set in motion, we drifted toward the seating area while he moved behind a partition, made some rustling sounds, and emerged with two full-sized paper cups. I realized I was thirsty and drained mine. Storie took a few sips and set hers down.

The air conditioning was heaven, and I felt my regular self re-emerging from the wilted version of me that had crossed the street from Mookie's. The humidity had curled Storie's blond locks. Wispy tendrils framed her face. There was something exquisite about her calm but pained expression. Something that drew me to her. Not in the sexual way I had been drawn to her before. The look in her eyes somehow conveyed the ageless struggle of the human condition. Maybe that's what was whispering to me. I couldn't be sure. I didn't have much more time to ponder before someone appeared in our little waiting area.

Chapter 12

"Hello," said a bright voice from behind me. Storie and I both stood up and turned toward the voice which belonged to a petite badass with spiky hair.

"Hey," I said, feeling the need to assume the responsibility of greeter/explainer, at least until my friend got her legs under her again.

"My name's Lily Barlow." Reaching beside me to touch Storie's elbow, I added, "And this is Storie Sanders. We'd like to talk with someone about an unidentified murder victim we saw online. Storie has some information for y'all that might help with the investigation."

"I'm pleased to meet you," the officer said. "I'm Detective Glory St. John." She shook my hand and then Storie's. "First, thank you for coming in. It's never easy to talk about a murder, especially if you have information."

She was kind. I liked that. I supposed she wouldn't be half so sweet if she rolled up on a robbery in progress, but in this situation, she was lovely. We followed her down a series of nondescript corridors to a room with a desk, a table and four chairs. I didn't think it was her office, or anyone's for that matter. There was nothing personal on the walls or the desk. No framed picture of anyone shaking hands with the governor. No autographed baseball in a Lucite box. No concert poster signed by Jimmy Buffet. I didn't expect a detective's office to look like a dorm room, mind you, but I thought it was reasonable to have a few sentimental items around. That's how I knew this was not the office of Glory St. John. Well, absence of personal items coupled with the placard on the door that read *Meeting Room C.*

I was about to poke my imaginary friend, Stephanie Plum, so she could marvel at my awesomeness but realized she was deep in conversation with someone who looked a little like Clint Eastwood, from one of the cowboy movies, smoking one of those tiny cigars and wearing dusty boots and faded blue jeans. Why those two were collaborating was beyond me. As I quietly backed away so as not to interrupt, I caught my reflection in a mirror above the table where they were working and took the opportunity to give myself a thumbs-up. With or without them, I would celebrate my ability to crack this meeting-room-office-space mystery wide opened.

After that, I advised myself to consider seeking professional counseling for my delusions. And for my over reliance on mediocre humor when stressed. May as well get my money's worth if I'm paying for therapy, right?

Thankfully, our host continued talking, which helped bring me back to the present situation. "I'm a detective on the force, but I may not be the person you need to speak with." As she talked, she set up a laptop computer on the table in front of her. No plug, I noticed, which meant this wouldn't take very long or she was sufficiently charged. "Let's start with me, though," she continued, "and we can figure out where to go from here."

Storie and I nodded in unison.

"I'm sure Clive offered you something to drink while you waited. He's always so attentive," she said. "But can I get you anything else? Coffee maybe? Oh! There's a homemade coffee cake in the break room. Ruby brings one in every Friday."

I perked up at coffee cake and was prepared to make Ruby my new best bud, but I was taking my cues from the person whose friend had been murdered. She declined, so I did as well.

"Thank you, Detective St. John," I said, "Sounds delicious, but I'll pass also."

"I'd like it if you called me Glory." She smiled.

I mentally registered the interesting use of a non-name for a name that rhymed with the other non-name in the room. Glory. Storie. Wait a minute. Lily. Lily is a non-name name, isn't it? It was a flower first, so, originally a non-name. Wrong vowel sound, but fascinating coincidence, nonetheless. Uh...I stopped myself. If that was fascinating, I was in for one long, humdrum life of boredom.

Clearly, these random distractions fed a half-hearted stall strategy. I didn't think I would be, but it turned out I was nervous about proceeding. Storie had to be way more nervous, though. I bossed myself with a firm, *Get it together, Barlow,* and reentered the conversation just in time to field Detective Glory's next question.

"Can you tell me what brings you to the Keys?"

"Yes," I said, easily. "I was on a website called the Doe Network."

"I'm familiar with it," she said in a neutral manner, careful not to criticize or endorse, almost as though she didn't want to lead us one way or another. An admirable quality in an investigator.

"Well, I saw a purple flower tattoo on a person whose body was found here in Key West. She was missing her head and hands, and the police had not been able to identify her," I said. Because I didn't want to sound like I was accusing Key West's finest of slacking on the job, I added, "According to the website."

"That's our Jane Doe," the detective acknowledged.

"The tattoo was the same one my friend Storie has on her ankle. So, I thought the victim was Storie, who I hadn't seen in a year," I said, glossing over the specific details of our torrid encounter last summer. "I had never met her family, so it took a little digging to find them. I wanted to let her dad and mama know in case they were looking for her. But she was…" I stalled for a second "…not the person on the website after all." I looked over at Storie who gave me a weak smile.

Detective Glory interjected, "Can I see the tattoo?"

Storie stood and moved around the table so her left leg was visible. She lifted the skirt of her filmy sundress, which had all the consistency of a shadow. It grazed the part of her leg just above the tattoo. Gracefully standing on one foot, she extended the other one sideways to give the detective a better angle.

Detective Glory seemed surprised by what she saw. She tapped a few keys on the laptop and studied something on the screen before looking down toward the floor as Storie shifted her leg again. The detective's glance bobbed back and forth between her computer screen and the tattoo while Storie stood perfectly still, balancing on one foot. I couldn't see the computer, but I imagined she was comparing Storie's ink to that of a crime scene photo.

"It's definitely the same," she acknowledged, "and it's a pretty specific tattoo, not just a generic flower." At this point she looked up and spoke directly to Storie.

She seemed to be connecting the dots that the women knew each other well. "I'm so sorry for your loss," she said quietly.

"Thank you," Storie replied with eyes that looked brighter than usual. It made me wonder if she was close to tears, but I had absolutely no idea what to say that would ease her pain. I sat quietly, trying hard to be her courage. Then, I did the one thing I could do, not only for Storie, but for the victim. I said, "Her name is Luanne."

"Luanne West," Storie added.

Detective Glory tapped the keys before speaking again. "Gil Dixon is the detective in charge of Luanne's case." I appreciated how she used Luanne's name. She continued, "Gil is off today and won't be back until Monday. I'm not as familiar with this case, but I can certainly take your statements. Would you be available to talk with Gil on Monday?"

"We can't," Storie explained, "We're flying back to Virginia on Sunday. The reason we came was to tell y'all her name."

"But," I added, in a burst of helpfulness, "Detective Dixon can call if he has more questions." Storie nodded enthusiastically.

"Sure," Detective Glory agreed. "Storie," she said, turning slightly, "can you tell me the details of how you know about this tattoo. And would you mind if I took a picture for the file?"

"Yes, you can take a picture. And yes, I can tell you about the tattoo." She launched into her account without hesitation. "Back in tenth grade, I was one of six best friends who decided to seal our devotion to each other by getting the same tattoo. It was almost impossible to talk all the parents into letting us do it. They thought we were too young." She smiled, remembering the teenaged angst, I assumed.

Interrupting to get clarification, the detective looked at me and asked, "You weren't one of the original six then?"

"No," I said. "I only met Storie last summer at a music festival."

"I gotcha," she said, then to Storie, "I'm sorry to interrupt. Please keep going."

"Once we got everyone on board, including Dana's grandparents, we had to decide on the design. Believe it or not, that was even harder." She chuckled. "We wanted it to be so unique that no one would have the same thing, but not something goofy. Funny. At the time, we thought choosing the right picture to link our sister hearts forever was the hardest thing we'd ever have to do."

Detective Glory nodded, and it felt as if she was expressing an understanding that none of the girls could have ever dreamed they'd end up using the tattoo to identify one of their own. She didn't rush, but eventually she turned her attention to the keyboard to capture the statement. She was an incredibly fast typist.

Storie kept going. "When Lily came to our farm store to show me the tattoo she saw online, I knew it was either Dana, Pauline, or Luanne. They were the three people from our group that I hadn't heard from since before the body was found. It was easy to track down Dana and Pauline. So, by process of elimination, Luanne is the victim."

"Have you spoken to Luanne's family yet?"

"No. I don't know where to find them, actually." Storie admitted. "They moved to Maine when we were in the 11th grade. Her mama found a good job up there. The six of us were together one more time the summer before twelfth grade; we met up with Luanne at Bethany Beach in Delaware. After that, communication became more infrequent. I can't remember the last time I heard anything from her. Maybe spring of senior year. It seemed like she was doing well. There was nothing that made me think she was in trouble. Then…I guess…you know…we just got too busy with our own lives…"

She paused, eyes on the table in front of her as she traced a finger along the rounded corner. Detective Glory glanced at me, and I responded by raising my eyebrows in a where-do-you-go-with-that look. It seemed more respectful and less invasive than shrugging my shoulders.

She gave me a thin smile and went back to Storie. "It's not unusual for people to lose touch out of high school. Life moves so fast these days, especially when you're young." She waited, not rushing us, aware this was hard.

After what felt like the perfect length of time, she added, "Can you remember anything about Luanne's family? The names of her parents maybe?"

Storie looked up, startled. "We only ever called her mama Ms. West. Her daddy was never in the picture. She didn't have any sisters or brothers." She sounded a little panicky when she added, "They had a dog named Whiskey."

Detective Glory patted Storie's forearm. "It's okay," she assured her. "We'll get her mother's name from the school records, and we'll track her down that way. People who move are usually not that hard to find."

I thought that was probably true. Unless you were going underground or off grid, there had to be a trail, right?

"We went to Culpeper High in Culpeper, Virginia. We graduated two years ago."

"Great," the detective said as she typed. "That helps." She asked Storie a few follow-up questions, mostly pertaining to the relationships in the circle. Finally, she asked, "Did any of the other four show an interest in coming to help identify the body?"

"No," she shook her head sadly. "Scarlet never could do funerals, even for her own family members. And while Shelby isn't at all what I would call squeamish, she completely freaked out when I told her about the murder. I didn't mention coming to Florida when I got in touch with Dana, and I didn't speak with Pauline personally. I guess I should have invited them all down for this. I kinda wanted to do it before I lost my nerve." She looked at me hesitantly and kept on rambling. "And I figured we'd have a memorial after. Right? That makes sense, doesn't it?"

"Yes," I assured her. "It makes sense." It had never dawned on me that the other four friends might want in on this. For the love of lopsided luminaries. Did I usurp a spot on this mission out of sheer perverted curiosity? I didn't even think to suggest she take the other members of the tattoo sisterhood. Wow. When even the most obvious course is lost on me, I had to question my ability to work in the field of forensics. And then my head snapped up.

"Is Storie a suspect?" I asked.

"No," Glory said plainly. "She's not a suspect. We'll use her statements first to identify the victim, and then we'll go from there. Is there anything else you can think of that you'd like me to share with Gil?"

Storie sat quietly. It looked like she was trying to come up with something else. Something that would help. In time, she slowly shook her head no.

"If you do think of something later, here's my card." She handed one to Storie and one to me. "Call me, okay?"

"We will." I nodded, then thought to ask another question. "Do y'all have any leads?"

"It's an active investigation," Detective Glory said, almost by rote, "so I can't give out a lot of details, other than the fact that the body was found by the salt ponds out near the airport."

"She was in the mangroves? Is that right?" Storie wanted to know.

"Yes," she said softly. "That's where she was found."

I got the distinct impression that it was the only fact we would be allowed to confirm, so I asked, "Do you need anything else from us?"

"I don't," the detective answered. "We're finished for now. But let me thank you both again for coming in. It was an incredible investment on your part to travel all this way so you could help give a victim her name back."

We all stood up, and she reached out to shake our hands again. Her grip was firm. I wondered if she knew judo. I was taller than her by six inches, but I had the feeling she could kick my ass while eating a hunk of Ruby's famous coffee cake and not get any crumbs on the floor.

Back outside, Storie sucked in a huge breath of salty summer air and said, "I want to go by the crime scene."

I was surprised that came up so quickly. I thought I'd have to seed it after a beer or two.

"Let's go back to the hotel and get the car," she continued. "I think I can remember how to get to the airport road."

"If we can't," I replied, "the magical global positioning system in the sky certainly can."

The only thing that might've stood in between me and the crime scene was the fact that I was famished. "How do you feel about grabbing a taco on the way?" I asked.

"I was hoping you'd say that. I feel like I could eat that last fish the boys caught. By myself."

"My kinda girl," I said approvingly, and we were off.

Chapter 13

Tacos were procured and consumed en route to the hotel. Sufficiently refueled, we made a beeline to the room for a costume change. Let's face it, a swamp habitat did not favor flip flops or a gauzy dress. While she changed into shorts and worn out hiking boots, I threw on a ratty pair of Keds, then we both reapplied our sunscreens of choice and headed out the door.

It was around three o'clock when we rolled up to the gate that had been locked the night before. It was wide open today, so I drove in, albeit at a comically slow rate of speed.

"Since we don't exactly know what we're looking for, let's just poke along and keep our eyes open," I suggested. Three fingers of her left hand were pressed tightly against her lips, so she agreed with a non-verbal gesture, never taking her gaze from the view out the window on her side. We were both intent on spotting something. I'm not sure what, but something. Maybe something that didn't belong, like a red balloon whose string was caught on a twig. How an out-of-place object like that would help on any level remained to be seen.

We passed what looked like the entrance to an actual park or bird sanctuary of some kind. There was a small lot with one car. The road continued, though, so I kept on driving past the sanctuary. My instinct said to follow it to the end, before deciding where we wanted to get out and explore.

That instinct paid off. We entered an area with a collection of buildings, some clearly in various states of abandonment, others clearly off limits. There was no one around that we could see, although I spotted a couple cars behind the chain link fences which surrounded the buildings that were meant to be off limits. The fences boasted no trespassing signs, but I saw nothing else to indicate we weren't allowed on this road.

"Wha'd'ya think?" I asked.

"Wanna get out here and take a look around?"

In answer to her question, I eased the car off the road onto a sandy patch of ground and put it in park. We were in the shade of an old, rundown, cinderblock building, the last one in the short series. It looked as if this one had been abandoned the longest based on the graffiti and garbage, but that could have been a matter of convenience. This was the empty building farthest from what little activity there was and closest to the swamp to boot.

We ambled over to a hole that used to be a window and peered in. From the collection of litter, it was best described, in its current state, as a mixed-use establishment for eating, sleeping, and various recreational activities. There was a ratty mattress pushed into one corner amidst a carpet of beer cans, fast food cups, and junk food wrappers. I'm pretty sure I saw a used condom from where we stood at the window. It wasn't unrealistic to think there were hypodermic needles for days, we just couldn't see them in the semi-dark interior.

Storie walked from our spot at the window to a gaping doorway. For the love of baby Jesus in the manger, I hoped she didn't plan to go inside. The rooms had to be dripping with Hanta virus.

"Anything?" I asked, mainly to arrest her progress. She stopped and looked.

"No," she replied, indicating the scenery was pretty much the same from that perspective. I had been holding my breath, and I blew it out when she made no move to enter through the door hole.

A ribbon of faded yellow tape fluttered, catching my attention. I saw the word *crime* and knew it was left over from an investigation. Judging from the surroundings, though, it could've been attached to any number of illegal activities, not necessarily the murder in question. The yellow tape was not our red balloon.

"Let's walk around back," I suggested. With the mattress and the used condom, the possibility that Luanne was raped descended rapidly. I knew Storie had wrestled with that likelihood, so before it had a chance to land, we left the front of the building and slowly picked our way to the back where the sandy soil glittered with broken glass. From there, I saw a path into the mangroves. We moved toward the twisted branches and stepped into the shady mass. I fought back my concern over spiders and bugs in order to see this through. As we moved into the vegetation, the sun broke into the pieces of a jigsaw puzzle strewn across the ground, making it even harder to see the narrow stumps and roots. I tripped, crashed into a thick branch, and Storie grabbed for me.

"I'm fine," I assured her, rubbing the spot on my shin where I expected the bruise to bloom. "I trip a lot."

"Be careful," she cautioned, but I didn't see the point. I lacked the basic understanding of how a body moves carefully. Still, it was sweet that she was worried.

We wound our way farther and farther into the trees, without any semblance of a plan, and the next thing I saw in the shade was what looked like the remains of a campfire in a cleared out, tamped down section of ground. The woods were noisy. There were birds calling, and the sound of water came from somewhere close by. I felt sure I heard the aggressive splash of a saltwater crocodile, but I tuned it out as I kicked at the bits of charred wood with the toe of my shoe, wondering who was out here roasting marshmallows. Storie bumped me, and I moved a little to get out of her way. When she bumped me again, I looked up. "What?"

She pointed deeper into the woods. I followed her arm to the end of her finger then moved my eyes beyond until I stopped at an organized, purposeful stack of rocks. The red balloon. When I fumbled over to it, I saw we were right beside a narrow waterway.

The cairn was obviously a manmade memorial of some type. "Do you think that's where the body was found?" Storie wanted to know.

Fighting every urge to jump to that conclusion, I slowly advanced another idea. "I'm not sure," I said, trying to keep us both from panicking. "A friend of mine at school builds those whenever she has sex outside. Maybe this is that kind of marker."

It sounded stupid, even to my own ears, but I didn't think it made sense for Storie to have an emotional breakdown, here, in the woods, when we still had to get ourselves back to the car. In my mind, however, I believed that the rocks were put there for a very specific reason—to mark, I was positive, the location of where a dead body was found, or, more gruesomely, to mark where a murder had taken place. I noticed there were no rocks lying haphazardly on the ground. This particular spot was rock-free, which meant someone went through the trouble of trucking these in from somewhere else. It was a decent stack. I supposed a Jack or a Joe could carry them in one trip. But a less muscled person would have to make at least two trips. And a person like me… probably five. It gave me a little shiver, enough to decide we should begin working our way back out with an appropriate amount of urgency.

Unfortunately, my co-investigator was deep in a sweep of the area, looking for anything else besides the campfire and the cairn that could give a clue to what happened here.

"You know," I started, "if this was the crime scene, the cops have already gone over it for clues."

"I know," she agreed. "But what if somebody keeps coming back here…" She trailed off. I really didn't want to know how that statement ended. To relive the murder? To commit other murders? I started to wonder if this had been such a great idea. Even I knew that the remains of a campfire from last February would be pretty well scattered by late August. Wind, water, daily meteorologic and atmospheric influences, right? These were current remains. This was an active campsite. Someone had been here within the week, or at least the month. We were up in someone's space. Someone who knew about this crime or committed it, one.

I heard a branch snap, and I whipped my head around. It was a woodland sound, and we were in the woods, but to my heightened sense of freak-out-ability, it was somehow different. That sound was far more nefarious than your average crocodile strolling through the swamp. I thought I saw a shape that didn't belong. Then there was a movement. Storie's body language changed, too. She felt it.

I whispered, "Maybe we should go for now. We can come back with the guys if you want." She had already grabbed hold of my hand and was pulling me along. When she realized we could move faster if she let go, she did indeed drop my hand, but she hissed, "Come on, Lily."

Retracing our trail to the best of our ability, we bumped along with the single-minded intention of getting the hell outta there. We eventually popped back into broad daylight. I reached around to my back pocket to check the time on my phone.

"Shit."

"What?"

"I think I dropped my phone."

"You didn't. We left them in the car. We were so anxious to look in the building."

"Thank the lucky Four Leaf Clover Association."

Storie laughed, "I like your stupid sayings."

That broke the tension, and I laughed with her. Hearing ourselves, it occurred to me that I hadn't heard us laugh much today. It was a sound I suddenly yearned for, like the sound of the Goody Goody Man coming up the road when you're ten.

"You want to lay this heavy load down for a bit and go get some tequila?"

"More than anything in the world," she said, smiling.

We started working our way up the path. That's when I saw it. The bike leaned up against the side of the building.

For fear we were being watched, I said it quietly, and without pointing, "Was that bike here when we went in the woods?"

Storie drew a sharp breath, clearly surprised. "I don't know. Once we came around the building and headed to the woods, I didn't look back."

It was a beach bike. Where it was parked, we wouldn't have seen it unless we turned around before we got to the woods on our way in. Which we didn't. It looked like the one I saw on the way out of Mookie's earlier. It was blackish, but when the sun hit it, you got a hint of dark metallic purple. Leaned up against the cinderblock wall, it just looked black. Big tires, not chained to anything, definitely not new.

"I think I saw that bike earlier today."

"*That* bike? That *exact* bike?" she asked.

"I think it was that bike. We were coming out of the bar. It sort of looked like the ones Stevie and Jimbo were on last night, that's how it caught my attention."

"No," she said. "Their bikes were red, not black."

"Red?" I applied all the disbelief I could muster. "Are you high? Those bikes were dark. Either black, dark blue or dark purple."

"No, they weren't." She was insistent. "Both were red, one was a little brighter than the other."

We were still walking, but much more slowly. "Alright," I conceded. "Whatever color the bikes are isn't the main thing here. The main thing is that we might have company. Let's just be on the lookout for Jimbo or Stevie."

"Right," she said.

We worked our way up the side of the building, turned the corner, and nearly ran into two beach bikes, leaned up against a rusty metal post. One was yellow and one was silver.

"Hey, hey pretty ladies," Stevie popped out of the window hole like he was in some kind of Western movie.

"Stevie!" We greeted him like we had missed him desperately. It was a pretty decent fake helped along by the use of his name. He was oblivious to the fact that he never told us his name last night.

He smiled, liking our enthusiasm.

"I thought that was your car." He pushed his head back, indicating the rental behind him.

"We thought those were your bikes," Storie chimed in, tipping her head toward the rusty post.

"Yeah, everybody in the Keys knows these two ponies."

Hmm. Weird that he used *ponies* when I just made that Western reference in my head. Had he said something that alluded to cowboys last night? I couldn't remember. That was weird though, wasn't it? I guessed I was talking to myself. Stephanie Plum and the Clint Eastwood look-alike had cleared out. But, if I remembered correctly, that Clint guy *had* been dressed like a cowboy.

"Where are your boyfriends?" Stevie asked.

"Fishing," I answered, and I deeply regretted leaving my phone in the car at this point. "Where's Jimbo?"

There was a three-second delay, before he said, "Peeing."

Just as he said it, Jimbo ambled around the corner, holding a cigarette precariously while making a show of zipping up the fly of his cargo shorts. It seemed just a bit calculated. Was he the shape I had seen when we were down by the campsite in the woods?

"Look who it is," Stevie shouted to his friend, "our favorite pretty ladies."

"Mmhmm." Jimbo nodded, taking a drag off the cigarette. "What are you two doing out here all alone."

"Their boyfriends are fishing," Stevie explained.

"Bored?" Jimbo asked with a leer that gave me the creeps.

In a move that literally could not have surprised me more, Storie took control of the situation. "Nah," she cooed, as she put one arm around my neck and leaned in to kiss my cheek. She pulled away, gave me a sultry smile and a wink, and still looking at me she said, "We never get bored."

It was perfect. They were floored. And any question about what we were doing here or in the woods was expunged. I put a little topper on the cover by grabbing her hand, palm to palm, then interlaced my fingers with hers. It was just intimate enough to seal the deal.

After a tiny space of shocked silence, the two idiots hooted.

Capitalizing on their admiration, and possibly laying the groundwork for our exit, Storie said, "We're looking for some weed. A girl we met in a coffee house said to look for Jordy out by the bridle path."

And then, with big innocent eyes, I played along. "Are we at the bridle path?"

"Not even close," Stevie said, shaking his head with what I perceived to be disdain for a woman's inability to follow directions.

Feeling like he was about to lose a sale, Jimbo jumped in, jabbing Stevie in the ribs. "I don't know who this Jordy jackass is, or where you're getting your information, but I got good weed right here, and I'm running a special for pretty ladies." His smile dripped with snake oil, and I could see him as a used car salesman on a two-bit car lot. Or as an inmate in a penitentiary, one.

We made the transaction, more to keep up the ruse than to buy the pot. Once we had the merchandise, Storie blew a kiss to each of them, linked her arm in mine and turned toward the car. I rooted around in my pocket for the keys and hit the button to open the doors. Right before we were forced apart by the car's fender, I slipped my hand into the back pocket of her shorts and let her pull away slowly, as I drew my hand back out.

The two beach bums who were watching hollered again, like they were on the actual set of an adult film, and started falling over each other as one shouted, "Let's party!"

From the passenger seat, Storie rolled down her window and waved, "We'll find you," she promised.

I kept it cool as I backed out and headed down the road. In the rear view I watched them make their way into the shelter of the abandoned building, probably to light up and talk about lesbians.

Meanwhile, the phone *cha-chinged*. Before I glanced at it, we both busted out laughing, riding the high of duping a couple garden variety murderers and living to tell about it.

"Who are we?" I wanted to know, "Double agents?"

"We should get Glory St. John to let us go undercover," she said when she could talk.

"Do you think they did it?" But before she could answer, I changed direction. "Wait. I thought you said their bikes were red?"

"Well, I thought you said they were black."

"We really have no business solving crimes if we can't even get the color of the bikes right. Yellow and silver? Seriously?"

Without warning, she changed direction again. "Was Jimbo really peeing or just acting like it so we wouldn't think he had followed us into the woods? Lily..." She stopped laughing. "We could have been at the crime scene, with the murderer."

We had just come through the main gate, and I pulled to the side of the road. I needed a minute to absorb that.

Cha-ching.

"Is it just me," I said, "or did that text sound more... impatient?"

"Jack?" She asked.

"Oh, I'm sure of it."

There were eight messages in all, which had been sent over the last forty-five minutes the phone had been locked in the car. I paraphrased for Storie's benefit.

"The fish stopped biting...blah, blah, blah...came in...at the hotel...where are y'all..."

"Where are y'all?" She asked.

"Where the *hell* are y'all?" I corrected myself.

"Thought so."

I quickly texted a message to the effect that we had taken a walk and left the phones in the car, but we were on our way. Fifteen minutes. Ish.

* * *

"We gotta play this cool," I warned Storie as I slid into the parking space at our hotel.

"Don't I know it," she agreed. "Is Jack gonna go bananas?"

I smiled at the banana reference. She caught it, too, and smiled along with me.

"Only if he finds out we put ourselves in some type of danger, which," I conceded, "in Jack's mind could involve using a curling iron or drinking something hot." I kept the car running with the air conditioner blowing full blast as I thought.

"Do we lie?"

"I don't like the term *lie*," I said. "It implies you're in the wrong. I prefer to craft true statements that don't exactly answer the question. It's part of my loophole philosophy. You know, always give yourself an out."

"You do this a lot?"

"Multiple times a day. Hard to spot if you don't know what you're looking for. But I can resurrect a loophole I engineered from a month ago when necessary," I confessed absently, then I looked her way. "He'll probably lean on me more than you for two reasons. One, you're emotionally saturated, and two, he tends to keep tabs on my long loophole rap sheet. Your out will be genuine sadness. When in doubt, be sad. A, it's true, and B, he won't tug at any loose threads because, well, you're sad."

"I think I can do that," she mused. "I am sad. That's the truth."

"Therein lies the beauty," I whispered.

A heavy object hit the window, and after demonstrating perfect execution of the startle response, accompanied by Storie's high yelp, I turned to see the heavy object was Jack's knuckle. He had squatted so he could peer in at us. I hit the button to roll down the window.

"Y'all gonna sit in there all day or what?"

"If the alternative is putting up with your nonsense, then yes, we'll stay right here."

He chuckled, stood up, flipped the door handle a couple times to encourage me to unlock, and when I did, he opened my door. I stepped out.

"You didn't wear this fishing," I said, referring to his nylon basketball shorts.

"No. I went for a run."

"That's why you smell like a fish." Catching a whiff, I added, "who just ran a marathon."

He moved in closer, bringing the odor with him, and threatened to grab me in a boogeyman-style hug.

"Ugh," I choked it out. "A fish running a marathon in week old gym socks! Go take a shower, Jack!" I dove back into the driver's seat while Storie stood on her side laughing.

He backed up three steps, threw his hands in the air, promising he would not do me any stink harm, and let me get back out. "Seriously," he said, the tone reflecting the word choice, "how'd it go today?"

"It was rough, but we did okay." I left it there. A true statement. I did an imaginary curtsy, because that, friends, was how it's done.

"Can you fill me in?"

"Of course," I promised, truthfully. "After you take a shower."

Upstairs we all disappeared into our appointed rooms. Storie, bless her heart, was suddenly crushed by a falling brick wall of exhaustion and laid down on the bed. I sat on the edge for a skinny minute before asking, "You okay?"

"No," she said honestly. "But give me half an hour, and I'll rally."

"You got it," I said and slipped out the door.

Joe was in the rocker, having already showered. He smelled great and looked surprisingly fresh after battling...permit was it? Those boys never seemed tired. I suppose it had something to do with their level of physical fitness. Maybe I should try it sometime.

"You catch anything?" I asked, plopping into the rocker beside him.

"I did." He seemed pleased with himself.

Jack and Joe fished and hunted together. I believed one was considered more accomplished at fishing and the other at hunting, but I didn't know which brother deserved which title. Didn't *know*? I weighed the word in my head. Or didn't *care*? Ah. Add that to the list of things I didn't care about. Right between ball-peen hammers and car tires. But, feeling the need to connect, I asked a follow-up question.

"Who caught more? You or Jack?"

"Don't you know Jack always catches more?"

Okay, so Joe was the hunter, Jack, the fisherman. Got it.

Just then the fisherman appeared. Damn, that boy could shower fast.

"Did you even get clean?" I asked, to which he answered by grabbing me out of the chair and draping himself on me like an ape would hang onto a tire swing.

"Oh, Lord." Joe stretched out Lord, almost turning it into two syllables. There was a deep chuckle in his chest.

"Smell for yourself," Jack challenged.

"Okay. Alright. You're good. You smell clean. Let me go."

He did, positioning me back in front of the rocker, while he took up a post leaning against the wrought iron railing. He swept me with a glance from head to toe, and in a flash he bent back down, cupping his hand behind my right calf. He ran a thumb along the outside edge of the new bruise on my shin. Looking into my face, he didn't question but smiled in soft sympathy. I shrugged it off.

"Storie okay?" he asked.

"She's closing her eyes for a few minutes," I shared. "Worn out."

"What happened today?"

I started the recap, and when I got to the part about wanting to see the crime scene for closure, he cut in.

"Did the detective take y'all?"

I didn't see a way around it, so I said simply, "No."

Jack shifted. "Y'all drove out to the swamp by yourselves?"

I pointed out that by myself meant alone, and since we were together, not alone, we were not either of us by ourself.

"God damn it, Lily," he said almost inaudibly.

"She wasn't by herself, bro," Joe piped in. I looked over at him with deep gratitude for taking my side.

"Joe, if you think Storie is any help at all, your whistlin' in the wind, son."

"Let me rephrase it," Joe said. "They weren't alone."

"What?" Jack asked.

"They weren't alone," Joe repeated. "I sent somebody with 'em today."

"*What?*" I demanded, whipping my head around to look at Joe as I took back all that gratitude I had just bestowed on him.

Then, with the same amount of accusation, I whipped my head back to Jack. "Y'all had us *followed?*" I was finding it hard to control the volume of my upsetment.

I glared at Jack who shrugged in a show of innocence. "Not me," he said, defensively, "but only because I didn't think of it."

I swung back toward Joe, and asked the same thing, except louder. "You had us *followed*?"

Jack, looking pleased as a snake in a hissing contest, nodded at his brother. "Smooth, dude."

"Com'on, girl," Joe snorted. "Everybody knows you're an accident looking for a place to happen. You wouldn't've let us come, and it didn't make any kind a sense to leave y'all alone under the circumstances."

"The circumstances?" I demanded.

"Drug dealers. Rape. Murder. Decapitation," he paused, looking at me flatly. "Pick one."

I turned toward Jack, "I find it hard to believe you didn't know about this." He started to shake his head.

"Jack didn't know," Joe answered for his brother. "I kept him in the dark, so you couldn't be mad at him."

With laser eyes, I burned a hole right through Jack. "I'm sure I can find a way," I said, marshalling all the saltiness I was feeling.

Then I turned my laser glare toward Joe, "Who did you get to follow us?" What that mattered, I had absolutely no freakin' idea. There wasn't a measuring stick where it was good to be followed by someone on the high end but bad to be followed by someone on the low end.

Joe shrugged nonchalantly. "I know a couple guys down here."

I sat there shaking my head at the two of them. The pieces slowly settled into place and things started to come together for me. The bike outside of Mookie's. That was the spy's bike. That shadow we saw in the swamp. That was the spy. The bike at the back of the building. Again, the spy's bike. We were never totally alone with Jimbo and Stevie, the alleged, in my mind, murderers. If I hadn't been outraged that we were followed, I would've been relieved, that, you know, we were followed.

As it were, I thought my fury was justified, and in that pathetic way, I wanted to get back at them. I stood, looked from one to the other and then delivered my bombshell. "So, I guess your *spy* told you we ran into Jimbo and Stevie, who we think were somehow involved in the murder. And we perpetrated a cover story that Storie and I are lesbian lovers running around together behind your backs. And we were there to buy some pot from a drug dealer named Jordy on the bridle path. And to make it stick, we kissed and bought the pot from Jimbo."

They seemed stunned, but not the way I was hoping. I knew I stretched the idea of "kissing" a little. Storie, giving me a kiss on the cheek was not exactly kissing, but they were in no position to cross-examine me at this point. With half smiles on their faces, they both mumbled something under their breath.

Making no attempt to decipher it, I stood up and turned toward my room. "I'm about ready for a banana daiquiri," I said over my shoulder, rekindling the banana bane on purpose. "Y'all think you can make that happen."

"Yes ma'am," they said in unison.

Chapter 14

I was glad Storie was up when I came in the room. "You'll never believe this," I said, walking over to the sink area to brush my teeth.

She was splashing water on her face, and as she patted it with a towel, she said, "Believe what?"

"Those two had us followed today. Well, Joe did. Jack conveniently didn't know anything about it, or so he says. They didn't trust us not to get in trouble."

"Thank God," she said with relief. "Was that who we thought we saw in the woods?"

"Yes, but aside from the fact that it could have been the difference between our little charade and a serious damn problem, aren't you at all upset?"

"Yeah, no, totally," she agreed with me, nodding vigorously. "But...thank God."

We looked at each other for a long moment. I didn't know what was playing out in her head, but playing out in my head was a scene where Luanne lost her life in or near an abandoned building. We communicated to each other through silence.

"Right. You're right," I said. "Maybe we were in over our heads. I hate it when I have to concede to Jack, though. I hate it when he wins. I want control of my own life. This is why Jack drives me nuts."

"But you said Jack wasn't in on it."

"I know. But I'm mad at him for being brothers with the one who masterminded it." I grabbed my toothbrush and directed my anger toward my own gums. Take that, plaque.

Storie changed back into her dress from this morning, and I put on a fresh going-out t-shirt. My feelings about being followed had ebbed a little, but filling that space was the fact I was half starved. Taken together, the combo qualified me for inclusion in the highly explosive category.

As soon as we opened the door, the Brothers Turner whisked us down the stairs and through the courtyard. Much like I had attacked my gums with the toothbrush, I kicked at a small coconut innocently sitting on the deck of the pool. Thanks to crummy foot-coconut coordination, the object barely moved, but I stumped my toe in the process. It was enough to remind me not to attempt that wearing flip flops next time.

Neither boy dared comment, but Storie said, "Ouch. Did that hurt?"

"Yes," I seethed.

Knowing I was both upset and hungry, Joe offered an olive branch, "Five minutes and you'll have a drink and a basket of chips."

Loving the sound of that, I eased my grip on my grudge. "Thanks," I said quietly.

We walked the rest of the short route without comment, arriving at a Mexican restaurant boasting outdoor seating on the main street. The hostess showed us to a table immediately, and Joe hadn't been lying. I had a perfect margarita and a basket of chips almost before my butt was comfortably positioned in the chair. I really wanted to follow through with the banana daiquiri request in order to flirt with the banana whammy a little longer, but it seemed wrong on several levels. First, banana as a flavor doesn't go with salsa and tortilla chips. Second, rum isn't my favorite kind of booze. Maybe I could work a banana into desert somehow, banana split or a milkshake. Ooh! frozen banana on a stick. Dipped in chocolate. Yum.

I didn't need a menu. My plan was to consume my weight in queso, then order chili rellenos; I was that hungry. Who knew crime scenes built up such an appetite? If I decided on a career in this field, I'd have to seriously think about working out. At least a walk now and then. Something. Captain Workout would love that. Another opportunity for him to be involved.

I stuffed a chip in my mouth before a blob of cheese could splat on the table and looked over to see him grinning at me. In response, I rolled my eyes and shook my head. When he gave me that wink of his, I gave in and cracked the tiniest smile. Then he bumped my ankle lightly with his shoe. Jackspeak for *Sorry*. I bumped his shoe back. Lilyspeak for *I forgive you, but don't piss me off.*

Our foursome slipped into a gently rolling conversation. The need to disguise the truth had disappeared with the revelation that we were tailed all day, so I wasn't actively fabricating loopholes. We ate and talked. Storie grieved among friends who could never know the depth of her sadness. We took our time with the meal, not worried about turning the table because the place was only half full. The waiter didn't rush us.

It was around nine when we left the place and headed back to our rooms. I knew Storie was ready to crash, and I probably wasn't far behind her. On the breezeway, Jack grabbed my hand and pulled me back as the other two went inside and both doors closed quietly.

"Thanks for not jinxing me with a banana meme on my phone today," he said.

"I thought about it," I confessed.

"I'm a little surprised you could exercise so much restraint."

"Well, you seemed intent on your silly superstition, and I didn't want to cramp your style."

"You know," he shared, "some sailors say you're not supposed to bring a woman on a boat either. Bad luck."

"Now that," I replied, nodding, "that's a version I can get on board with." I smiled because I had used a nautical phrase without intending to.

He tucked a strand of hair behind my ear in that newly familiar way attached to the recent change in our friendship. "I wouldn't bring a banana," he said seriously, "but I'd bring you. You're worth every bit of trouble you'd cause out on the water."

I smiled. It was comforting knowing that someone valued me in spite of my unbridled tendency to be a pain in the ass. Still, I felt compelled to reiterate the ground rules. "I'm not going out on your stinky fishing boat."

"Is that because of the sharks or because of the name?"

"Yes," I answered, smiling. It was really the sharks, but the name on the boat, *Touching Bottoms,* was outrageously annoying. "Both. The sharks and the name. I mean, seriously. Why not just call it *Grab Her Ass?*"

He waited a beat, then said, "I'd like to."

I detected a not-so-hidden message in that answer, and I looked up to see if we were talking about the boat or about something else. Damn it. I fell right into that trap, landing in a tractor beam of direct eye contact. I looked away. There were times when I challenged myself to engage. But I was caught off guard, and I just let it go. With his free hand, he traced a line down my throat. In spite of the fact that it was still eighty-nine degrees out, goose bumps that I could not explain popped up on my arms.

Holding my hand, he said, "I can't really say I'm sorry Joe had y'all followed today, but I'm sorry it bugged the shit out of you. It was a good idea. You mean a lot to me."

I had no response for that. Over the course of the evening, I had realigned my previous anger and privately acknowledged that Storie and I could've been in a tight spot. The difference between us and Luanne, was simple—we had overprotective people in our lives, and she was dead because she didn't. I didn't have the ability to share this verbally, as it amounted to saying he was right, so I did the next best thing. I leaned onto his chest and let him fold his arms around me. I thought he was smelling my neck, but I could've been mistaken.

I don't know how long we stood there; it might have been minutes. Eventually I pulled away. "See you in the morning for the coffee run?"

"Yep. See you in the morning," he said. "Good night."

I stepped into my room and he went to his. Storie, surprisingly, was not fast asleep. She was sitting cross-legged on her bed, toying with the little baggie we got from Jimbo.

"Want to?" She asked, holding it up and giving a little shake.

"I very much want to! And it's perfect," I said, spreading out my arms. "We're here in our own space free from the boys."

She and I both had a nice buzz from the tequila at dinner. The guys nursed beers, but I guessed that was because...actually I don't know why they only had a couple of beers. No one was driving. Odd, but, to each his own.

While I slipped into a pair of pajama bottoms and a tank top, she fiddled with her phone and pulled up a music app. The bluesy tune floated through the room. I dropped my head when I recognized the lyrics of a song by Gravel in the Whiskey. Was it just a few days ago when I had approached the band's bass player, Ditch Miller, because I thought he had murdered Storie? I didn't point out the irony to her.

After fifteen more minutes of puttering around, I joined her on the bed. We positioned ourselves so our backs rested against the headboard. The two of us had bonded pretty well over this tragedy. It was clear we had a good chemistry, and I could see keeping her in my life.

"I liked being your girlfriend today," I said.

She nodded and admitted she liked it, too. "I wish you were gay," she said.

This time I nodded. "Maybe I'm bi," I offered, as a compromise.

"Maybe. Or maybe you're just a person who's not afraid of experiencing life, which I think is more the case." She lit the joint. "See, I'm not that person."

"What do you mean? You hiked the Appalachian Trail from top to bottom. You embrace life."

"I do, on my terms," she took a drag and handed it to me. "But I'm not so open that I would sleep with a man just to see if I liked it."

I felt like she was giving me a compliment, and at the same time, laying groundwork that would allow us to separate from the complication of pursuing a relationship.

I was holding the joint when someone banged loudly on the door, making us both jump.

"What do y'all want?" I hollered to Jack and Joe.

No answer. "I swear those two never outgrew elementary school."

Three minutes later, there was another knock. Storie took the joint from my hand, and I went to the door. Flinging it opened, I was not expecting nobody to be there. A quick look to the left and right, and I closed the door again.

"Jack," I assured her, "goofing around."

"He's in luuuuv," she drew out the word and laughed at my predicament. I took the joint she offered.

I was aware we were in a non-smoking room. Hopefully we'd have time to air it out before Sunday. If we decided to smoke the second joint in the bag, we should plan to do it outdoors. The mystery knocker struck again, and this time I fairly ran to door. At least what I would consider a run. Maybe a left-leaning trot was a more accurate description.

I jerked the door opened again, and again no one was there. Storie hopped up and came to inspect for herself. We both stepped onto the breezeway in bare feet and moved to the railing to peer over. In the courtyard below, tucked behind some leafy bushes, I saw the blackish-purple bike that belonged to the spy, and I knew we had 'em at their own game.

Returning to the room, Storie stood guard at the window while I texted Jack.

"Cut it out."

Cha-ching: "Cut what out?"

"Knocking on our door. It's immature."

Cha-ching: "I'm not knocking on your door. We're at the bar on the corner."

"Then tell Joe to tell his spy to stop knocking on our door. We see his bike."

Expecting a text response, it startled me when the phone actually rang. It was Jack. I put him on speaker.

"What are you talking about?"

"The guy who followed us into the swamp, Joe's spy. His bike is in the courtyard. Tell him to stop banging on our door."

"Lily," Joe was on the phone now, "my spy drove a car. He didn't ride a bike."

"No, he did," I insisted. "We saw a bike on the way to the police station and the same bike was behind the empty building near the swamp."

"He didn't. I don't know whose bike you saw or who's knocking on your door. Just keep it locked. We're on our way."

Just then the heavy fist knocked again. I dropped the phone.

"Shit."

"Lily," I heard Jack's voice coming from the phone on the floor. "Are you okay?"

"Yeah, yeah. I dropped the phone. He knocked again."

Storie shifted into a loud whisper. "Let's don't panic," she said. "We couldn't even say what color Jimbo and Stevie's bikes were. This bike might not be the same one at all."

"Lily," Jack said calmly, "we're in front of the hotel. I'm gonna hang up now. Do not open the door until I call you on the phone, okay?"

My mind felt clouded by these odd instructions. "Okay?" He repeated, still in his calm way.

"Okay," I said back into the phone, and he hung up.

I looked at Storie. Instead of a knock, a voice said, "I know about your friend. The dead girl."

I could not reach her before she threw opened the door. We were standing face to face with Ball Cap, the guy we saw at Mookie's earlier in the day.

"My name's Simon."

In spite of Mookie's high opinion of him, Simon was one of the people suspected of committing the murder. We stood frozen. Simon repeated, "I know, I know about your friend. The dead girl."

Storie engaged him by asking, "How do you know her?" And as he stood there awkwardly, making me very uncomfortable, I saw Jack and Joe enter the courtyard below. They moved smoothly without making a noise. Joe bent and grabbed two of those baby coconuts. He silently tossed one to Jack, who of course snatched it easily then moved across the courtyard. Joe stayed on this side.

Storie saw them and made a noise of recognition which alerted Simon. He jerked his head, looking up the breezeway, never suspecting the danger was coming from below and behind. I fought the urge to dive and yank Storie down with me, so we wouldn't be bombarded by accident. However, I willed myself to remember their perfect accuracy on the baseball diamond and stayed statue-still.

Just then, two coconuts sliced the night air, pelting Simon with heavy thuds almost at the same time. Both landed on large muscles, not bone, one on the back and one on the outer thigh. I wondered if that was on purpose or just a happy accident.

Jack, standing much farther away had a straighter shot, right above the railing. Joe's coconut came through a narrow space where the wrought iron stopped and a concrete pillar started. I judged both shots to be incredibly hard to make, but that was from the perspective of a person who couldn't have hit the target which was standing two feet in front of her.

The fallout was loud. Simon made an unusual half-moan-half-yell sound that put me in mind of the bellow you might hear from a baby yak. He stumbled forward, into me and Storie. And before we could push him off us, Joe was already up the stairs, grabbing him in some kind of wrestling hold. Jack came from the other direction only a few seconds later. With the murderer out of the way, he assessed us, pushing us back into the room before turning to deliver a punch.

Simon protested loudly, "It's, it's not me. I didn't do it. I didn't do it."

Joe tightened his hold. "Then what the hell are you doing up here harassing these two women?"

"Looking for your next victim?" Jack asked, as he got the pending punch under control.

"I didn't do it," Simon repeated. "I didn't do it."

I finally found my voice and said, "We saw this guy at Mookie's Bar today. He's the guy who found Luanne. The one Jimbo and Stevie told us about. His name is Simon."

Joe grunted then said to Simon, "Are you carrying a weapon? Gun? Knife?"

"I have a pocket knife in my, in my left pocket."

Jack pulled the knife out and tossed it through the door onto the bed. He said to Joe, "Move him into the room." Then to Simon, he said, "I swear to God, man, if you so much as lift a finger, we'll beat the livin' shit outta you and worry about the mess later."

"I, I won't," Simon muttered. "I won't."

Still in Joe's hold, the two made their way into the room. Jack closed the door, and Storie and I stepped as far back as we could, just shy of shutting ourselves in the bathroom.

Jack moved a chair and motioned for Joe to let Simon sit. Joe did not relax, every muscle on standby to take down Simon if he tried to run. Jack sat on the bed across from the perp. It appeared he had done a little mind game and emerged calmer than he was a minute ago.

"What are you doing here, Simon?" he asked.

Simon's eyes darted around the room. You could tell he was struggling. I remembered how Mookie said he didn't relate well to people. I didn't know if it would help, but I pulled Storie into the room and we both sat down on her bed. She reached for her phone and turned off the music which had been playing this whole time. I rubbed out the joint that was still burning.

Simon regurgitated his very first statement. "I know, I know about your friend," he said to me and Story. "The dead girl."

"What about her?" Joe asked, his voice still thick with tension.

"I, I didn't hurt her," Simon stated. "I have an alibi. The cops, the cops checked it out."

I wanted to know more about his alibi, but I didn't interrupt. I figured we had a limited window with a guy like this, so I let the boys move the interrogation forward.

Simon continued, "I found the body. That part, that part is true."

"How'd you find her," Jack wanted to know.

"I work in the salt ponds."

"Work?" Joe asked.

"I do research." Simon said. "On an endangered, an endangered species."

Jack and Joe didn't dig into that any farther, but Jack asked, "Your research takes you into the swamp then?"

"Yes. Sometimes for days at a time. I camp in the, in the salt ponds."

Simon rolled his shoulder and winced, and suddenly Jack realized he was in pain.

"Dude," he said, "we're not done here, but you need to ice your shoulder and your leg."

"I'm fine," he said. I sensed he did not want to belabor the visit longer than necessary. "I found the girl's body. In the water. Caught on the roots. She was so little, I thought, I thought it was a kid."

Storie stood up abruptly. "You're lying," she said quietly. "You killed her, didn't you?"

Joe moved just a little, just enough to look like he was closing in.

"I'm not lying," Simon said, a strained note tainting his already agitated voice. "I didn't kill her."

"Then why are you making shit up?" Storie demanded.

"I'm not, I'm not making it up."

"Luanne was five feet ten inches tall. She wouldn't have looked like a little kid."

"No," Simon said firmly. "This person, this person was short. Four feet and a couple, a couple inches. She, she would have been under five feet."

"No way," Storie denied it firmly.

"I swear," Simon said, checking to see that Joe hadn't moved any closer.

Jack assessed Storie the way he does when someone might be in danger of having an attack of some sort. Keeping his eyes on her, he said her name.

When she looked, he continued. "Is it possible the victim is not Luanne?"

"No," she said. "It's not possible. She has the tattoo."

"Okay," Jack said. His voice was soothing. "Okay. Maybe the artist was so thrilled with the design y'all came up with, maybe he sold it to someone else without y'all knowing."

Storie was stunned. She looked at me to help her synthesize this information. "If the victim is too short to be Luanne," I said, "Jack's idea could explain how she has the same tattoo."

While Storie wrestled with that, Joe took over. "You didn't come here to tell us the victim wasn't Luanne. You wouldn't have known that. Why are you here?"

"I came, I came to tell you I know who killed the girl."

"Did you tell this to the cops?"

Simon looked flustered. "I don't..." He paused, before finishing his sentence. "Interview well." He took a breath. "They didn't..." Another longer pause. "Believe me."

It seemed like two things were at play here—the homicide itself and the victim's identity. We came down here strictly to be of service where the identity issue was concerned, not to solve a murder. However, if a clue was handed on a silver platter, I, for one, did not see the point of ignoring it. Plus, I felt bad that this possibly innocent suspect was struggling. "Simon," I said as kindly as I could, "tell us what you know."

He took a deep breath and started to rattle off a list of events without using any transitional words.

"I found the body. Not where you two, you two were looking. That campfire and that, and that rock stack aren't connected to the body. Stevie and Jimbo built that."

Jack looked at me. With my eyes, I told him I would explain later. With his eyes he told me damn right I would.

"The cops watched the area for a, for a while. They cleared out in a couple weeks. I stayed close. To work. I watched. I know who goes back there. Homeless mostly. Some kayakers. I paid attention. I saw a, saw a dark blue pickup truck in April. Georgia plates. That guy, he didn't belong. I told the cops. Gave them the license number. The cops ran the tags but nothing, but nothing came up. The cop said most witnesses don't get the, get the license plate right. I have a pretty good memory. But he could've, he could've altered it. Made threes into eights or maybe an *H,* an *H* into an *I.* Something like that. That guy was at the, at the spot where I found her."

I remembered in the bar, Mookie had called Simon "off-the-chart smart." If that was true, I thought the part about him having a good memory sounded reasonable.

"That truck was here again, here again in June," he continued with his account. "I saw the guy."

"You saw the guy with the Georgia plates?" Joe asked.

"Yes. He was in the, in the spot where I found her."

"Wait a minute," Storie interrupted. "He went to the place where you found Luanne?" She still wasn't willing to accept that a stranger had her same tattoo.

"Yes. He stayed there for a, for a while. He looked at some, at some pictures he brought with him. Then he left."

Jack interjected, "You told all this to the police?"

"Not the part, the part about him coming back."

"Dude," Jack said, his voice a perfect balance of concern and encouragement, "that's important information."

"I know it's tough," Joe added, his body language had softened considerably, "but you gotta go back to the cops."

"I have a, I have a theory," Simon said. "But if she's, if she's not your friend, it won't matter to you."

"She's still a person," I said quietly. "She may not be our person, but she still matters."

We waited, and after a short silence, Simon shared his theory. "I think, I think the man in the pickup will come back. I saw the truck the end of, the end of April. Again the end of June. I think he does something that brings, that brings him down here every couple months."

It landed on me like a honey bee on a dandelion that it was now the end of August, two months after the suspect last visited the spot where the victim was found. If he was on a two-month cycle, he could be here, in Key West, now. I looked at Storie, who seemed to be doing the math in her head, too. Jack and Joe, both better at math, had completed the problem and already jumped ahead.

"Simon," Joe said, "There's a lot at stake here, brother. You gotta take this to the cops."

"They don't, they don't believe me," he protested.

"Would it help if we went with you?" Jack asked. "Storie will need to update the detective on some specifics like Luanne's height, so they can compare that with the description of the victim. Joe and I can fill them in on how we met you, minus the coconuts, of course." He smiled and added, "Sorry about that, man."

Simon nodded his head and rubbed his outer leg.

"We were a little rough," Joe agreed. "Sorry, man."

"It's okay," Simon reiterated.

"The point is," Joe added, circling back around to the crux of the problem, "we can do a lot of the talking. All you need to explain is when you saw the truck and the guy, and your theory about his timeline."

I slipped Detective Glory's business card from my back pocket. "The detective in charge of the case is gone until Monday," I informed the three guys, "but we shouldn't wait that long." Holding the card in one hand and flicking the edge against my opposite index finger, I said, "I bet if we call Detective St. John right now, she'll be able to meet us at the station tomorrow."

Simon didn't say anything. Jack's voice got one notch quieter as he said, "It'll feel good to get this off your shoulders. I know they didn't believe you the first time, but it'll be different this time."

Eventually we reached a consensus and everybody bought in. I dialed up the detective as the other four sat quietly.

"Detective St. John," she answered professionally but with a touch of friendliness.

"Hey Detective Glory. This is Lily Barlow. Me and my friend…"

"Hello Lily!" Her tone was bright and fully friendly now. She didn't sound perturbed that I was calling her at, Lord, was it ten thirty?

Regardless, I apologized. "I hate to call so late."

"No worries. How can I help you?"

"Storie and I struck up a conversation with one of your town folk." I shrugged my shoulders and raised my eyebrows at my little audience, knowing that I was putting a very benign spin on it. "After talking," I continued, "some things came up we'd like to share with you. Could we all come in tomorrow morning?"

"Absolutely," she said, with the grace of a hostess who might be having people over for brunch. "Say, nine thirty? Would that work?"

"Yes, ma'am, nine thirty would be fine." I was speaking, but my eyes were on Simon. He seemed distracted, so I gave a little half-wave to get his attention. When he noticed my hand, he looked up and nodded to confirm that he was available. "We'll see you then," I added.

"Be safe," she said by way of ending the call. I thought it was quaint that an officer of the law would sign off with those words. I hung up and looked at the group, feeling strange. You could've thrown in a twist that involved an elephant wearing high tops and carrying a sign that read *Free Tibet*, and that wouldn't have surprised me more than what had just unfolded in this hotel room. An hour ago, Storie and I were listening to music and smoking a joint, now our group had grown, and we might be on the brink of cracking a murder. What were the odds?

"Simon," I said, coming back to the present, "where would you like to meet us?" I figured with his social anxiety he'd prefer to go in together under the protective strength-in-numbers format, rather than rolling into the police station alone and unsupported. I also figured there was a good chance he'd stand us up.

Chapter 15

Lying there staring at the texture in the ceiling, it was apparent I hadn't slept much since Simon left and the boys cleared out. I picked up my phone. Again. Only thirteen minutes since the last time check at four thirty-seven. That's it? Thirteen stinkin' minutes?

With my eyes wide opened, I went back to the ceiling swirls where I had already identified an ostrich, the Washington Monument, and King Tut's...what's the Egyptian coffin called...sar-something? You know... that thing Tut was buried in. Sarcoffinus?

Shrugging off Egyptian kings and their coffins, I focused on the designs in the ceiling. What I didn't see edged into the plaster was a pictograph outlining the secret steps for falling asleep. Bored and now fully awake, I got up, took a quick shower, threw on some clean clothes and jammed my phone in my back pocket.

When I opened the door, the first order of business was to move directly to the railing and scan the courtyard below for Simon's purplish-black bike. No bike, but he could've moved it. Sure, he walked us down the garden path of his innocence, acting all awkward and nervous, telling us he wasn't involved, but let's be honest, a lot of serial killers probably did that. And we didn't know this guy from…

When the rocker to my right creaked, two things happened. First, I nearly peed my pants and next, I entered a state that was just shy of catatonic. Shit. Either the haunting I had feared all along was happening. Or, if it wasn't a dreaded haint, I was about to come face to face with a known killer. At last count, that could have been one of four people—Simon, Jimbo, Stevie, or the man from the pickup truck who for now would be known as Georgia Plates. Too scared to move, I saw with my peripheral vision, the form of a person. All I could distinguish in the dim light was the bill of a ball cap. That didn't rule out ghost entirely, but Simon wore a ball cap. My mind screeched around that curve, and it became obvious we had badly misjudged Simon, who was now planning to kill his next victim. Unfortunately, it seemed I had drawn the short straw.

"Looking for somebody?" The spirit or the criminal wearing the ball cap asked quietly.

I slowly blew out the breath I'd been holding. Relief bubbled up like an artesian well, replacing the fear that had been gurgling there seconds prior. It was neither ghost nor killer. It was Jack.

"You scared the Jujyfruits outta me, you jerk."

"I know," he said with a snicker in his voice. "You're so easy. Which way did you go? Haunted rocking chair or murderer?"

"I was split fifty-fifty," I said, my heart still pounding.

"If it makes you feel any better, I looked, too. In fact, I took it one step farther and walked the grounds."

Well, it eased my suspicious mind a smidgeon to know I wasn't the only one jumping to unfounded conclusions. Instead of pondering Simon's involvement in this or any other murder, I turned my attention to something else.

"What are you doing out here?" I asked. My voice settling back to a more normal cadence as I got a grip on my nerves.

"I'm guessing same as you," he said. "Can't sleep."

"I tossed from the minute my head hit the pillow," I confessed. "This whole thing is a lot closer to a murder than I expected to get this weekend."

"Second guessing your criminal justice major?" He smiled in the half light.

"You know, JT, there are other crimes besides murder. You know that, right?"

"Ones that would interest you? Let's see. How 'bout the high stakes world of tax evasion? Maybe a robust case of insurance fraud? Identity theft should be good for some laughs."

"No," I said, ignoring his wisecrack while shaking off those options as too bland. "I'd want something with a little more *oomph* than that. Something like human trafficking. How does that sound?"

"Dangerous," he said flatly. Then, in case I didn't hear him, he reiterated, "It sounds dangerous."

"Well, I'm not volunteering to go undercover as bait."

"That's a relief," he mused and reached over to grab my arm, "because I'd hate to take off work every time I had to kick the ass of a trafficker who threatened you. Just like I would've kicked Simon's ass."

I elected to hop on that train, mainly to lure Jack away from his potential involvement in my potential career choice. "Simon. He's a weird bird, isn't he?"

"Yeah, buddy. He reminds me a little of that kid from middle school who had a crush on you."

"Jake? What was his last name? Young? Jake Young?" Jake Young had moved to town in the seventh grade and moved out in the eighth. I don't know if I'd go so far as to say he had a crush on me, but I was nice to him and he needed that. Middle school stinks when you're not in tune with your peer base.

We sat there for a few more minutes, rocking companionably, until he hoisted himself out of his chair. Standing, he offered me a hand. I accepted but did nothing with it, hoping he would give a good heave ho and pull me up, which he did. We headed down to the car. Although it was still soundly outside the hours of operation at Nine-O, I hoped this little jaunt would involve coffee, and the sooner the better.

Within sixty seconds he was pulling into a gas station, and I smiled to myself, even as I managed the expectations of my taste buds. I knew this wouldn't be like yesterday's *café con leche;* however, the tiny convenient store portion of the establishment smelled great, like a coffee roasting factory.

I enjoyed the process of working my way around the little island. In a self-serve situation, where there's more than one kind available, I take a splash of each. It's called a suicide. Insensitive? Very possibly. But it was one of those things I picked up from my Uncle Dave, and I wasn't likely to let it go at this stage in my life. As kids, Uncle Dave and Dad used to make suicides by mixing Coke, Mountain Dew, Dr. Pepper, Sprite, Pepsi, Orange Crush, root beer, ginger ale, Cheerwine whenever they were a little farther south…basically whatever was available to them. He taught me how to do it when I was little, and I did it at every fast food restaurant that offered a drink machine. As my palate matured, I abandoned the carbonated beverages and started applying the suicide method to coffee instead.

Jack waited patiently as I sorted through the condiments looking for the real raw sugar and the full fat creamer. The results were worth the time it took. Strong and good with the caffeine bump I craved. He paid for our coffees then held the doors for me: store and car.

Buckled safely back into my seat I said, "Part of me wants to ride back over to the salt ponds to show you what we saw down there."

"Too early," he said. "That gate'll be locked." He eased the car into the street and added, "But we can go later if y'all want."

This statement confirmed a suspicion. "You and Joe aren't fishing today?"

"Nah," he said with a shrug in his voice. "Weather's changin'. Cap'n doesn't think we'll have much luck." He glanced at me and something about the line of his jaw made me think he was waiting to see if I'd buy it.

"That's the reason y'all aren't fishing?"

He shook his head, keeping his focus on the road. "No. We wouldn't have gone anyway. With all these new developments, we both want to be…" he hesitated, hunting for the right word.

In my mind, I supplied *in charge*. The corners of his mouth lifted, almost like he was reading my thought, and he finished his sentence with, "supportive."

My eyes couldn't have rolled any farther back in their sockets, but I didn't let him see that.

"These last couple days have been tough on Storie. She's pretty raw right now. Simon, if he even shows up, will be jumpy as a long-tailed monkey at a lawn mower convention. You…" He looked at me again, and when I raised my eyebrows in a challenge, daring him to say something derogatory, he reined it back in with a semi-sweet reversal. "You," he said, "will have your hands full with those two, and it's the least Joe and I can do to offer an ounce of moral support." He put his heavy hand on my knee and squeezed. I let him get away with it. I doubted he thought I was capable of managing this interview, but the fact he didn't say that bought him half a point.

Arriving at the destination he had in mind, he parked the rental in a space that bordered Smathers Beach. We got out and crossed the street to the bridle path which ran parallel to the road and the ocean. I chuckled because this was the spot where Storie and I were planning to buy imaginary drugs from imaginary Jordy. As we strolled, my mind wandered to the night of the murder. If the vic wasn't Luanne, who was she?

"I guess I need to start calling the victim Misty again, since we know she's not Luanne."

"Mmhmm," he said. "It seems like that's how this is playing out, but I wouldn't push Storie too hard yet. After she talks to the cops about it this morning, she might have an easier time."

Jack reached down and took the hand that wasn't holding the coffee cup, forcing me to shelve Misty for the moment and focus on him.

"Can I help you?"

"Oh," he said, "you could if you wanted to." His eyes narrowed, and I felt like the thing he wanted my help with was getting undressed.

In classic Lily Barlow fashion, I responded with a stammer. And in classic Jack Turner fashion, he responded to my response with a laugh.

"I just want to talk about it," he said. "Yes, I want to do it again. But first I want to talk about it."

"We don't have a lot of time," I offered up in a calculated delay.

"That's okay," he said, pulling me to a stop. "We don't have to finish the conversation."

"I don't like the standing, face-to-face format you've selected for this conversation." It was honest and at the same time it provided another roadblock.

"Would you rather sit?" He gestured to an area across the street over on the beach. There was a collection of large rocks providing seating options. We could sit and look at the ocean. Relocating would further delay the conversation, which appealed to me, but sitting seemed too restrictive.

Perhaps he sensed my turmoil, because he added, "Or, we could keep walking."

Weighing the options, I agreed to keep walking, minus the hand holding. Movement eased my anxiety over things like this. And we didn't have to look at each other. Changing scenery offered security in the form of distraction. I could look at the ground, the birds, the occasional passing car. I bent to snatch a twig, and as I fiddled with it, I glanced over at a car on the road. A pickup truck. A pickup truck with Georgia plates.

"Jack, is that the truck?"

"Truck? What truck?"

Jack, who up to this point had done a yeoman's job of accepting and adapting to my stall tactics, sounded baffled by this one. He looked up as an old, dark blue truck pulled into a parking spot on the ocean side of the road.

"The guy's truck. The guy Simon saw back in the swamp." My nerve endings were abuzz like I just finished a fourth cup of coffee. Jack, on the other hand, was cool and controlled as he started taking in the information.

Distressed that he wasn't taking it in fast enough, I heaped on more. "Didn't Simon say the guy drove a navy pickup with Georgia plates? The killer?"

"He did say that," Jack answered abstractly and pulled his phone out of his pocket. "Come here," he directed as he draped a heavy arm across my shoulders and held the phone up to snap a photo of us.

"Jack," I hissed, "this is not the time for selfies."

"I can't think of a better time," he said, pulling me back to him and holding the camera higher. When he released me, he pointed to a spot where he wanted me to stand. I was not amused, and the look on my face proved it.

"Smile," he coaxed. I didn't, so he tried a different tact. "Say *naked*." That succeeded in getting me to flap my left arm against my side in frustration. He looked at the resulting picture on his screen and nodded. "Perfect," he crooned. "You're sexy when you're agitated."

"Will you please stop goofing around and pay attention to the truck?"

"I did," he assured me. "It's in each of these pictures. There's a clear shot of the license plate in that last one. Call your lady detective and tell her you want to text her some pictures."

I was so impressed with what he'd just done, I decided not to blast him for using the slightly offensive phrase, *lady detective*.

He kept walking, his hand plastered to the small of my back. I believed he was using the cutesy couple-on-vacation act to keep his hand on me, but I couldn't be sure. We stopped walking when I tapped the screen to call Detective Glory, and he took another picture of me. I glared at him, but he winked and smiled. "Appearances," he said by way of assuring me.

The phone rang once, and she picked up. "Good morning, Lily," she said. Already knew my number or had added me to her contacts, one. That was interesting.

"Good morning, Detective Glory. I hope I'm not bothering you."

"Not at all. Are we still on for this morning?"

"We are. And what I'm about to share would make a lot more sense if we had already filled you in on a few things, but we might not have time for that."

"Are you okay?" She asked.

"Yes. Fine. Just trying to figure out how to give you this lead in a way that won't make me sound crazy."

"Well, you didn't come off as crazy yesterday, if that helps."

"Okay," I said, relaxing a little. "Okay," I repeated and took a deep breath. "I'm with my boyfriend, Jack Turner, on the bridle path." I made an effort to twist in such a way that prevented any eye contact with the alleged *boyfriend* before continuing. "We talked with Simon, the guy who found the body in the swamp. Simon is some kind of biologist studying stuff in the salt ponds. He says there's a pickup truck with Georgia plates that's been coming to the swamp every two months since the murder. Last time the truck was here, Simon saw the driver at the exact spot where he found the victim's body. He planned to tell you about it this morning when we all come in, along with the fact that he expects the truck back down here any day now. End of August will be two months since he last saw it." I paused, trying to gauge if she was with me or not.

"Go on," she said, encouragingly.

"An old dark blue truck with Georgia plates just

pulled into a parking space on the main road."

Jack leaned in and clarified in my ear. "South Roosevelt Boulevard at Smathers Beach."

I shared that with the detective, adding, "I have pictures of the truck and the license plate. I can text them if you want."

"Yes, please do that," she directed. "Has anyone gotten out of the truck?"

"No," I said.

"Lily, please do not approach the vehicle or engage the driver in any way. Tell Jack the same thing."

I repeated what she said to Jack who nodded understanding.

"We won't," I said. Mainly I was thrilled that she was taking me seriously.

"Can you give me a landmark? What are you near?"

I looked up and down the bridle path, searching for something that would serve as an identifiable marker. Palm trees mainly. Nothing really stood out.

Meanwhile, Jack was tapping and scrolling on his phone, and in a matter of seconds he came up with something. He took a screen shot, then sent that along with the other photos to my phone.

"Tell her you're texting GPS coordinates."

She was pleased by this, and I wished I could've found a way to take credit. I wanted to be the helpful one.

I paused the call long enough to text the information,

and she let me know she had received it.

"I'm heading out now. If the truck moves, do not follow it. Do you read me."

"Loud and clear," I assured her.

She hung up, and I looked at Jack, who snapped my picture.

"Stop it."

"Just trying to look natural," he said.

We walked further along the path, until we discovered a hidden side trail that led toward a salt pond and a little wooden pier of sorts. The trees provided some cover, but they weren't dense, and we could still see the street and the truck. We would know if Georgia Plates got out or moved. Jack tested a dilapidated railing to determine if it would hold his weight. Too bad he decided it wouldn't. Instead of leaning on the railing, he circled me in a hug and kissed the top of my head.

"You okay?" he asked.

"Yes. You don't need to hug on me."

"Appearances," he said, falling back on that lame excuse.

"Georgia Plates can't see us from where he is."

"Then call this my consolation prize since we never got to have that conversation."

I tried to slip out, but he snugged his arms tighter, and I didn't see the point of struggling further. Although, if I had to guess, I bet he was hoping I would give it one more shot.

I stayed still, waiting for him to tire or get too hot. It took longer than I expected, and before either of those things happened, a police cruiser pulled in beside the pickup. Georgia Plates panicked and threw his truck in reverse, slamming into an oncoming car that was in his blindspot. It wasn't Detective Glory who exited from the cruiser but a uniformed officer. He barked instructions to Georgia Plates to stay in the vehicle.

Georgia Plates ignored the instructions and opened his door to make a break for it on foot when another unmarked car whipped in front of him. He tumbled into the fender; Glory jumped out, gun drawn. Showing me I hadn't underestimated her bad assery, she took down the perp in a clean, smooth motion, cuffing him and hauling the dude, who outweighed her by a good hundred pounds, to his feet. She patted him down while the other cop assessed the driver of the oncoming vehicle for injury. He spoke into a radio on his shoulder, and I assumed he was calling for an ambulance as a precaution.

Watching this whole thing unfold, I lost complete control, running up the dock to dry land before turning and running back to Jack. I grabbed him out of pure excitement. And he let me. Our faces were close. I noticed the intensity of his blue eyes. I moved my head in, closing the last little space between our mouths. It was meant to be a kiss of celebration after witnessing what could have passed for an action scene out of any cop show on Netflix. And, in my defense, it started that way. Slowly, though, the kiss transformed into one of passion. I pulled away, embarrassed, and turned my back to him. At the moment, that was the closest I could come to a disappearing act.

He stepped up to my back and whispered, "It's okay." Putting his hands on my shoulders, he added, "Me too." Then he stepped away again, giving me space to collect myself. In another few seconds, we ambled off the dock and headed to the rental car with me pretending nothing had happened.

As Jack turned the ignition, my phone rang. It was Detective Glory. "Hey there," I greeted her, "nice job!" I raised my hand from the passenger side to wave.

"All in a day's work," she said, and I was touched by her modesty. "I'll be a while, but it's more important than ever that I talk with you and Simon."

"We're planning to meet up with him for the nine thirty appointment. My gut tells me, if he shows, you might wanna talk to him while you have him. He's flighty," I warned her.

"I hear ya," she said. "Okay, keep it the same. Try to get him to the municipal building. I'll be there."

"Ten-Four," I said and ended the call. Jack just shook his head at my cop lingo and backed us out of the parking space.

Chapter 16

I sat in the passenger seat, feeling stunned. "What just happened here?"

"Are you talking to me or Stephanie Plum?" He asked.

"You," I said aloud, but the speech bubble above my head referred to him as *nitwit*. And a second speech bubble extended an invitation to Stephanie that she could join in if she wanted.

"Well," Jack started a recap, "we took a walk, and I had the bright idea to talk about our relationship. You dodged the difficult conversation by identifying the vehicle of a murder suspect, based on a very thin description from a squirrely eye witness, and you subsequently got the suspect apprehended. Best I can tell...you *really* didn't want to talk about our relationship."

I laughed. Hard. And once the amusement part was over, I couldn't seem to stop. Monitoring my level of hysteria, Jack soothed me, "You're okay, Lily. Slow down. Easy."

My laughter morphed into a chocking, gasping sound as I tried to draw air. That's when I started to cough. He kept talking quietly. I kept coughing dramatically. He must not have been too concerned, because I noticed he wasn't pulling off the road, which was reassuring. My death from asphyxiation was not imminent. Once I could breathe normally again, I thought it best to ride the rest of the way in silence. Holy jicama slaw on a hamburger. Storie would not believe this.

* * *

Barreling through the lobby near the buffet, I spotted the other two deep in conversation at a table near the window. By the looks of their plates, they were on the backside of breakfast. Jack and I grabbed some food before plopping down to fill them in. My pancakes weren't cold before Jack had delivered the whole story; that boy was nothing if not succinct. We were to the Q&A portion of the presentation, and Storie had a million questions. Jack carefully responded to each one until she was completely satisfied, helping her understand that right now, the only things Georgia Plates could be accused of were causing an accident when he backed into the other car and attempting to leave the scene of the accident.

"Yes," she agreed, "but he did it. Right? Simon said he did it."

Feeling compelled to clarify, I made a tiny contribution by refreshing an important detail. "Simon said he saw Georgia Plates at the spot where the body was discovered. He didn't see him commit the murder."

"You're right, Lily," Joe said. "We need to stick to the facts when we give this information to that lady detective."

Again, with the *lady detective* crap. The depth of the Turner boy chauvinism was beginning to gnaw at me. "Detective," I corrected Joe.

"What?"

"Detective. You don't need to say *lady* detective."

He looked at me in a doofus kind of way, unclear what I was getting at, so I added, "You wouldn't say gentleman detective, right? It's just plain detective, whether it's a man or a woman."

Catching my vibe, he nodded and offered a lukewarm apology. "Yes 'um. My bad. Detective."

The lesson in biased language was enough of a segue to give us all a breather from the murder. Jack checked his phone and reported that we'd better think about heading out if we wanted to be on time for Simon.

* * *

As we neared the rendezvous point at Mookie's Bar, I saw our fifth wheel waiting out front with his bike. Joe's plan was to take advantage of the parking at the municipal building, but as I watched Simon's gerbil-like nervousness, I had a feeling he might bail before we parked and made it back. At the light, I told the boys we'd meet them inside, then Storie and I jumped out. Not the safest transfer, and maybe not the most legal, but I didn't want this guy to get away.

"Hey, Simon!" I greeted him cheerfully as we crossed the street. "You been waitin' long?"

He shook his head, but he looked disappointed. I felt like another minute thirty and he would have talked himself out of it. I could tell the way his face lost a little light, kind of like when you unplug the computer from the charger and the screen gets one degree darker even though there's plenty of juice.

"The boys are parking. They'll meet us inside." In my mind that was a pretty clear invitation to proceed, but Simon didn't pick up on it. So sweet Storie took over.

"You ready?" She waited until he nodded, then she swished to the side so he'd have room to push his bike between the two of us. We entered the cross walk, with the signal, three abreast.

There was a more business-like woman at the reception desk this morning, and I immediately missed the guy from before, even though I couldn't remember his name to save my life. The five of us bunched into the waiting area. Simon was the only one who didn't sit, and when Joe realized it, he manufactured a reason to stand. He walked over to a fountain for a sip of water. Sauntering back, he didn't return to his chair but approached Simon. Before long, Joe had coaxed Simon into a conversation about the endangered species he was studying in the salt pond. Surprisingly, I didn't think Joe was faking interest in the subject. Even more of a shocker, Simon turned out to be exquisitely articulate. That was the key; he needed to be the expert. I rolled this idea like a hunk of orange Play Dough in my palm, wondering how I could help him become an expert in the interview scenario, in like five minutes.

I pulled a "Joe," nonchalantly wandering over to the water fountain first and looping back to the two who were standing. I gave Joe a little head jerk to let him know I wanted a minute with Simon. He read my message, nodded, and gave me an introductory greeting to get Simon to turn in my direction. Then he slipped back to the chairs.

"Hey, Simon," I started.

He nodded. Then my idea came tumbling out, and I didn't waste any time tying it with a bow.

"I doubt they'll interview us all together. They'll probably split us up, which might be nerve wracking."

"I would prefer to do it as a, as a group."

"Me, too. But here's the thing. I overheard you telling Joe about your work, and you didn't seem nervous talking about that at all."

"Well, that's because I know, I know what I'm talking about."

"Don't forget," I advised him, "that you also know what you're talking about when it comes to the guy in the blue truck. You saw things. You have a good memory. Just tell them what you know, because you *know* what you're talking about. You're the expert of your eye-witness account."

Just then, Detective Glory appeared. I turned back to Simon and gave him a last parting reminder, "You're an expert." He nodded, but he was already shifting his weight looking around, so I didn't know if it registered or not.

As it turned out, they did interview us separately, even though none of us was a person of interest. Joe and Jack went pretty fast, probably because they were the farthest removed, accentuated by the fact that they can both keep a discussion short and to the point when necessary.

Storie took longer than me, I figured because she was giving pertinent information about Luanne, height and whatnot. But I also imagined she was struggling, which might've slowed her down a tad.

Simon took the longest. We waited for him, because, well, it'd be plain mean spirited not to. We kind of got him into this, and he was walking around with a bruised leg and a bruised shoulder because of us. The least we could do was wait on the guy.

When he appeared, he looked like an old rag, wrung out and draped over a fence post to dry. "How'd it go?" Jack asked as Simon approached us in the waiting area.

"I think, I think they took me seriously."

"You done?"

"They may want me, want me to answer some more questions. Maybe make an identification."

"You okay with that?" Joe asked.

"I have information that could, that could help catch the guy." He looked at me as he said this, and I think he was implying that he found a way to capitalize on his expert status to survive the experience. I smiled at him, and in return he gave me the closest thing to a smile he may have ever managed. I was exceedingly pleased with myself for being of service. Maybe this was my career path, coaching socially awkward witnesses on how to interact with investigators.

As a group, we nodded approval of Simon's involvement, and then I said what was on everyone's mind. Or at least what was on my mind. "I'm starving. Wanna eat?"

Whether it had been on their minds before or not, they all whole heartedly bought in. We let Simon pick the spot, and he took us to a quiet diner that was walking distance from the police station. Joe and Jack kept the conversation going. Falling behind those three as we made our way up the sidewalk, I grabbed Storie by the arm to show I knew her world was flipped upside down again. She looked at me with a calm, tired expression, and squeezed my arm in return.

We all decompressed over the food. I stuffed myself with a burger and one of the best chocolate milkshakes I'd ever tasted. We didn't delve too deeply into the mystery that was Simon, but a few tidbits floated to the surface as we chatted. He was home schooled, which explained a lot. He started a biology program at one of the Florida universities but dropped out for reasons he didn't share. He was now one of several people collecting data for a research project at Florida State.

When we got to the end of the meal, I asked if he wanted my phone number in case anything came up about the investigation. I tried very hard to make this sound like an ordinary thing people would do, not like I expected he would eventually be accused of accessory to murder, and to be honest, I was surprised when he accepted. We parted ways in front of the diner, Simon waiting for us to pick our direction before committing to his. He had had his fill of us, and who could blame him?

Walking toward the car, I asked, "What do y'all wanna do now?"

Ding and Dong were uncharacteristically quiet, but then I guessed why. They wanted to see what Storie had in mind. I turned toward her and asked the question again. "Is there anything you'd like to do?"

"I know Luanne wasn't murdered, but, I'm still kind of sad about the woman who was."

I nodded, thinking she wasn't yet finished.

"Would y'all mind if we drove over to the swamp again?"

"No problem," Joe said.

I did not think it necessary to point out that we never learned from Simon where exactly the body was found. It didn't seem as if that was relevant to her plan. I did think it necessary to request a stop by the hotel so I could get my sneaks. Storie approved and decided she wanted a pair of shorts instead of the frothy skirt she wore to talk to the police. Joe and Jack waited in the parking area with the chickens while she and I ran upstairs.

On our own, away from the aggravation that all men bring to every situation, I asked, "You doing okay?"

"This last week has just been so crazy," she sighed. "I haven't cried this much since my pet donkey died when I was fourteen."

Pet donkey? As tantalizing as those two words sounded, I did not take the bait that was dangling there in front of me. Instead I filed it away for another conversation and focused on her feelings. "It's been a roller coaster."

"Here's one thing I know for sure. I need to find Luanne. It took a murder to get my attention…but I'm listening now." The way she said that last part, with her head tilted up and speaking toward the ceiling, it was directed more to the universe than to me.

Intrigued, I followed that dotted line. "You think all this was engineered so you would reconnect with Luanne?"

"Yes," she said, completely committed to her conviction. "Do you think that's weird?"

"No." I scrunched my mouth. "Not weird, exactly, but definitely extreme."

"There's so much we don't understand about our existence," she explained. "I try to stay opened to all the possibilities."

"That sounds, um, reasonable."

I slipped into the bathroom to pee, and when I came out, she was already in her shorts. Flinging my flip flops across the room, I decided to put on sunscreen, since I hadn't done it this morning when I got up at that crazy early hour. Once I was fully protected against both UVA and UVB rays, I found my Keds and declared myself ready.

The guys had moved to the shade and were both actively scrolling on their phones by the time we worked our way back to them. "What the hell took so long?" Jack asked, faking frustration.

"You will never understand the power and mystery of two X chromosomes, so don't even try."

"Give me a chance," he pleaded as he reached for me. I twirled away, just ahead of his grasp, and moved myself to the passenger side of the car where the other brother was standing. Using his tongue, Joe made a sympathy cluck, which sounded like he was commiserating with Jack's dilemma of being bamboozled by a crazy person. To me, however, he simply smiled and opened my door.

The car had heated up to the point of melting plastic, and we rolled the windows down and blasted the AC to get the cooling process started. It didn't seem like anything was too far away on the island of Key West, and in a matter of minutes we were passing the gate, the bird preserve and the first of the rundown buildings. When we got out, Storie and I assumed the peculiar role of tour guides, explaining our interpretation of what we had uncovered here yesterday.

I saw no bikes, and we glanced in the window holes of the last building to make sure no one had arrived on foot and taken up residence in the lounge area. Standing there, it occurred to me that this spot was out in the open, and the main reason a crime could take place was more because there wasn't any legitimate commercial traffic, not because it was especially well hidden. This made me wonder about something else.

"Hey, Joe, why didn't we see your spy down here if he followed us in a car?"

"Well, for starters, the guy's an ex-Army Ranger," he said. "And, don't take this the wrong way, Barlow, but you have a twisted sense of awareness when it comes to your surroundings. It's not that you're completely oblivious, because you usually tune in to some obscure detail. The type of collar on a dog, or the color of red in somebody's tie-dyed t-shirt."

As much as I would've liked to defend my ability to be observant, I knew I didn't have a leg to stand on here, so I gave a nod and a one-shoulder shrug. "Can't argue that, I guess."

Joe felt the need to share with us a little more of the intel he had received from the spy. "My guy had y'all in his sights the entire time. He knew y'all stopped for a beer before talkin' to the cops. And he knew Jimbo and Stevie were here."

I was both offended and amazed at the complete and total invasion of our privacy. "Why didn't he come to assist?" I demanded, remembering how creeped out I felt around Jimbo and Stevie.

"I gave him strict instructions not to interfere unless he felt y'all faced imminent danger. I also warned him he'd risk death by yammering if he intervened before his services were legitimately required." Joe smiled;

Jack laughed; I huffed; Storie strangled a giggle with a cough.

Feeling like he could take it one step farther, Joe added, "Oh, and Nick did mention that your little... charade...made the whole day worthwhile." He stood there with a smirk on his face, nodding his approval, and I tried to stare him down but lost my nerve. Maybe it was the blue eyes that won every time. Maybe I had a blue-eye aversion and I'd never win a stare down with a Turner boy because their deep blue eyes had some kind of voodoo sorcery thing that prevented me from engaging. In my head, I cursed the wizardry of genetics, then bowed out.

It was a relief when Storie came to my defense, linking her arm around my elbow. Side by side, we headed toward the corner of the building, and she said over her shoulder as she tossed her blonde hair, "Y'all wanna see what we found in the swamp?"

Our foursome proceeded, and I slowed at the back of the building so we could scan for Simon's bike. Nothing. It appeared the entire scene was deserted, but who knew for how long. While the area lacked business traffic, there seemed to be a constant flow of locals down here, plus the odd out-of-town sightseer, like us...and Georgia Plates.

"Hey," I wondered, "do y'all think the cops will tape this place off again after they question the new suspect?"

"Probably," Jack answered. "Makes sense they'd go over it again. Might ask Simon to show them where he saw the guy. Stuff like that."

Entering the path through the undergrowth, Storie and I gingerly picked our line. We were still in the lead, but that didn't make any kind a sense at all. Why not let American Hero Number One and American Hero Number Two knock down all the spider webs and scare off all the snakes? There was only one real path to speak of; it wasn't like we had to show them how we got to the fire ring and the rock cairn.

I sweetly suggested to Jack that they move to the front. "This is the path we were on," I said. "It's pretty straight forward from here."

"You want us to lead?" he asked. "Why? Y'all are doing such a bang-up job out front."

I could tell he was teasing me. "Just go," I demanded.

He and Joe stepped to the front and he squeezed my hand as he moved past. Small price to pay for spider web removal.

When we got to the place, Storie and I were shocked to see someone had tossed paint on the rock cairn. Lilac. Yellow. Carolina Blue. The colors ran into each other in a way that implied the task was conceived and/or completed in haste. "What happened here?" I asked, my voice edged with excitement that could've been mistaken for panic.

"Looks like a unicorn threw up," Joe offered.

"This wasn't painted yesterday," Storie explained, her voice echoing the note in mine.

"Really?" Jack asked, touching a spot of lilac. "Tacky," he reported.

"Yes, it's tacky," I agreed, "but it's not a question of taste, it's a question of motivation."

"Tacky, like it's seventy-five maybe eighty percent dry. So, it didn't just happen."

Oh. That kind of tacky.

"And with this humidity," Joe chimed in, "could've happened a while ago. Early this morning?" He looked at Jack who nodded.

"I doubt it was done last night."

"Yeah," Joe agreed. "Probably be a lot more gnats and mosquitoes hung up in it, don't ya think?"

Waiting for the Home Depot paint department to finish its analysis, I broke in, "But who painted it?"

"And why?" Storie wanted to know.

"Not a clue," Jack said.

"Simon told us the body was found somewhere else. Not here. This wasn't the place where he saw Georgia Plates," I added, going over everything in my head.

"Is this on the way?" Storie wanted to know.

"I don't remember hearing Simon say where the spot was," Joe answered her, seemingly aware she was referring to the spot where the body was found.

Jack took out his phone. Snapped a picture of the colorful cairn, then snapped a picture of me. I decided the picture thing, much like the kissing thing, was getting out of control, but I knew he was doing it to push me into a conversation. I tried to send a telepathic message that it wasn't going to happen, this conversation of his, not before we got back to Virginia anyway. He either didn't receive the message or ignored it, and instead took another picture of me.

"When I get a signal, I'll text this to the l—." He caught himself before he completed the word *lady*.

Knowing he was about to use the term *lady detective*, I whipped around and asked, "To the *who*?"

"To the detective," he replied firmly and accompanied his answer with a smoldering look meant to ignite passionate desire.

"You are tap dancin' on my very last nerve, son."

"I know," he said, "it's my absolute favorite pastime."

Meanwhile, Joe had discovered an empty quart-sized paint can that matched the light blue color. "I bet the other cans are around here somewhere," he said, looking beyond the one can further into the tangle of mangroves. "You know, y'all saw Georgia Plates this morning. Timing-wise, he coulda done this little art project before y'all ran into him."

"Do you think he did this?" I was getting a distinct Stephanie Plum vibe, and I said, "Shit, Jack, you stuck your finger in the paint. Your perfectly preserved fingerprint is now recorded at what could be a crime scene."

"I guess you're right." He showed little concern that he would somehow be tied to this whole thing.

"When we tell Detective Glory about the paint," Storie chimed in, "we'll explain about the finger print."

Joe walked over to the rocks, found Jack's fingerprint clear as a Do Not Disturb sign hanging on a doorknob, and opted for a more pragmatic approach. He obliterated any connection to his brother by blotting out Jack's print with his own, making it virtually impossible to decipher even a partial from the resulting smudge. "I'd still tell the lady detective about it." He winked at me, but more than his use of the gender biased language I honed in on the fierceness with which he looked after his younger brother. In spite of the egregious manipulation of evidence, I was intrigued that the trademark Turner Overprotectiveness wasn't only reserved for those of us belonging to the fairer sex. Yes, I realized my use of the term *fairer sex* may fall within the limits of gender biased language. And no, I didn't care.

Before departing, Storie suggested we stop to think of Misty for a few seconds, so we did. We sent our energy out toward the spirit whose human life had been violently snuffed out, and call me crazy, but it seemed like the surrounding woods got quiet as we stood there reflecting. Was Storie onto something with her abstract philosophy regarding the connectedness of everything?

Before I could spend too long on it, she made her way to the edge of the water, undid a silver charm from a clip in her hair and tossed it into the channel. It landed in the middle with a lonely plunk. I decided not to obsess about the fact that now a piece of evidence tied her to this spot, and instead just beheld the token and the gesture as a memorial to Misty.

Chapter 17

It was around five in the evening when we relayed our report about the paint and the fact that someone in our group touched it. Detective Glory was extremely interested to the point of asking what color paint we saw, where we saw it, how it was applied, and so on. Ending the call with her, I asked my friends, "Do y'all think she wanted to know the colors because she noticed paint on Georgia Plates? On his hands or maybe on his blue jeans?"

"That's a real possibility," Storie acknowledged. She was eager for some hard evidence tying this guy to the crime scene, something that would put the wheels of justice in motion.

From the driver's side, Joe said, "The sad part is they still don't know the girl's name."

"Yeah," Storie agreed. "How're they gonna figure that out?"

Level-headed Jack offered his view. "I'd say her identity will take a back seat to finding her killer, especially if they have a new lead to work with. But, find the killer and you might get the name that way."

I had come to a very similar conclusion on my own, that the killer would be the focus, not the identity. However, the need to give this person her name back tugged at me hard. To that end, I had already hatched a plan to visit the tattoo parlor where the girls got their ink. Couldn't hurt to talk with the artist, right? I did not, however, see the benefit of putting my idea to any kind of committee vote at this time, so I held my tongue.

Joe pulled into the hotel lot and gave brief but pointed instructions for everyone to change into our swim suits. "We're going swimming?" I couldn't keep the glee out of my voice.

"Yep."

"Wait. Where?" I asked.

"In the water, Lily."

"I'm not swimming in the ocean."

"Just put your damn suit on," he insisted, "and for once, don't give me any damn grief."

I grabbed Jack's arm and twisted him toward me. "I'm not swimming in the ocean," I informed him.

"Why you tellin' me? This is Joe's thing."

"I'll put my suit on, Joe Turner, but I'm going on record now. I am not swimming in the ocean."

"That's fine, girl. You can watch my wallet for me while you're sittin' on the beach."

So, we were going to the ocean. Fabulous. I felt the glee deflate with a slow hiss, and in its place, a heavier, darker dread started sharking around me.

"Don't worry," Storie whispered, "maybe there's a pool. And if not, we can walk on the beach. It'll be pretty at sunset."

I was touched by her willingness to be my buddy on this excursion, so I grabbed my suit, jumped into the bathroom, and came out ready for the dual opportunities of a dip in a pool or a walk on the beach.

Driving again, Joe took us to an unpretentious oceanside bar that was popular with the locals. Not especially busy, we had our pick of tables. The bar seemed to be informally attached to a house. It was an open-air arrangement. All the tables were outside, but there was a floor made of boards over top of the sand. Meandering across the plank decking toward the table I had chosen, Joe put his hands on my shoulders and pulled me to a stop. "There's a pool through that gate," he said, "for people who... how do you put it...don't like things touching their legs." He gave me a friendly I'm-looking-out-for-you squeeze, and I thanked him.

"It's the least I could do," he said. "After all, I kinda feel responsible for your phobia."

"What do you mean?"

"Remember when you were in the sixth grade and you came to the beach with us?"

I remembered multiple trips to the beach with the Turners, so I wasn't sure which one he meant.

"This was the time you actually made it into the water for about five minutes before you ran back out screaming, *Something touched my leg! Something touched my leg!*"

"Yeah," I said as the memory surfaced. "I remember that trip." It was the beginning of the end of my relationship with the ocean.

"That was me," Joe confessed. "I touched your leg. I knew it would scare you, and that's why I did it."

"That was you," I said, barely managing to contain the tentacles of my accusatory tone. "You colossal jerk."

"Guilty," he said and smiled lazily. "I'm a nicer guy now, but I don't expect you to forgive me for that. It was a pretty messed up thing to do."

I looked at Jack for some kind of confirmation. He shrugged, indicating that he may not have been in on it but that he could certainly see it happening.

I shook my head at the two of them. What the hell was I supposed to do with that information at this point in my life? To this day I was living in a perpetual state of fear when it came to sharks, and sea life in general for that matter. Finally, I said. "I forgive you for being a jerk to me when I was in the sixth grade." More quietly, I added, "And I'm still not going in the ocean."

We ordered drinks, beer for me and Storie, sweet tea for Jack and The Jerk. When they learned that the tea was unsweetened but there was sugar on the table, they both changed their orders to Coke. No sweet tea drinker worth the ice cubes in his glass would settle for sweetening cold tea. No deal. Not the same. You gotta add the sugar right after you brew the tea, when it's still warm, so the sugar dissolves completely and hangs in glorious suspension instead of collecting, undissolved, at the bottom like so much wet sand.

We worked our way through a variety of appetizers, including hush puppies, fried fish nuggets, boiled shrimp, and something called gator bites. I grabbed one of those, plunged it into a tub of pinkish sauce, and bit it in half. It was definitely meat. Having no idea what an alligator tasted like, I couldn't verify with certainty that it came from the reptile family, but it didn't change my life as a food item, so I stuck with the less unique options that were fresh off the boat and remarkable in their own right.

The baskets and plates of food were pretty well empty when Joe said, "Okay, that's the end of round one. Now we jump in the water to cool off and let our food settle before round two."

I smiled big. Stomach satisfied. Mini beer buzz generating that happy, easy feeling. And now a dip in the pool. Pushing back from the table, Jack said, "I'll go with Lily. Storie, you going ocean or pool?"

She looked at me for direction. Knowing she wanted to swim in the ocean, I released her from the obligation of babysitting me. And I knew now why both Jack and Joe drank Cokes instead of beer. They were the lifeguards, and they were splitting the responsibilities between chlorine and salt.

"If you don't care," she said with a lovely lilt, "I'll take a swim in the ocean."

"Go have fun," I told her.

She jumped up and quickly came out of her shorts. She was on the beach before the rest of us were officially up from the table. Jack and Joe exchanged glances. "I got her, bro," Joe assured his brother. "You'll have your hands full with this one." And he swatted my pony tail as he moved behind me.

Jack stood and waited for me to get up, which took a minute as I gathered people's phones and Joe's wallet, dropping them in Jack's knapsack. He signaled to the bartender that we'd be back. From the look on the guy's face, it never would've occurred to him that we might skip out on the bill. Island life was so easy going. Unless you were getting murdered, of course. Why did that little detail keep getting in my way?

Jack led me over to the gate separating the pool from the bar, and to my deep disappointment, it was locked. A passing server saw my puzzled expression and said, "Sorry, sweetie, pool's closed for repairs this weekend."

My smile, heart and spirit all fell. Jack put an arm of friendship around my shoulders and gave a little hug. "I'll go swimming with you in the hotel pool later," he promised.

The urge to pout was unexpectedly attractive, but I pretended to be more mature and settled for releasing a sigh accompanied by, "Aww."

He took my hand and pulled me past our table, which I noticed had been straightened up but not completely cleared, to the sandy beach. We walked a short way, just beyond where people might be entering or leaving the bar area, and plopped down on the sand.

Loose strands of hair had fallen around my face, and Jack reached to tuck one piece behind an ear. Locking eyes with me, he said softly, "Come be my mermaid."

"I can't. The pool's closed." I knew he wasn't talking about the pool.

"Come be my mermaid in the ocean."

"You can go be a merman with them," I said, pointing to Storie and Joe.

"Without you, Lily, I'm just a guy in the water. You bring the magic."

That was a load of bunk if I'd ever heard one. "Well," I answered, "you'll have to enjoy the magic on dry land, because I'm not swimming in the ocean, especially when The Leg Grabber is lurking out there."

He laughed. "Alright. Alright. Suit yourself. But I'll warn you now, since you're a captive audience, I plan to talk about our relationship."

Knowing I'd never make it to my feet with any kind of speed, he took his time circling my wrist with his hand to secure me in place.

Mouth opened in a look of disbelief, all I really seemed capable of doing was shaking my head no. Which I did. Repeatedly.

"I can't make you talk," he acknowledged, "but you'll at least have to listen."

What he had to say about this whole scandalous dilemma scared me as much as being forced to reveal my own feelings. Realizing this, I quickly rethought my position.

"I'll go in to my ankles."

"You'll go in the ocean?"

"I said I'll go in to my ankles."

"So, you'll go in the ocean."

"Are you listening to me?"

"Correct me if I'm wrong, but up to your ankles is *in the ocean*."

"You're not wrong; I just don't want you getting any ideas about tricking me into swimming."

"Look at me," he said with a sudden seriousness.

I glanced up long enough to see the sincerity scribbled across his features then dropped my eyes again.

"I swear to you, I will not push you on this. I swear it. And if you freak out, I'll carry you in my arms back to the beach."

That type of water rescue seemed unwarranted given the fact that ankle-deep was probably four or five steps in, but I understood his intent. He wouldn't test the boundaries associated with the legitimacy of this particular fear.

"Let me know that you hear what I'm saying." He waited. And I noticed he didn't try to get into my line of sight or move my head so he could see my eyes. He just waited patiently.

"I hear you. You won't make me feel uncomfortable."

"I promise I won't make you feel uncomfortable in the ocean."

Damn it. He ferreted out my loophole and effectively cinched it closed by adding *in the ocean*. He knew me too well.

I gave him a half smile half sneer. He knew why I did it, and he gave me his own half smile. Jack was the only person I'd ever met who could demonstrate a superiority complex using only half a smile.

He stood with the ease of an athlete and reached a hand out to me. I was intrigued that the amount of strength he used to pull me up was exactly the amount needed. He didn't over-pull me so I'd crash into his chest or under-pull me so I'd thrash around spastically giving him an opportunity to swoop in and assist. He also didn't hold on to my hand once I was up, letting me set the pace on this death march to the water.

I glanced over my shoulder at the backpack full of valuables which was now unattended.

"It'll be okay," he assured me.

Striped of my last possible delay, I carefully and slowly walked to where the sand stopped feeling loose and dry and started feeling packed and damp. Scanning for any dark shadow that would indicate a shark, I paused, still as a loblolly in a stand of pines on a hot July afternoon.

"Do you wanna hold my hand?"

I did, but I didn't want him to know that. Joe and Storie watched me for a second. Neither waved, and they kindly turned away so I didn't have to deal with an audience. I opted for grabbing his arm instead of holding his hand. He exhibited more restraint than I gave him credit for, keeping his own hand from taking hold of mine.

"Only up to my ankles," I whispered to myself.

"Only up to your ankles," Jack repeated, showing his comprehension of the ground rules.

I gulped a big breath and stomped out to where my ankles were submerged. Fully prepared to stomp right back to the beach, I was surprised when I didn't. Instead, I lingered, letting the salty water wet my skin, finding the feeling I always missed when I was in the air instead of in the water. Maybe I was a mermaid after all.

I suddenly had an uncontrollable urge to go deeper, I just couldn't make myself do it. I was stuck, halfway between where I was and where I wanted to be. Looking for some kind of bridge, I fell back on language. "It feels good," I said as I dug up tiny shells with my toes.

Jack smiled at me. "Yeah," he said. But I couldn't tell if he was talking about the water feeling good, my hand on his arm, or the fact that after all these years I had finally stepped foot in the ocean again. Showing more confidence, I dropped my hand, took another step out, and kicked my foot, producing a spray that blew back on me in the most refreshing way.

"I want to go deeper," I said while I was actively scanning the low waves. Even I could hear my voice sounded unsure.

"What can I do to make you more comfortable?"

"For starters, you could round up all the sharks. Maybe pen 'em up about five hundred miles offshore."

"So you want to do it the hard way." He laughed and bumped me so that I would laugh, too. "What if I walk out ahead of you, you know, to check for sharks."

I searched his voice for any shard of mockery. Finding none, I agreed. He started walking and checking.

The way he checked for sharks reminded me of the way he checked for spiders on the dock whenever we went swimming at the lake back home. He moved his head to and fro in an easy rhythm. When he found a spider, he'd smash it with his foot. I wondered if he planned to use that same stomp-and-kill method when he found a shark. Once he was out to his knees, he turned around. "All clear," he announced.

He stood where he was. Waiting. I stood where I was. Debating. He never beckoned or even held out a hand. He just smiled from his post in the knee-deep water. Finally, something in Storie's connected universe nudged me forward. I don't know if it was Misty, or maybe my mama, heck, it might've even been Jack's love.

Jack's *what?* Did I just use the phrase *Jack's love?* Why in the name of teepees and toaster ovens would I use a phrase like that? I faltered, and I'm sure there was a look of mortification on my face, because the expression of relaxed encouragement on his face changed slightly.

"Lily," he called to me, "you okay?"

Before I could answer, he began closing the distance between us.

I held up my hand, "No, stop. I'm okay."

"Are you sure? You look like you're struggling."

"I'm okay." It was better to soldier on at this point than try to explain what had just crossed my mind. "I'm okay. I'm coming." And I did. I walked out to him. It occurred to me that I was walking away from

Jack's love toward the source of said love. To escape that conundrum, I thought about sharks. When I got to where he was standing, I accepted his high five, slapping his hand as I took another step beyond. I was scared, but exhilarated. Five more steps and I stopped.

There I was, waist deep. I pulled my pony tail lose, snapped the band around my wrist, and made Jack hold my hand so I could dunk my head and not get swept away by a riptide while underwater. I couldn't seem to go out any farther than that, but hell, it was already a win. I hadn't realized that the last time I was in an ocean was back in the sixth grade. I didn't feel that it was entirely Joe's fault, but for sure some of it was. I was about to whip out an imaginary happy dance I had choreographed for just such a momentous occasion as conquering the sea, when, you guessed it, something touched my leg. I jerked frantically and Jack was immediately beside me, ready to enact the promised water rescue.

"It was seaweed," he assured me. "But I'll walk you out if you want."

"Seaweed?"

He reached down and pulled up what looked like a thin brownish strip of rubber. I took it from his hand to examine it more closely.

Feeling stupid, the only thing I could really do was own it. "Well," I said, "this seems harmless."

We laughed, and he hugged me. I flashed back to the wet skin from the lake just last week. Luckily, Joe and Storie were splashing their way over to us, giving me a good excuse to separate from JT. He let me, but not before he squeezed a little tighter.

Joe moseyed his way to me and put his hand up for a high five. "Glad to see the damage I caused doesn't appear to be permanent."

I smacked his hand and told him he was not entirely off the hook, but that I'd come around eventually. He grabbed me in a big hug, lifting me off the sandy bottom, and then carefully put me down, letting go only when he was sure I had my balance. The sun had set. I was sharing the ocean with the sharks. Luanne wasn't murdered. The cops were one step closer to finding Misty's killer. There was another beer waiting for me back on land. That's pretty much all anybody could ask for in life. Right?

Chapter 18

The next morning, we got up slowly, meaning Jack waited until almost seven to text me. He and I started the day with a coffee run to Nine-O. I worked diligently to keep him away from anything that smacked of relationship nonsense. It wasn't easy, but basking in my new Viking status after taking back the ocean last night, I was up for the task.

"Since the plane doesn't leave until three, I was hoping we could swing by Hemingway's house to see the six-toed cats before we leave."

"Hemingway as in Ernest?"

"Yes."

"What the hell is a six-toed cat?" He asked.

"Special cats with six toes."

"Don't all cats have six toes?"

"I don't know how many toes regular cats have," I confessed. "But these ones are special. The original cat was given to Hemingway by the captain of a ship. The extra toe sticks out like it's the thumb on a mitten."

"How do you know about these special cats?"

"Hey," I said defensively, "I know stuff, too."

"Stuff? Or useless stuff?"

"It's not *useless* since I just *used* it, birdbrain. If I held my knowledge of the six-toed cat in perpetuity, never contributing it to an active conversation, then you might get away with calling it useless. But as you can see, I used it."

Jack seemed not to know where to go with that, so he conceded. "Well constructed litigation, counselor."

While I got the concession, I didn't feel like I got the W as far as the cats were concerned. You know, W meaning *the win*.

"I know you're not a fan of the feline, but there's history, too." Granted, literary history probably held as much interest for him as cat toes, so I played the curiosities card. "I read that when they tore down Hemingway's favorite bar, he rescued one of the urinals. He supposedly claimed ownership, since he had put so much money into it over the years."

That made Jack laugh, and I added, "They say he used it as a watering trough for his famous cats."

Opening his eyes a little wider, he said, "No freakin' way."

"That's how the story goes."

Still no bite. I might've gone too far with the watering trough image. I was clearly striking out with the cats and the interesting artifacts. Haphazardly I threw out one more idea like it was my last try at a carnival ring toss. "What about fishing?"

"What about it?" Visually, Jack appeared to have moved on from the cat portion of the conversation, but fishing got his attention.

"Did you know Hemingway was a big fisherman?"

"I did not know that. But, if you want the truth, the extent of my knowledge on this guy covers the fact that he wrote a book about a whale. I've spent more time discussing Ernest Hemingway in the last five minutes than I spent on him in all my high school English classes. Total."

I weighed the need to disabuse him of the notion that Hemingway wrote a book about a whale. It was a marlin. And it was in *The Old Man and the Sea*. He was obviously confusing that book with Herman Melville's *Moby Dick*. While literary accuracy was somewhat important to me, it wouldn't advance my agenda in this case, and I could pretty well guarantee it'd be another twenty years before Jack found himself needing to access the writing achievements of the one called Papa. I privately apologized to Hemingway's ghost, hoping the oversight wouldn't get me haunted later, and presented my pitch about fishing.

"Ernest was a famous fisherman; he went after the big boys." When Jack zoomed in, I knew we were getting somewhere.

"Please," he said, totally engrossed, "tell me more."

"He fished for marlin."

"Mmm," he hummed, warming up.

"They have pictures of him on the boat. And pictures of the huge fish he caught." I wasn't lying because I knew for sure these photographs existed. My statement had the taint of a fib, however, because I did not know whether the museum housed any of these photographs. It seemed like a thing you'd find in a museum, though. Right?

Here was a secret when dealing with Jack Turner— offer something that he found irresistible then let him chew on it for a while in the privacy of his own teeny brain. Known for my need to pound away at a topic until I got resolution, it took great restraint not to hammer this home, and admittedly, I was delighted when I managed to back away.

He told me some ridiculous tidbit about a marlin, which I pretended to find fascinating. Dunking my *pan Cubano* into my *café con leche,* I smiled inwardly and shifted the conversation to a series of unrelated points, not lingering too long on any one subject. I went from marlin to murder to murder suspect to college major to the Florida Keys to Jack's dog.

"What about Largo as a dog's name?" I asked. "I'm putting that on my list of possibilities."

"Largo," Jack tested it out. "Like the Bertie Higgins song."

Then, because Jack grew up on a steady diet of old sappy songs constantly playing in his dad's garage, he recited a lyric from memory, without the tune. *"Honey can't you remember? We played all the parts. That sweet scene of surrender, when you gave me your heart..."* He looked at me with exaggerated longing, but I could tell he sort of meant it. So close, Barlow. So close to getting through a conversation without giving him an opportunity to pine.

"On second thought, I don't like Largo that much."

"Really? I love it," he said and winked.

Putting an end to it, I declared, "I have to pee."

"I'm sure you do."

Alright, so I didn't, but I removed myself from the love song serenade situation anyway. When I got back, he was scrolling on his phone.

"The Hemingway Museum opens at nine, and it's not far from here. Let's go see these polydactyl cats."

"Now?" I figured I had a chance after the fishing connection, but I didn't consider it a slam dunk.

"Why not?"

"Aren't you hungry?"

"This'll tide me over." He gestured toward our empty plates and cups. "Come on. You want to check this place out. Let's go."

* * *

There was no one, and I mean NO ONE, visiting the Hemingway House & Museum at nine a.m. on a Sunday morning in late August. I asserted myself at the register when he reached for his wallet.

"My thing, my money," I said firmly, as I fished cash from my back pocket. I didn't think he'd make a big production over it since he and Joe had paid for practically every single expense on this trip so far.

He studied me for a second and then said, "Thank you."

I was shocked, and gratified, and on guard for the inevitable blitzkrieg. Surely he'd leverage this to get something he wanted. I'll let you pay if I can kiss you in the garden…something along those lines. I checked, but his blue eyes were clear, not calculating. I let it go, warning myself to stay alert.

We skipped the guided portion of the tour and ambled through the house. I'd read a great deal of Hemingway through high school and college, so this brought it full circle for me. Jack wasn't enamored with the house, but he was genuinely interested in the swimming pool. Come to find out, it was a huge construction accomplishment in the 1930s because it was dug into a bed of coral. Pool construction didn't light my fire, but the pool itself…spectacular. I had a vision of me skinny dipping in that pool, after hours, when the place was closed up.

Moving on, the gardens were gorgeous. And the cats, with their little mitten feet, adorable. I was relieved to see framed photos of the marlins and the fisherman in question. Whew. Jack soaked in the past energy of a kindred spirit, and that seemed to make the whole visit worthwhile for him.

We were done in less than forty minutes, but before we left, we swung through the gift shop where Jack passed over a marlin-shaped bottle opener in favor of a refrigerator magnet cast from the paw print of a six-toed cat. I took it from his hand and looked at him with amusement. He was very close to revealing some deep dark secret, but he must've thought better of it, because instead he offered a simple explanation. "Some things you wanna remember." To avoid that quagmire, I grabbed a marlin bottle opener and threw myself into the transaction as the docent rang me up.

* * *

It was around ten when we got back to the hotel. Storie had taken a swim and was getting showered. Joe was reading a local paper in the rocking chair outside the room. The four of us were packed and checked out before eleven, and with time to spare we went to a touristy place to grab a bite. By now that piece of bread I'd eaten had long been digested, and I was famished.

After lunch, Storie wanted to take a quick walk on the beach. Jack found a place where he and Joe could sit in the shade while she and I strolled for a few minutes. It was hot, and I was damp with sweat by the time we got back to the car. The AC didn't start to cool the vehicle until we pulled into the rental lot, but the fully refrigerated airport concourse brought me back around.

On the airplanes, the group paired off in a boy-girl-boy-girl seating arrangement without much drama. Frankly, I think I was too tired to argue, a point underscored by the fact that I slept through all turbulence on both legs of the trip. When we landed in Virginia at eight p.m., I woke refreshed. Back at Miss Delphine's, I offered to let Storie stay over if she was sleepy and didn't feel like driving back to Culpeper.

"I'm good to drive," she assured me. After she took advantage of the bathroom, she hugged and thanked each of the boys but saved her longest hug for me. When she was gone, Joe made his goodbyes from the kitchen.

"Great fishing, bro" he said as he and Jack snaked their arms and quickly bumped shoulders in some warped male version of affection. I received a more traditional hug and noisy kiss on the cheek. "Girl, what can I say?" He laughed and released. "You always keep it interesting."

We stood on my little porch in the dark, waving bye to Joe. Once his truck disappeared around the garage, Jack turned to me. "I'm staying," he said with an authority that struck me as odd. Up 'til now, it had been more a question of whether or not I was okay with him staying. I was about to pin him down on that point and get some clarification as to what he had in mind, when he cut in again.

"I want…" He stopped, correcting himself. "No. I *need*. I need to kiss you. Can I? I promise I won't do anything else. Not unless you want me to." He had moved closer to me, which was hard to reconcile since we were already pretty close. It was a small porch to start with, further crowded by the two Adirondack chairs.

He kept talking. Either his voice was getting softer or I couldn't hear him as well over the blood rushing in my head. "Can I?" He asked. "Can I kiss you?"

Caught off balance by the urgency he was expressing, I worked to untangle the knot of emotions I encountered. My mind and my libido were trying desperately to explain themselves to one another, and neither came out on top. Based on the evidence each side presented thus far, I was looking at a hung jury. Meanwhile, without making any sudden moves, I found Jack had positioned himself so I was in the sink hole created by his body heat. And he kept talking.

"Since we kissed in the hotel room, I haven't stopped thinking about you…" He was even closer now, "in that way. Can I?" He finally broke the plane and laid his hand on the side of my neck, thumb resting in that little pocket at the base of my throat. Not trusting myself, I stayed quiet while I considered my options. The chair behind me let my calf know there was no room to back up.

"Lily, I realize we're a long way from figuring it out. This kiss won't change that. I promise I can stop," he whispered, then added, "if you want me, too." That last part wrapped around me like smoke. It was there, but it wasn't.

I couldn't decide if I'd want him to stop at just a kiss. The one thing I could say for sure was that I wanted the kiss. I mean, I really wanted it. What I didn't want was the associated havoc. I knew myself well enough to know accepting the one would make me freak out about the other. And, in the name of the long-forgotten tan-colored M&M, I decided right then and there I did not care about the havoc.

Shifting to my toes, I touched his lips softly with mine. He moved his hand so he could wrap an arm around my back. We stood there, mainly because I was afraid to move.

He sensed it and pulled apart by half an inch. "You okay?" The heat of his breath was irresistible, and I answered by touching lips again.

He didn't accept that gesture as an answer, though, and repeated the same thing over again, moving another half an inch and asking, "Are you okay, Lily?"

I nodded, but that didn't satisfy either. "I want you to say it."

What was it with this guy and verbal consent?

"I'm okay."

"Can I keep going?"

I looked up, not sure exactly what he meant. "With the kiss," he said, answering my unspoken question.

"Yes." I nodded, feeling barely strong enough to manage the fireworks of the kiss, but wanting the fireworks anyway.

He stopped talking and gently put his lips back on mine. When I didn't sound any kind of Mayday, he opened his mouth and slowly traced the tip of his tongue along my bottom lip. I sighed. He used his arm to bring me more tightly against him.

It was incredibly sensual. I heard a trumpet playing. The notes were long and sultry. I was lost in the song or the kiss, one. Or maybe the song was the kiss. I didn't know for sure. He was a good kisser, and I made a little noise of disapproval when he broke the spell by reaching back to open the door. I let him pull me into the apartment.

The air conditioner was making its version of white noise, and it tried to drown out the trumpet. Why was a trumpet still playing? Where in the hell was that music coming from? The source of the sound was intriguing, but not nearly as intriguing as the kiss, so I closed the door behind me and leaned against it, inviting him to pick up where we left off.

He didn't. Instead he stood looking at me in a way that made me feel like he could see what I had on my mind. *SexwithJack*. I had pushed the idea into an imaginary corner, and in my mind I was trying my best to hide it from view by standing in front, hands on my hips. That worked about as well as hiding a jukebox blasting *Great Balls of Fire* by standing in front of it, and I think he saw through my pithy attempt.

The moment dragged on to the point where I was compelled to speak. "What?" I often used this one-word question when I couldn't win a staring contest but didn't want to reveal anything relevant.

"I'm just taking you in."

"Well, stop," I said and reached a hand out to draw his attention in another direction.

He didn't stop, and he refused my hand to boot. I let it drop back down to my side, trying to unravel what he was up to. He turned and walked to the couch where he sat. I blew the breath I had been holding.

"Want a beer?" I offered, taking a different avenue.

"Nah. I want you to come here."

Making my way into the living room, I debated where I should sit. The safety of the easy chair made sense, but accessibility to the thing I wanted to kiss won out. Libido one, logic zero. I plopped on the far end of the couch, grabbing the pillow from behind me for something to hold.

"I get you want this for protection," he said, pointing to the pillow. "But you know you can trust me."

"I know." I was still recovering from the rush of endorphins, and it reflected in my voice.

"Show me."

"Show you what?"

"Show me you trust me."

I squinted, trying to figure out his end game. It made sense when he reached for the pillow and tugged. I released, not because I wanted to, but because I didn't want him to think he was more in control than I was. He moved the pillow from my lap to the coffee table. I followed with my eyes and fought the urge to take it back.

Trying to come out on top, I tossed my hands in the air to indicate I didn't care one wit about that ol' pillow. "Happy?" I asked, in an effort to sound breezy.

He held the word and my eyes for a few seconds before nodding. "I am," he confirmed. "I'm happy you trust me. I'm happy you let me kiss you. I'm happy we're here together."

Oh, good Lord. This had the makings of a conversation. I weighed my choices—start the kissin' again and gamble on whether or not I could stop before it got out of hand or let him have his freakin' conversation. Damn, I wished I'd gotten me a beer before I sat down. For one, I'd have something to hold, and for two, I could get back to the kissin' knowing he wouldn't let it get out of hand if I was drinking.

Needing to say something, anything, I offered a very weak, "I'm glad you're happy."

In one smooth motion he moved in so he was sitting much closer. We were both angled sideways on the sofa and our knees were now touching. He put a heavy hand gently on my leg.

"Tell me what you're afraid of."

It was trepidation that made me shoot for humor, and being well acquainted with my fears, I rattled them off in a spitfire fashion. "I'm afraid of spiders. Ghosts. Sharks. Root canals. Public speaking. Bats that suck your blood or get tangled in your hair. Running out of toilet paper. Ticks. Snakes. You getting hurt in a fire. Chromium toxicity. Railroad crossings with no crossing gates. Skin cancer…"

I paused too long between skin cancer and the last item on my list which was a newly discovered fear of chickens, allowing him time to lean in and redirect me with a kiss. It was a short one, just long enough to shut me up. With our faces still close together he asked his question differently. "Tell me what scares you about us." He followed that with another chaste kiss and pulled back to wait.

As always, when confronted with a distasteful discussion, I started by stalling. "Jack," I said, using his name to buy time. If I could think of some way to dodge long enough to clear my brain, I could get out of this.

"I know you don't want to talk about it, Lily. I have to, though. I have to talk about it so I can understand what's going on in your head. I'm moving this thing forward one way or another, and I want to do it right. If you tell me where you're stuck, I can figure out how to help."

Shocked at his declaration that he intended to move it forward, with or without me on board, I stammered. "I…I don't know where I'm stuck," I finally said, getting more flustered by the second.

"You do."

I stared at him, marshaling up as much defiance as I could with what little emotional reserve was available to me.

He wasn't put off by my ferocity, and he repeated, "You do. You know what scares you. You're just afraid to tell me because it'll make you vulnerable."

With a huff I blurted, "I've already told you, Jack, and all the stuff I said is still true because I'm afraid this is a game to you and you'll get tired of it when you win but at that point it'll be too late for me because I can't control my feelings so easily and if I fall for you I'll fall hard and I won't be able to recover and then I'll lose my heart and my best friend which would devastate me in a way I could never get over and that's why I think we should just pull the plug now before anybody gets hurt and call it an experiment that was fun but didn't work and—

Jack laid his cheek against mine, put his hand on the opposite side of my face and quietly hushed me with a soft *shhhhhh*. "Use a period, for God's sake."

It was funny, and I smiled long enough to take a breath. Once I had new air in my lungs, I was ready to start again, but he laid a finger on my lips. "I want you to tell me everything that's got you worked up. I do. But slow down, girl, so I can get it all."

He moved his finger down my chin and replaced it with his thumb, which he used to graze my lips. Caught up in the sensation, I kissed the thumb. After I did, I realized I had completely lost my place in explaining why I was so against the idea, which was probably how he designed it. Regardless, I felt compelled to summarize. "I'm afraid I'll lose you as my friend. I can't do it."

"I understand." He dropped his hand to my lap and played with my fingertips. "It scares me, too."

"Then let's don't risk it," I pleaded.

"We have the opportunity to turn the greatest friendship of all times into the greatest romance of all times," he said, watching me.

"This is what they call an impasse, JT. I'm satisfied with the greatest friendship of all times. You want it to be more than that. There's no way to meet in the middle because there is no middle."

I broke the eye contact, but as usual, he kept talking. "Tell me one thing."

Supremely self-assured, I was inclined to tell him *thirty* things. Squaring my shoulders, I prepared to re-engage.

"Tell me that day we made love at the lake wasn't some of the best sex you've ever had."

Well, I wasn't prepared to tell him *that*. His use of the phrase *made love* was a point of contention, and he knew I spurned its application in terms of our physical encounter. That technicality aside, calling up the memory was a maneuver devised to topple me. And it worked. I squirmed, feeling suddenly modest, and adjusted my position on the couch, but it did nothing to ease my discomfort. By means of escaping, I devoted my full attention to studying the hem of my shorts where I identified a loose thread which I scrutinized thoroughly.

"You don't have to answer," he said. Nice of him to afford me that courtesy, since I wasn't going to anyway.

When my refusal to speak stretched on, he took over. "I bet it was in your top three, though. I can read the signs. The only reason it wasn't number one on your list of the best sex ever is because I need a little more time to learn which buttons to push." The smile he flashed was lecherous as he added, "And how much pressure to apply when I push 'em."

His confidence paired with my confusion created an internal chaos the likes of which I did not feel prepared to handle. My only option was to reach for the pillow, but he intercepted my hand. "I know this is more than you can digest right now. I'll stop talking. You don't need the pillow. You don't need to run to the bathroom. We can sit here like the great friends we are and hang out."

I couldn't have explained why, but I was embarrassed by the fact he had carnal knowledge of me. I mean, I had knowledge of him, too. We were both present for the activities. But when I tried to recall his reaction to anything we did that day, I drew a blank. Was I so self-absorbed that I didn't notice one thing he liked? And all the while he was over there making a flow chart of my reactions and behaviors.

He stood, maintaining possession of my hand, and brushed my knuckles with his lips before letting go. "I'll take that beer now," he said. "Want one?"

I couldn't be sure he was smiling, because I refused to look up, but it sounded like there was humor in his voice. I nodded. I wanted the beer, but if he went to the fridge, it would also get him out of my personal space for a minute, giving me an opportunity to collect myself.

By the time he returned with my beer, I had activated my innate ability to ignore the obvious, pretending the conversation we just had never took place. He played along. We listened to music and kept the conversation safe. I drank two beers, he drank three. When it came time for bed, I invited him to sleep in the bedroom, but he chose the couch. I admired his ability to draw a line when it meant honoring a resolution. There was a long, moody, magical kiss before we went to our separate areas. I might have started it.

Chapter 19

When I finally rolled out of bed the next morning, I was confronted with the paradox of feeling both relief and disappointment, swirled together like the chocolate and vanilla in a soft serve cone. I didn't have to face Jack, hence the relief, because he was already gone, hence the disappointment. There was coffee in the pot, and I poured and prepped a cup before sitting down to read his note.

Don't shut me out, Lily. You are my oldest and closest friend, and I promise I'll protect that above everything. I'm asking you to trust me, like you did last night. Please.

—Jack
p.s. I fed the chickens

The postscript was accompanied by a drawing of a chicken, which bore an uncanny resemblance to a toad with a duck's bill. That was Jack's way of making me laugh so I wouldn't get too caught up in the seriousness of the first part of the note. The boy had a gift for using humor to put people at ease.

My list of things to do today did not include thinking through the ramifications of this note, so the note got folded into a temporary coaster for my cup. I wanted to track down Storie's tattoo artist and possibly transfer from UVA to Shenandoah University. But first, I'd have to check in or the mob of townsfolk tracking my whereabouts would be marching up the lane with their pitchforks any minute. That meant Dad, Mercedes, and Miss Delphine.

Miss Delphine was first because she was the closest, so, obviously, the easiest. I grabbed the small bag from my suitcase and tromped down the wooden steps, flip flops clacking on the boards. Checking my phone for the time, I figured she'd be out digging in a flower bed, or burying a body, one. It was already nine a.m. And I was right.

"Child," she said without turning to see it was me. "I saw Jack this mornin'. Y'all get that business in the Keys sorted out?"

I wanted to scratch at that a little, see if he said anything I could use against him later, but I let it be. "Yes, 'um, we did. But it had a surprising twist to it. The dead body wasn't my friend's friend after all. If you want to come up for dinner later, I'll tell you all about it."

"I'll take a rain check on that, but thank you much."

Curious as to what else an old woman had going on that she couldn't come for dinner, I asked, "Whatcha doin' today?"

"Today is the F day," she reported. It was a weird answer to my question and confirmed my suspicion that her grasp on reality might be a little wobbly.

"What? Friday? No...today's Monday...the M day."

"No, child," she sounded exasperated with me already. "The F day. The day I do my chores that start with F—floors, fur, and feet."

Waiting for her to elaborate, I added a few more obvious tasks that should be included—*foul play* and *falsify* jumped to mind. Then, to impress myself with the breadth of my knowledge on murder and forensics I introduced *fratricide* (to kill one's brother) and *fusilation* (death by shooting).

The murder words must've given me a blank stare. She clucked her tongue and provided a more detailed explanation. "I mop my floors. I wash the dog. And I get a pedicure."

"A pedicure!" Toenail polish trumped murder suspicions every single time, and I couldn't contain my joy at this new found connection I shared with my landlady.

"What color are you getting?" Trying to guess what a senior citizen would favor, I visualized a palette of pretty pastels.

"I haven't decided yet. I like the black one called The Dark Side. But there's a vermilion one called Crime Scene that caught my eye last week."

Shocked by the new information and not knowing how to proceed, I bailed. "You get your toes done every week?" What I really wanted to ask was what color she was currently wearing. Hemlock? Which I envisioned as a dark, smoky green. Or maybe Blunt Object....a mahogany.

"Every Monday for the better part of my life," she said, in answer to the fake question I had asked first.

"I change my toenail polish all the time, too. In fact, I've been wearing this shade for about two days too long. I just didn't have time to do it down in Florida. Which reminds me, I brought you a present."

"Lordy, Lily, you didn't have to do that!" She sat back on her heels and then carefully pushed herself up. I hovered a little closer, in case she needed a hand, but she didn't.

"I was sad you couldn't come with us, and I wanted to thank you for letting me stay here." I gave her the marlin bottle opener, still folded sweetly in bright yellow tissue paper. I had taken the price tag off when I paid for it.

She commented on the cheery color and rustled the thin paper until the marlin popped out. "Well, I'll be. Sword fish?"

"Um, if a sword fish is the same as a marlin, then yes. That's really more of a Jack question. He's the one who could tell you everything you never wanted to know about any fish in the water."

"Fisherman, is he?"

"He is. And did you know you're not allowed to bring a banana on a boat because it's bad luck?"

"I didn't know that," she humored me. "I don't believe it ever came up when I was a child." I remembered Miss Delphine told me a neighbor used to ferry the local kids around on his boat when she was little. That was one of the few things I knew about her. That and the fact that every Monday she gets her toenails polished.

The bottle opener was stamped with *Hemingway House & Museum* on the back. When she read it, she commented, "Ah, Hemingway. I never cared much for him. Too stingy with the description. But he was one of the greats, they say."

I was practically falling in love with Miss Delphine on the spot. Nail polish and an opinion on literature? I really needed to get to know her better.

"Someone once said Hemingway *got the most from the least*. I don't know who gets credit for that quote, but it's probably on Wikipedia."

"Lily, I adore it. Thank you, darlin', for thinkin' of me."

She flipped the opener in her hand, feeling its weight, and tested the sharpness of the marlin's bill with her index finger. Goose feathers in a ski jacket! Did I just give her a murder weapon?

Handing the item back to me, she said, "Wrap this in the tissue and set it on the table by the door, would ya, child?"

"Sure."

I did as she asked, then to kind of close out the conversation, I posed one more question. "Chickens do okay without me?"

Miss Delphine chuckled and shook her head. "They did fine. Just fine." And she was back to her flowers.

"See ya later!" I waved as I headed upstairs to shower.

Something occurred to me as my left foot touched down on the bottom step, and I turned to ask over my shoulder, "Did you hear a trumpet last night?"

"I did," she answered. "I occasionally play a record. It soothes me."

"It was nice." Jazz music? Literature? That old gal was an enigma.

* * *

Mercedes and Uncle Dave were busy working out the decorations for the reopening. I didn't hang around, first because I didn't want to, and second because they didn't want me to. I couldn't catch Mercedes up on anything with Uncle Dave hawking around, anyway, so I headed over to see Dad. He checked out okay, happy I was back safe and glad I had a nice time with Jack and Joe.

"The boys caught a lot of fish," I told him, reinforcing the storyline.

Cha-ching. Ah, the conjured Jack. I had forgotten about it over the past few days. Maybe my powers were stronger in Virginia. I didn't reach for the phone. Since his heart attack, I felt the need to make sure Dad knew he was my priority whenever we were together.

"Aren't you gonna see who that is?" He asked.

"I imagine it's Jack," I assured him. "He probably left something over Miss Delphine's when he dropped me off yesterday." I was taking a wide berth around the physical piece. Dad knew Jack stayed over with me hundreds of times without any hanky-panky. And even though I was sure he also knew I'd slept with boyfriends before, this new dilemma was so highly sensitive to me, I went out of my way to deflect attention, a maneuver that, in and of itself, often draws the exact attention you're trying to avoid.

"Well, if he left something important, like his wallet, you might want to get it back to him."

"Jack doesn't forget important stuff. It's probably the magnet he bought as a souvenir."

"Don't leave that boy hanging too long," he admonished me.

Sheesh. Take his side much?

When I was in the Jeep, after I cranked the ignition to start the rush of air but before I took it out of park, I checked the message.

"Thinking about you." That was a many pronged fork. I waved bye to Dad who was standing on the porch, drove up the road until I was out of sight of the house, and pulled over to send my reply. Best to have this electronic conversation once and get it out of the way. Otherwise he'd be *cha-chinging* me to pieces.

I replied, "Shouldn't you be thinking about putting out fires?"

Cha-ching: "Some fires you just can't put out."

To end it quickly, I texted, "Dad says hey."

Cha-ching: "How's he feeling?"

"Better every day."

Cha-ching: "See you tonight?"

"What time?" I didn't want to commit in the event I was off somewhere tracking down a tattoo artist.

Cha-ching: "9ish"

"Sure."

Cha-ching: "Your place or mine?"

"As if." I needed the advantage of being on my home court.

Cha-ching: "Yours it is."

"And thanks for feeding the chickens."

In response, he texted a chicken emoji.

See, easy-peasy. Now that was done for the time being. Note to self: Don't conjure Jack.

I had texted Storie before I left Miss Delphine's to see if she was free any time today. She was working the store on their farm, so she had all the time I wanted since Mondays were slow.

* * *

The bell on the door jingled as I entered. In a second Storie rounded an aisle and came up with outstretched arms. I hugged her like we were two strangers who had just learned we'd been separated at birth. When we let go, she pulled me by the hand to a corner of the store where there were a couple rockers for customers to sit and take a load off. Since the place was void of customers, we sat, and I didn't pussy foot around.

"I had an idea down in Florida, but I didn't have time to talk to you about it with Mr. Get-All-Up-In-My-Business inserting himself."

She laughed. "What's your idea?"

"Let's go talk to the tattoo artist who did y'all's tattoos and ask him if he gave the same design to someone else."

"Lily," she exclaimed, "that's a great idea! Want to go now?"

"Aren't you working the store?"

"Aunt Clemmie is here today. I'll get her to cover."

* * *

As it turned out, Aunt Clemmie was an aunt of the family-friend type vs. the family-tree type, and she was happy to cover for Storie while we headed out on our "errand."

"The tattoo parlor is called Mermaids & Octopus Ink," Storie said. My eyes got wide at the mere mention of mermaids, bringing back my evening in the ocean with Jack. "It's in Charlottesville. One of the hoops we had to jump through was finding a place that all the adults considered unequivocally clean and safe. Our first six suggestions were unanimously voted down. This place boasted a tattoo artist who was a registered nurse. We didn't have to use her, but we couldn't get the work done unless she was on the clock that day."

"Y'all kinda lucked out on that front, didn't ya?"

"We would not be denied." She stood taller when she said this. "Anyway, we didn't like her style as an artist, too cartoonish, but we discovered that she worked the same days as another guy whose style was perfect for us. His name was Wyatt Crabtree."

Storie suggested we call Mermaids & Octopus Ink and ask if the guy was still there. Chagrinned I didn't think of it first, I agreed. He was still working there and by the good luck of all that is considered lucky he was working today. She dug for a few details like how long he'd be there.

"You could start your own detective agency," I said when she hung up. "If you do, hire me."

"Uh, I basically did the secretary's job. So I could start my own secretarial service. You still wanna work for me?"

"Do I have to file? I hate filing?"

"Well, of course you have to file. What kind of secretarial service am I running here?"

"I was hoping the kind that pays a lot of money for people to answer the phone. Maybe you could subcontract the filing piece."

"I'll think about it."

* * *

The tattoo parlor was in an area I had been to on multiple occasions. I considered it the part of town where you could find Charlottesville's soul. Great restaurants that didn't advertise or take reservations, bars with live music, eclectic and peaceful neighborhood streets. I hadn't been to this particular block, however. From the outside, it was nothing special, other than the fact that the sign had the most glorious iridescent mermaid tail I'd ever seen. I loved it immediately.

Inside, it was a cross between a hermetically sealed clean room and a yoga studio. The only thing missing was the scent of bleach, but that could've been masked by the diffuser flooding the air with a mist of essential oil that smelled a little like grass with a light lemon accent. There were salt lamps pumping out the good negative ions. Every accessory seemed handpicked to reduce stress in customers. I felt better walking through the door, and I wasn't in the position of being anxious about coming in to get a tattoo.

We were greeted by a receptionist who had the air of someone working as the concierge at a world class spa. "Welcome, friends," she said in an octave suited to the tranquility of the establishment. I began to speculate that tattoo parlors had the same level of patient anxiety as dentist offices. Brilliant strategy from a business perspective if you were courting middle-aged women who fancied themselves upscale hipsters on a quest for a tramp stamp. They loved the idea of a tattoo but not the grittiness of a traditional parlor.

"Hey," Storie returned her greeting sweetly. "We're here to talk with Wyatt Crabtree about a tattoo. I called earlier."

"Of course," the woman said, nodding as if Storie had just confirmed what she herself had already deduced. "Please make yourselves comfortable while I get him for you. Would you like some jasmine tea?"

"Ice tea or hot tea?" I asked.

"Whichever you prefer, of course."

"On second thought, I'll have water," I said. The chances were slim a place like this would offer sweet tea, so better to avoid the disappointment altogether.

Storie then said, "Make that two."

"Certainly,"

She brought the water in trendy glassware on a pewter tray with delicate cloth napkins.

As soon as she delivered our refreshments, Wyatt Crabtree walked through the door. Shaggy reddish-brown hair and matching goatee, one of those open circles in his left earlobe, muscles for days, and tattoos. As he introduced himself, we stood and took turns shaking his hand.

"Hey Wyatt, I'm Storie. You probably don't remember me, but you tattooed me and five of my friends when we were in high school."

"Storie Sanders," he said. "I never forget a tattoo. You, Shelby, Pauline, Luanne, Dana and Scarlet. Purple flowers on a stem. I loved that piece. How's it look?"

I was amazed by his memory. Storie smiled and nodded. "You do remember!" She lifted her skirt so he could see her ankle.

"I do. Are you here for your next tat? I love repeat customers."

"Tempting," she said, "but no. At least not right now. Is there some place we could talk?"

"Absolutely. Come on back to the consultation room."

The facility was larger than it appeared from the outside. We passed private rooms with chairs and what looked like massage tables. In the hallway there were pieces of art that seemed to dominate the cool blue/green/purple side of the color wheel. We peeled into a small room with comfortable chairs and a table that held volumes of professionally bound books filled with ideas.

As we sat down, Storie launched into the saga of what had transpired. Wyatt listened carefully, asking questions to flesh out the details.

"So as it turned out," Storie summed up, "the person who had this tattoo was not Luanne after all. The victim wasn't tall enough to be Luanne. So somebody else got our same tattoo."

"Every one of mine is an original, but I'd like to see a picture if you have it."

Storie looked at me. "Can you pull it up on your phone, Lily?"

Finally, I was able to be of service. "Yes." And in two taps, I was there. I blew up the photo as much as I could before handing the phone to Wyatt.

"If you look carefully at the six tattoos, you'll see they're exactly the same. This one is obviously somewhat degraded," he noted, referring to the fact that it was on a corpse, "but if you look at the lines on the stems, you'll notice they're not the same. It's a pretty good knockoff, but it's not my work."

Storie glanced at it but didn't immediately clue in.

Wyatt noticed and said, "Here, let me take a picture of your tattoo on my phone, then you can compare the two side by side." It was a great idea, and it made it very easy to see what he was talking about. Several of the lines were just a little thicker.

"Are you sure that didn't happen as the body went through the decay process?"

"I'm sure. This artist has a heavier hand than I do. Could be a matter of experience."

I was moving these puzzle pieces around in my head, but I needed to repeat it out loud to make sure I understood. "So you're saying that someone looked at one of the six tattoos, maybe took a picture of it, and showed it to an artist who copied it?"

"Yep. It's poor etiquette, but it happens all the time. There used to be honor among artists, but like everything else in this life, that dissolves over time."

Turning to Storie, I asked, "Did anyone ever take a picture of your tattoo?"

"A couple girls took pictures when we got them done."

"Anybody post it on social media?"

"I'm sure they probably did. Doesn't everybody post everything on social media?"

"There ya go," Wyatt chimed in. "If it's on the web, it's out there. But start with your inner circle and see if anyone has a connection. One of them might know exactly who lifted my design. If that's the case, you might be able to figure out the name of the chic in the swamp."

We nodded.

"In the meantime, when you two are ready for some new ink, I'll make a deal—buy one get one."

Storie glanced at me with an enticing smile. I agreed to think about it, but I was making no promises.

"Take your time," Wyatt encouraged. "The offer won't expire."

"Thanks," we said in unison.

As we exited through the lobby, we waved goodbye to the receptionist. Inspired by the meditative vibe, I pressed my hands together in a prayerful pose and gave her a tiny nod of gratitude. She smiled.

"That's a lot to chew on," Storie noted as we climbed into Sandi-with-an-i.

"Speaking of chewing, are you hungry?" I asked.

"I could eat."

"There's a pizza place near here that makes the best oven-fired crust. Seriously. And it's early enough we won't be waiting in line."

With our margherita pizza ordered, we rehashed the next steps. "So," I said, "I guess the thing to do now is ask the others if a person ever showed enough interest in the tattoo that she—"

Storie cut in. "Or he—"

"—might try to copy it."

"Agreed," she said. "I'll get hold of the other four. And of course I'm planning to track down Luanne."

"Can't hurt," I said. I knew she believed the universe was pushing her to locate this missing friend, so even if the tattoo question wasn't looming, she'd do it regardless.

After we had the next phase of our investigation worked out, she shifted, "If you got a tattoo, what would it be?"

"Lord, I don't know. My mama's favorite flower was the daisy. Mine is the zinnia. Maybe a daisy and a zinnia growing together? Or a mermaid. Seems like mermaids keep surfacing in my psyche just now for some reason. I loved the mermaid tail on the sign at the tattoo parlor."

"Wyatt did that," she remarked. "You should look at his work."

I had the distinct feeling we were moving toward tattoos, and surprisingly, I wasn't panicking about the needles or the hepatitis. I mean, it was just a conversation at this point, right? No need to get worked up over a daydream.

Chapter 20

After dropping Storie at home, I had time to run by the drug store for a new nail polish. Deciding on the shade was as much about the name as it was about the color, and I spent time reading the tiny labels on top of each bottle. Kentucky Moon was a beautiful rich blue. Incrimination was a deep blush red, and I considered buying it for Miss Delphine. Lilac Whisper was the palest of purply pinks. Flour Power was stark white, but it made me think of bakeries, or correction fluid, one. Mudd Redd was a dirty brick color. All fine contestants, but the winner was…drum roll, please… Metallic Mermaid. Something in a parallel dimension was putting out a strong mermaid vibe, and who was I to ignore the insistence of a parallel dimension?

Nail polish paid for, I skipped the bag, tossed the receipt and stuffed the bottle in the front pocket of my shorts. It made me happy just having it. Was that weird?

Miss Delphine's car was not in the drive when I pulled in, and I assumed she was off to the salon for her pedicure. I was dying to know if she picked the red or the black. Pondering Crime Scene and The Dark Side, I gathered my supplies to start my own pedi. The only things missing now were a good playlist on my phone and a beer, both easily procured before going outside to the porch.

I'd been doing my own toes so long; I was pretty fast at it. Fast and precise, hardly ever touching the cuticle accidentally. I always bought the quick dry formula, always, and the polish was dry before I decided the skeeters were winning and I should move indoors.

It was eight pm; Jack was due around nine. I could either prepare for his arrival by practicing the rebuttal I had been formulating all day, or I could go on the Doe Network. What the hell. That speech would practically give itself.

Planning to look at just two or three victims, I lost all track of time as I worked my way down to the last profile under Texas. Case 1312UFTX showed what looked like a computer-generated image of a female in a t-shirt that read *He Smurfs me, He Smurfs me not* with a picture of the girl Smurf plucking the petals off a daisy. That's what this 15-to-17-year-old adolescent was wearing when she died of an undetermined cause. If you're thinking the cause of death might've been natural, since it was undetermined, think again. Her body was found in not one but two black garbage bags and tossed near a gated drive not far from an oil field. Nothing natural about that. She may have been biracial, and a single bobby pin held back her shoulder-length hair. She only had twenty-two ribs. The rest of us have twenty-four. Her skull was asymmetrical, and there were growth-arrest lines in her bones. Many of her teeth were decayed and some infected. I hadn't seen this before—they determined she grew up in Austin or San Antonio based on isotope testing. I sat quietly thinking about her last day and the single bobby pin in her hair. I named her Rachael.

Jack's knock, when it came, wasn't louder than normal, but lost under an October sky somewhere in Texas, I jumped nonetheless, proving my startle response was still in good working order.

"Come in," I hollered.

"Why is the door unlocked?" He quizzed me upon entering.

"To give you something to fuss about." I retorted, disturbed by the surprise, or rather, disturbed that I allowed myself to be surprised. I clicked out of the screen I was in and closed the computer, momentarily forgetting I had a speech prepared.

Jack swooped over, pulled out my chair so I could stand, and wrapped me in hug. Not the standard white bread variety, either. I would've had trouble pinpointing the specific traits that made it different, but I could tell. Standing there, he pulled my ponytail loose, so there was that, too, in case I needed additional documentation.

"What are you doing?"

He annoyingly used my own words and said, "Giving you something to fuss about."

By then his hands were tangled in my hair, and that speech was quickly slipping beyond my ability to grab hold of it. The kiss was next. I tried to tell him I wanted to talk, but he swallowed all the syllables. I caught a quick glimpse of my imaginary mentor, Stephanie Plum, throwing her hands up in disgust as she turned on her heel and headed out the door. With nobody watching me judgmentally, I sank down into the kiss.

When I surfaced again, we were both breathing hard. "Um," I stammered. "That was fun."

"If you liked that, you should see my next trick."

"I'd love to," I said, with a sincerity that wasn't forced or fake.

"How many beers have you had?"

I wanted to lie and say one. One beer. The follow up trick held promise, and I suddenly wanted to pursue it. The second beer wasn't completely finished, anyway, which sounded like a reasonable loophole to me. "Here's the thing," I started, as he pushed me to the fullest extent of his arms' length while still holding onto my shoulders."

"What's the thing?"

"The thing is, the alcohol loosens the grip on my worry function and makes me more open."

"Mmhmm," he said, but I could tell he wasn't buying it.

"So wha'd'ya say we try it with a little alcohol?" I whipped out my best seductive smile to drive home the point.

"Not gonna happen, babe," he said definitively, "But I'm diggin' that come-hither look."

"Why not?"

"When you're straight up sober, you're not ready to take the leap. Physically, maybe, but not emotionally. True, the alcohol gives you a little liquid confidence, but you'll still have to wrestle with the ripples once the alcohol blows off. And from the point of view of getting you to take the chance on us, it'll be a lot harder to walk that back. You'll regret it, dig in, and I'll be starting from zero again."

He drew me in via a half twirl so my back was up against his chest. I knew immediately he was thinking about *SexwithLily*. "I'll get you there," he promised. "It'll just take a minute."

Disappointed, I asked, "So what now?"

"Let's go get my dog." By the smile in his voice, I knew he considered this an ace that I hadn't seen coming.

341

Not even trying to disguise my excitement, I asked, "Is it too late? Will your folks be up?"

"They're up."

"I haven't decided on a name yet!" The declaration was tinged with the faintest trace of hysteria.

"Well, you better get on it, girl. There's a puppy coming over tonight, and if you don't give me a name by morning, I'm calling her Dog."

On the drive to his parents' house, I caught him up on Wyatt Crabtree, his assurance that he didn't sell the design to anyone else, and the offer of half-price tattoos for me and Storie.

"Sweet," Jack said, approvingly.

To test the limits of this support, I said, "I'm thinking about getting a skull and crossbones, to celebrate my bad ass side."

"Yeah," he nodded, "or you could get a mermaid, to celebrate your mermaid side."

"What?" I jerked my head in his direction.

"A mermaid."

"Why did you say that?"

"Because I have this fantasy where I'm on a fishing boat and I see you in the water as a mermaid."

"Jack, that's not funny. Did you talk to Storie?"

"It's not a joke, and no, I didn't talk to Storie. Why? And why are you getting worked up?"

Worked up was a stretch, but mildly addled may have been accurate. "Because Storie and I thought about tattoos over dinner, and I told her I'd either get a zinnia and a daisy—"

"For you and your mama," he interjected.

"Or a mermaid," I finished.

"No shit?"

"Don't you think it's a bizarre correlation?"

"No, I think it's an interesting coincidence."

"Mermaids keep coming up." Pulling my foot up to the dash, I pointed to my toes. "This new polish is called Metallic Mermaid."

"Pretty," he said about my toes. "Mermaids are probably coming up because you're aware of them right now. Somebody said it well on Instagram—*Easy to spot a yellow car when you are always thinking of a yellow car.*"

"Who said that?"

"Who knows? But there's some truth to it, right?"

"If I was thinking about yellow cars all the time, you believe I'd be considering a tattoo of a taxi cab, or maybe a school bus?"

"I hope you'd go in the direction of a yellow Jeep Wrangler, but yes, that's the idea."

I filed it for later consideration, because he was pulling up to the Turner house. The porch light was lit, so I knew they were waiting on us. Mrs. Turner came to the door holding Jack's dog before we even got up the porch steps.

"Here she is." The puppy was thrust into my arms as Jack's mama stepped back into the house. "Does she have a name yet?"

"She will by tomorrow morning," Jack said as he hugged first his mother and then his father. They were a very affectionate family. Kinda like my own. I knew families that preferred not to hug or give goodnight kisses, and if they ever did, the bodies were always stiff, like rigor mortis had already set in.

"Oh? There's a deadline?" His dad was curious.

"More like an ultimatum wrapped in a deadline," Jack offered. "Lily picks a name by tomorrow, or I'm calling her Dog."

"Don't be ridiculous," his mama chided. "You simply cannot rush a name. It took us a long time to settle on yours."

"Well, it took your mama a long time," his dad clarified. "I wanted to call you Boy Number Two."

"Nice, Dad," Jack mused. "So Joe woulda been Boy Number One?"

"Nah," his dad said with a chuckle, "He was always gonna be Joe."

At ease with what I considered my extended family, I joined the game. "You know, Mr. T," I started, "Pain in the Keister would have been a good name, too."

Both his parents laughed, forcing Jack to go on the defensive. "Oh, I get it, three against one."

"Four," I corrected, holding up the drowsy puppy. "Four against one."

"Look at that girl," Mrs. Turner said. "She's so laid back."

"You are talking about the dog, right?"

"I am, but it also applies to this lovely young woman."

"Have you been drinking, Mom? This lovely young woman is anything but laid back. Troublesome. Squirrely. Mule-headed. Take your pick."

"You keep him on his toes, Lily," Mr. T. said, smiling at me.

"Alright, alright. We're outta here. Y'all go back to whatever you were doing before we interrupted."

"Night," I said, holding the now sleeping puppy.

"Night, honey." She squeezed me from the side, then said, "Jack, you drop that dog back by if you need babysitting."

"Yes, 'um."

We put the puppy in a box and I rode in the back seat to keep an eye on her. Obviously we were going over to Jack's haunted house on Wisteria. So much for my home court advantage, but the puppy would keep us appropriately distracted, and she might also pick up on any spirit energy, which would help me out tremendously. Otherwise, it was mainly me making wild guesses about the activities of the haints. Dogs, and maybe animals in general, supposedly had a sense. I thought back to the story of when my mama was leaving this earth; Dad stayed by her side in the hospice room night and day. I don't remember being there, but Dad had our dog, Molly, up on the bed. The last night of mama's life, Molly stayed awake, slowly sweeping her head back and forth as she gazed at the ceiling. Dad thought Molly could see the angels that had come to escort mama home.

Not wanting to go any farther down that lane, I asked Jack, "Did your parents find families for the other two puppies?"

"Didn't I tell you? They're keeping them," he said, as he looked at me from the rearview mirror.

"They'll have three dogs? Lucy and two puppies?"

"Yep. Dad says Mom can't bear to part with 'em, but to tell the truth, I think it's him. Since Joe and I each have one, he wants the pack to stay together."

I smiled as I considered it. That would be something meaningful to him.

"How's your mama feel about it."

"I don't really know if she wants to or doesn't want to. She puts up with all manner of nonsense from that ol' man."

I almost made the mistake of comparing how I myself put up with all of Jack's nonsense. Barely catching myself in time, I blew out a breath. Whew. Dodged a bullet there. Comparing us to his parents, who had been together since…I drummed my fingers on the cardboard box, looking for an appropriately ancient analogy…The Beatles became popular? Give or take a few years. When I looked up, Jack was watching me in the rearview. Feeling exposed, I pretended I didn't see him and glanced back in the box to check on the sleeping puppy.

He reached a long arm into my area, and because his wingspan was so impressive, he easily grabbed my knee. "You okay about sleeping over my place? I know you were kind of set on Miss Delphine's."

"I'm okay. We need to get the puppy set up in her new home."

"Yeah," he agreed, but his voice sounded weird. I chose not to give chase and relaxed into the seat with my hand resting on the dog's back paw.

When we arrived, I waited for Jack to open my door, then I stood by ready to receive the box. He handed it carefully to me, and I carried it in my arms, firewood style, the way I might carry four or five logs. Who was I kidding? Two or three logs, max.

When we got into the kitchen, Puppy was fully awake after her power nap, and she went skidding across the linoleum. The first project was to design a barricade to keep her restricted to a defined area. While Jack got to work on that, I broke out the purple collar and leash we bought for her and took her outside in case she had to pee, which she did not. When we got back indoors, she promptly peed, but at least it was on the newspaper Jack had spread out. I replaced the paper with fresh and filled her water dish.

"What will you do with her tomorrow?" I asked.

"Take her to work with me. I'm off at the firehouse for a couple days while they train a few new recruits, so I'll make up the difference at the garage. I think Dad's gonna start bringing those other two."

"It'll be a regular rescue down there," I pointed out. The image of the daily antics at Turner's Auto Repair compounded by three puppies made me laugh. "If y'all want me to watch 'em for a while so you can get some work done, I will."

"Thanks," he said as he reached over and squeezed my hand. "I'll let you know."

So as not to get sucked into a tender moment, I stood up and went to the fridge for a beer. The magnet of the cat paw from Key West was holding up a picture of me and Storie, arm in arm, down at the abandoned building near the salt pond. Magnet in one hand, picture in the other, I turned to Jack for an explanation.

"Joe's spy took it," he said. "I thought it was hot."

"So he followed us *and* photographed us?"

"He did. It's his gig, the whole surveillance package. He didn't save any of the photos. Joe showed 'em to me before he deleted them. I kept this one. And one more of you by yourself, which I framed."

I could tell he was trying to get something started. And just as I was about to plunge in, I looked down at the magnet in my hand.

"That's it," I said, suddenly distracted. "That's her name."

"What? Surveillance? Kind of a weird name, Lily."

"No, not Surveillance. What did you call the cats?"

"I may have called them stupid. Please don't tell me you're naming my dog Stupid."

"No. What's the fancy word for six-toed cat? The scientific word?"

"Polydactyl?"

"Yes! Polydactyl! Your dog's name is Polly, but with two l's. Do you like it?"

He was either smiling because he was amused that my tirade had been upended or because he thought it was a good name. "Polly-with-two-l's," he said, rolling it around. "A little long," he teased, "but, I love it. She's definitely a Polly. And that's so much better than Dog."

I put the photo back on the fridge, blank side out, picture side in and reattached the magnet with a firm snap, smugly taking the point even without concluding the verbal argument. I got my beer, got him one and handed both bottles over as I bent to scratch Polly and whisper her name. She swung her head around in the spastic way puppies move, but I took it as a sign she was already connecting with her new name.

Chapter 21

Sleep had been hard to come by at Jack's house last night. Polly, away from her mama and siblings for the first time whined the entire night. We tried soft music. We tried a ticking clock sound Jack found on his phone. We picked her up. We made a nest of pillows and soft towels. Nothing seemed to soothe her. Plus, there were pee runs out in the yard all night long. We dozed in fits and starts, and when I woke up at whatever crazy hour it was, we were all three piled on the bed in Jack's bedroom. He was in a deep sleep.

I yawned and grabbed the dog, rushing her out before she decided to pee on the bed. The sky was changing from black to charcoal gray, so it was still pretty early. Letting Polly pull me around the back yard, I decided I'd give Jack a chance to sleep in. Unfortunately, I didn't get credit for that gesture, because he was leaned up against the back door, watching us when we finally turned back toward the house.

"Why are you awake?"

"I heard y'all get up."

"Well, go back to bed," I instructed. "I've got Polly."

"Nah. Not the same without you in there." He smiled and winked, and I flashed back to my proposition from last night about us having a roll in the hay. I appreciated that he didn't accept. He was right. I would have had trouble this morning. Still, when I maneuvered past him to get back inside, I went slow on purpose, but I pulled away before he could lock me in place.

"If you're up, you can take a shower while I fix breakfast."

"Cereal," he said flatly. "Yum."

"Or toast," I said, amping up the sarcasm, "your choice."

"Let me fix you a western omelet," he offered.

I wasn't one to dismiss a western omelet, but I felt compelled to be considerate. "Do you have time?"

"I do."

"I'll accept under one condition."

"Oooh, a negotiation," he said as his blue eyes got a shade darker, "my second favorite way to start the day."

"I'll let you fix me breakfast if you let me do the dishes after."

"Hmm. Tempting. But I feel like I can get a little more. I mean, everybody knows dishes are your jam.

That's something important to you. And I know you love my omelets…ah, I've got it. I'll agree, under one condition."

Here it comes. "You let me give you a single deep wet kiss."

I found it hard to reject his counter offer, being that I wanted all three of those things, the omelet, the dishes and the kiss. I held up my hand to indicate that he wasn't allowed to pounce the second I accepted the deal. I wanted to be clear about something.

"If I say okay, can we brush our teeth first?"

He smiled. "Wouldn't have it any other way."

I felt like he might have been lying, but I breezed past the snark in his comment. "Alright, you have yourself a deal."

I held out my hand to shake; he took it but instead of a firm pump, he brought it to his mouth in slow motion, and landed his lips all the while searing me with a steaming hot stare. Since he seemed intent on keeping his lips on my skin, I turned my head. His next move caught me completely off guard when he drew his mouth across my hand and down the length of my index finger, stopping to lightly bite the tip. I pulled against him and muttered something about toothpaste. All at once he released, and said in a husky voice, "Yes. Toothpaste."

It was awkward standing side-by-side at the bathroom sink. I kept my eyes on the porcelain bowl and cut my tooth brushing cycle by fifty percent just to avoid looking at him in the mirror. There was toothpaste in the corner of my mouth, but I addressed that with a handful of water from the spigot.

It struck me as disquieting that I was rushing through one uncomfortable moment just to dive into another. When I stepped outside of the bathroom, I took a deep breath, and waited for the kiss. Seconds later, he joined me in a minty fresh moment before I suffered an attack of vertigo where everything slid sideways on me.

Jack had snatched me up and was carrying me into the bedroom. The sudden loss of balance had me clutching his shoulders, and when he tossed me on my back on the bed, I was grabbing madly. "You said a kiss," I squeaked.

"I did."

"We can kiss standing up."

"We can also kiss lying down. You didn't specify, so I choose this way."

"Jack," I whispered. How could I have let him get that one over on me?

"You know I always keep my word, Lily. You're afraid this will turn into something else. It won't. A kiss. That's all. One deep wet kiss."

He positioned himself from the waist up across my body. While he kept most of his weight off me through the magic of upper body strength, I was still pretty well pinned. He didn't do anything for a second, other than smell my neck. Then he asked if I was okay and could he have his kiss.

I knew he would stop if I told him to. The sneaky grab, the supine position, the pending kiss, all culminated in a strong physical craving on my end. I told him I was okay and that he could kiss me. That launched an admirable lead up, making me think he was probably great in the foreplay arena. He whispered sweet nothings close to my skin that literally caused chill bumps. I felt my body being wound tighter one tick at a time, and I secretly thanked the reigning rodeo clown that Jack would be able to stop, because it was becoming clear in my own mind that I couldn't have if I tried.

Polly got tired of the game way before I did, and she started to serenade us with an amusing little song. I'm not sure how much longer Jack would have plied the "one wet kiss," but when he finally took his lips from mine, there was a haze in his eyes that indicated he was completely caught up in the moment, much like me.

He flopped over on his back, took a deep breath, then stood up. Walking around the bed to grab my hands, he helped me to a sitting position, and when I swung my legs over the edge, he pulled me to my feet. Still holding one of my hands, he led me to the kitchen, reached down for Polly, and placed her in my arms. Without words, I took her outside. She peed pretty fast, but I lingered, trying to calm down from the excitement on the bed.

Jack was in full sous chef mode when we came back inside, chopping onions, peppers and ham. I let Polly have the run of the kitchen as I got her bowl ready. Once she was fed, I started working on the coffee. The three of us were uncharacteristically quiet. I couldn't seem to put a sentence together, and Jack was also pre-occupied. With a full belly, Polly went over to her box and snuggled into the blanket for a morning nap.

After we ate, Jack honored his end of the agreement and let me clean up the kitchen, no questions asked. He went to take a shower, and with him out of my hair, I made quick work of it. We finished about the same time.

Freshly showered, he presented himself in a pair of gym shorts and no shirt. For someone who had supposedly dragged a towel across his body, his skin was surprisingly damp. I shook my head ever so slightly. "What?" He asked, smiling because he knew exactly what. When he winked, it was all I could do to keep my own clothes in place. Damn his sorcery.

Trying not to give any hints that he had me unnerved, I asked what the plan was. I had to get home, and he had to get to the garage.

"I thought I'd leave Polly here while I run you over to Miss Delphine's. Expose her to a little solitude a few minutes at a time. Then I'll swing back and pick her up on my way to the garage."

Sounded reasonable to me. "Hopefully she won't get out," I said.

"Hope is not a strategy, Lily," Jack responded as he tightened her kitchen barricade, ensuring she had no holes. I put a few extra layers of newspaper down. Lastly I grabbed the chew toy and put it on the kitchen table. I didn't want her choking on anything while he was taking me home.

* * *

The drive over to Miss Delphine's was subdued. We were both tired, and at least one of us was consumed with an internal struggle. He got out to open my door. Standing on the passenger side he reached for and held my hand as we walked around the front fender of his truck. With my free hand, I spun the key on the orange starfish keyring. Out of nowhere, McNugget made a bee line toward us.

The streak of white startled me. "What's she—," I started to ask but abandoned the question in favor of a strangled scream when she dove at me. Using the only weapon at my disposal, I threw the starfish at her, which had no impact since it landed nowhere close to the threat. I kicked a leg out, leaving me balanced badly on one foot that was halfway on and halfway off its flip flop. She dodged my kicking foot and pecked my standing foot. I hollered again.

Jack scooped her up before she connected a second time. "It's your toes," he said, but he was talking to my back as I darted up the steps. I didn't have time to interpret the sound of his voice. Was he in firefighter mentality? Was he laughing at me? I couldn't tell and frankly, as I ran for my life, it didn't matter.

"What?" I hollered from the safety of the porch at the top of the stairs.

"Your toes," he repeated calmly. I glanced at my beautiful Metallic Mermaid toenail polish. The iridescence made the bright green burst into glints of dark purple and teal blue. "She thinks she sees something to eat," he explained.

"Chickens eat mermaid scales?" I was totally confused by this information, compounded by the fact that I was also totally freaked out by the assault.

"No. But they eat frogs and lizards, shiny stuff like that."

"What are you talking about? They eat corn. You feed them corn."

Jack was standing at the bottom of the stairs, holding McNugget, and the look on his face said he had decided to handle the problems in the order of importance, and a chicken's diet was not the most important. "You dropped your key," he pointed out.

It was kind of him to refer to my erratically wild pitch as a simple drop, and the distinction was not lost on me. The key was in the dirt, where the chickens were scavenging. I either had to retrieve it or he had to bring it to me, which meant he either had to put the chicken down or carry her up the steps. None of these options really worked for me.

Still holding the chicken, Jack walked over and picked up my orange starfish, which he stuffed in his back pocket.

"I'll grab some feed from the garage, then I'll take her to the coop. She'll be so happy about the scratch she'll forget all about your toes. Then I'll bring you the key. Alright?"

I played the scenario out in my head several times to make sure there wasn't a potentially dangerous outcome he was overlooking. When I couldn't find one, I nodded my approval of the plan. To his credit, it worked exactly as he said it would. Up on my porch, he unlocked the door and we went in.

"You okay?"

"I still have all ten toes, if that's what you mean."

"Thank, God," he said, his tone edged with sarcasm. "I know she surprised you."

"Surprised me?" I said with gusto. "She nearly pecked me half to death! Do I need a tetanus shot?"

He assumed the classic pose of an athlete taking a knee as he sank to the floor and dramatically examined my foot. Seeing nothing, he asked, "Did she break the skin?"

"Didn't she?"

"I don't see anything." After inspecting the other foot, he added, "I think you'll live."

Not believing him, I kicked off my flips and studied my own feet. There wasn't so much as a red mark.

"Don't take it personally. She's just a chicken exhibiting natural chicken behavior."

"Wait'll I give her a taste of my natural anti-chicken behavior. It involves an ax."

"That would worry me, for your safety not hers, if I thought you could get close enough to take a swing." He smiled and added, "If it's any consolation, your Metallic Mermaid toes are super hot."

At the moment, that was not a consolation.

"Don't change the color yet," he said, gazing down at my toes, "just wear your sneakers when you go outside."

In my head, I calculated the times of day I could safely come and go with the chickens roosting for the evening. If I had to become a vampire, operating under the cover of darkness, so be it. Besides, I might stumble on whatever Miss Delphine was hiding.

He hugged me. I hugged him back. The truth was, I liked having him around for chicken emergencies. Did that make me a sniveling, yellow-bellied, can't-take-care-of-herself coward? Possibly. Did I care? Yes. Would I change? Nope. I gave myself an imaginary thump on the back and mouthed, *Good talk, Barlow.*

Chapter 22

Jack gone and sneakers on, I headed downstairs. I may not have a degree in poultry science, but the earlier debacle made one thing crystal clear—chickens have reasonably good eyesight, which is why I broke my cardinal rule of summertime footwear by adding socks. I needed an extra layer of security to hide my appealing frog-like toes, and regardless of what Jack said, toes that resembled frogs were not *super hot*.

Miss Delphine was relaxing in a rocker on her shady porch. I noticed there were two glasses beside the pitcher of tea on the little table. One was full, but the other just had ice.

"You expecting company?" I asked as I sidled up the steps.

"I was hopin' you'd have time to sit a spell," she said, handing me the empty glass. "Drink that down before I pour." The ice had started to melt, and I was happy to drain the little bit of water so it wouldn't dilute my tea.

"Aw, that's nice of you," I said, referring to her invitation and to the fact that she didn't let my tea get watery. Holding out the glass, I let her fill me up before I took a big refreshing gulp and parked my butt in the rocker.

"You alright?" She asked me. "I saw that little dance you did with Wanda. You got green toenail polish on?"

"Wanda?"

"The chicken."

"They have names?" I was mystified.

"Well of course they have names, Lily. They're not livin' in the wild."

"I call her McNugget," I said, sheepishly.

Miss Delphine chuckled. "Because you'd rather eat her than tend her. Funny. I don't blame ya. She certainly is the boldest of her brood, the whole flock for that matter. I'll make it her last name."

"Wanda McNugget," I savored the sound.

Not lingering on the name, she moved the conversation forward. "Lily, I have a favor to ask."

"Anything you need, Miss Delphine." She was, after all, letting me live here rent-free, and I was about to beg her to extend that lease should I enroll at Shenandoah University, a move that seemed more and more plausible. Privately, I hoped this favor wouldn't involve disposing of a body or covering up a crime.

"I don't have any family," she started.

"You don't have any kids?" I blurted, not bothering to disguise the surprise in my voice.

"I lost my baby" she said matter-of-factly.

"Oh, Miss Delphine!" I was shocked, both at the loss and the fact that she was sharing it with me. I wasn't really good at finding the line between expressing proper condolences and overstepping, so I said as little as possible. "I'm sorry you lost your baby."

"It was so many years ago, Lily," she said quietly. "Funny thing about grief. It doesn't go away, but in time, it grows more graceful." After a still pause that stretched on and on, she moved her hand, dispelling the vapors of this memory, and I was left to fill in the blank as to the child's tragic end.

"Not that I'm plannin' on keelin' over anytime soon," she added with more of her usual spunk, "but I'd like to know if somethin' were to happen, somebody'd look after Cro."

"Oh, for the love of the yellow honeysuckle blossom! Of course I'd take Cro." At the second mention of his name, he thumped his tail once from behind her rocker. I took that as his endorsement of this arrangement. "And I'd look after those chickens, too!" I was far less comfortable with this clause than with the first, and I hoped I wouldn't wake up one of these days, a newly minted legal guardian of a flock of mean chickens. Jack's words from earlier in the morning echoed in my head—*Hope is not a strategy, Lily.* Great. So how 'bout I give the chickens to him. He'd do nearly anything if I offered him a kiss. How's that for a strategy?

Then, because health issues were squarely in my scope of awareness after Dad's heart attack, I asked, "Are you sick, Miss Delphine?"

"Lord, no, child. Just thinkin' ahead." She set her glass on the table, and I noticed she looked a little pained, probably from reliving the devastation that comes with losing a child.

"Well, you don't have to worry about anything," I assured her definitively. Figuring now was as good a time as any to pitch my idea of extending my current living arrangement, I gently opened the discussion. "I have a favor to ask you, too."

When she didn't indicate that I should continue, I looked at her more carefully. Her pained expression was now accompanied by a light sheen of sweat. It was hot out, but I hadn't noticed her sweating before. "Are you okay, Miss Delphine?"

She lifted her hand to her chest. "Are you having a heart attack?" I asked. Fully frightened at this point, I stood, setting my glass down.

"I have angina," she said, "which is not necessarily a heart attack." She reached in the pocket of her pedal pushers. "Must've left my nitroglycerin on the bathroom counter. Fetch it for me, girl?"

Dragging my feet across the mat as I darted into the house, I pulled my phone out and dialed 9-1-1. Angina or no angina, I wasn't taking the chance. Primarily because I didn't know what angina was.

One ring and the operator answered, "9-1-1, what's your emergency?"

I explained that I was with an elderly woman suffering chest pains who had prescribed medication for angina, but I wanted to get an ambulance on the way. The operator told me to administer the medication. I gave her the address, and she dispatched an ambulance then waited on the line.

Having never been beyond her kitchen and front foyer, I relied on the fact that I was generally more attuned to bathroom location than most of the population at large. My instincts were right on as I swung through her bedroom and entered the attached bath. Pausing for a fraction of a second, I took in the space then grabbed the first bottle I came to. After quickly confirming it was the right one, I ran back out.

On the porch, I greeted her with as much cheer as I could muster. "I got 'em!" I had opened the bottle on the way, and I placed a tiny pill in her hand then reached for her tea so she could wash it down.

"No tea," she said, refusing the glass. "It's sublingual."

"What's sublingual?" I asked. Both Miss Delphine and the 9-1-1 operator who was on speaker said, "Under the tongue."

In minutes, she looked a lot better. "Is the pain receding?" This from the operator on the line.

Miss Delphine nodded. "Yes. A minute more an' I'll be right as rain."

Cha-ching. I checked the incoming text. Jack. I might have inadvertently conjured him when I contemplated dialing his number before the ambulance. Or…he might have gotten word from his secret channels of communication.

"What's going on?"

"Miss Delphine has chest pain. Just took a pill for angina. Says she's fine now."

Cha-ching: "Let the paramedics check her out."

"Ok"

Cha-ching: "If they take her to the hospital, I'll meet you there."

"Ok"

Cha-ching: "You alright?"

"Yes."

I was fairly certain the last message had to do with his concern that I might be having flashbacks to Dad's heart attack. I wasn't the one on the scene for Dad, but this was indeed stirring some angst. Jack was thorough in his sweep of crisis situations.

The ambulance pulled in sans siren. Given the fact that this was a desolate road with no need to warn traffic, it was not unexpected. I disconnected with the operator when the paramedics jumped out. There were two, and I knew them both, Jenni and Cooper.

"Hey, Lily, Miss Delphine," Cooper greeted each of us as Jenni pulled some more equipment from the back. "You got chest pains, Miss Delphine?"

After taking her vitals and talking with the hospital, it was determined that she should get checked out more completely. I offered to drive her, but they wanted to continue monitoring, so she went in the ambulance.

"Can I ride along?" Feeling like I had some sort of role in this whole thing, I thought it was the least I could do.

"Sure," Jenni said. "Miss Delphine, do you need anything from inside?"

"My bag. Lily, can you grab it?"

I knew she kept her purse on the table in the front hall, so I dashed in, checked that the front door was locked, picked up her purse and her keys, and locked the back door as I came out. She was already loaded in the ambulance by then. Cooper was with her, so I climbed in the seat beside Jenni.

While I suspected he already knew this, I texted Jack to say we were going to the hospital.

Cha-ching: "On my way."

* * *

It might have been a foregone conclusion, but I was hugely relieved when I saw him standing at the entrance to the ER.

"Everybody said you did great," he reported, sounding half surprised. Who could fault him, really? I was known more for my keen ability to panic than the other way around. "Maybe this is your new career path."

"Right. So you have one more way to keep tabs on me."

"Hadn't thought of that, but it would make it more convenient on my end." He circled me with his arms and offered a firm hug, releasing when they pulled the gurney from the ambulance.

"You doin' alright, Miss Delphine?" He asked, tipping his ball cap to her.

"Jack, honey, sorry for the trouble."

"No trouble at all, ma'am." He took off the cap, preparing to go inside. "We'll be right here for ya."

I kept track of her purse, tagging along behind the paramedics. Inside Jack went to rustle up something to eat as I chatted with the patient. Small talk was one of my specialties, and I could have gone on for hours. When the doctors decided to keep her overnight for observation, I told her I'd be happy to stay and sleep in the chair, but she insisted Jack take me home so I could take care of the animals.

In his truck, he said, "You look stressed. You sure you're okay?"

"Jack," I started, "this whole thing is very weird. Miss Delphine had just asked me if I'd adopt Cro in case anything happened to her. She had literally just said it. I asked if she was sick, because her request came out of the blue. She said she was healthy as a horse; the next minute she goes and does this."

"Are you telling me you think you caused this episode?"

"Well." I weighed the craziness factor before continuing. "Maybe. And that's not the only thing. I can practically make you text me just by thinking about you. It's been happening a lot."

"So you believe you have some kind of supernatural power?"

"It sounds stupid when you say it like that."

"Remember when we talked about the yellow cars this morning? That explains the text messages. I'm in your head right now because of this new..." he paused, looking for the right word. "development. Of course I'm on your mind when I text. I'm probably on your mind a lot. Which, by the way, I like."

I looked at him and shook my head. He kept talking. "As for Miss Delphine, that's one hundred percent coincidence."

We tugged on this like an old fashion taffy pull until the gravel crunched as he turned into the drive. He got out, reached in the back for his ever-present backpack, and walked around to get my door.

Standing beside the truck, I said, "There's one more thing I want to show you."

"Ah," he answered, "there's one more thing I want to show *you*, too." He leaned in and whispered, "Me first." Then he gently kissed my cheek before working his way to my lips.

When he pulled away, I could do nothing but offer a dreamy expression I wasn't particularly proud of. "Your turn," he said.

Shaking my head no, I said, "Let's keep going with yours."

"Fair enough." And he re-engaged.

This time, when we stopped, I was a little woozy, in a good way. "What is it you wanted to show me?"

"That?" I assured him it could wait, and I headed up the stairs to the apartment. He followed without comment. When we got inside, I found myself struggling to put my thoughts into words. Even though I was sure he already knew, I had the feeling he'd want me to say it anyway, so I scrounged around for some courage. Reserves were low, to say the least.

I came toward him, and he let me rest my head against his chest. "Tell me what you want, Lily. Just say it. I want you to feel comfortable just saying it."

It was barely audible when it came out. "I want to…" here I was confused as to what to say. *Have sex* is where I was going, but that would likely generate a conversation that did not interest me at the moment. *Make love* was what he wanted to hear, but the term was miles outside my comfort zone. I landed on what I hoped was a decent compromise. "I want to be with you. Like before."

He breathed out a slow long breath, and waited.

"I don't want this to be any kind of final decision, though. I'm still trying to figure it out." I kept my head on his chest when I said it.

"Are you sure you want to add this part before we get it figured out?"

At that, I pulled back and gave him my best eye contact, held it for an eternity, and then whispered, "Yes."

He searched my eyes before he slid his hands under my shirt, starting a domino effect you might see at the competition level, where the dominoes race back and forth creating amazing zig-zagging images. In time he drew my hands to his hips. I held them there lightly while he untucked his shirt. I knew it was a signal, but I was feeling bashful, and I did nothing until he gently placed my left hand under his shirt on his bare stomach. My right hand soon caught up. Shortly we were both shirtless. And shortly thereafter we were both naked.

"Do you have a condom in your backpack?"

"What kind of question is that?" He whispered into my hair.

"Can you get it please?"

"Yes ma'am." One zipper and three seconds later, he handed me the shiny purple square. "I want you to know you're calling the shots here. If you're in over your head, tell me, and I'll stop. Okay?"

"I'm not in over my head. I mean, I am, but I very definitely want to do this." He pulled me into my bedroom, and like before, it was intensely passionate. And this time, I paid more attention to what he liked, just in case.

* * *

When we finished, I was two things—starving and satisfied. Not necessarily in that order. Jack had fallen into a light doze and when I moved, he rolled over and draped his naked self across me.

"Are you hungry?" I asked.

Without lifting his head, he mumbled into my neck, "For you? Yes. For food? Yes."

"Me, too."

He chuckled. "Excellent."

"For food." I scrambled to clarify.

"Whatever," he said with that little bit of fake contempt, "but we can start with food."

"Oh, and I need to check on Cro." I tried to extricate myself from the weight on top of me. "Which reminds me, where's Polly?"

"I sent her home with Dad when I headed over to the hospital."

"Oh." It made sense. I continued to struggle to get up.

"Take a shower with me."

"What?"

"Take a shower with me, and I'll let you up."

It sounded too intimate and was associated with too much pressure. "No." I flat out refused.

"Suit yourself." He made no move to let me up. "I'm hungry, but I could literally stay here all night."

Trying to reason with Jack was like trying to reason with a hamster. Same brain capacity. "Jack," I started, "if we do everything now, what will you have to look forward to?"

"I have a list of ideas that'll take 'til your eighty-seventh birthday to get through. After that, we'll just have to start over." He kissed my ear in a provocative way. "If you suds me up with your special orange soap, and let me suds you up, I promise I'll give you an appropriate amount of space and time so you can do your freak out thing before I push again."

"And I can determine the amount of space and time necessary? Do you swear? No loopholes?"

"Oh, it's fine when you do it, but not cool for somebody else to engineer a loophole?"

"You're finally getting it."

"As long as the amount of space and time would be deemed reasonable by a jury of your peers, I swear. No loopholes." To my displeasure, I wasn't getting a carte blanche on my definition of the space and time I would require. He held up a pinky to make it official, but instead of the traditional pinky shake, he brought mine to his mouth for a seductive pinky suck. It almost, *almost* made me lose my resolve.

Fulfilling my end of the bargain, we sudsed each other in the shower. The water, the soap, the fragrance, and of course the nakedness created a new level of hotness for me. Surely I'd taken a shower with a guy before. It must not have been too special, though, if I couldn't pull it from the back issues of my memory. I was pleased with myself for noting that the shower scenario seemed to give him an extreme amount of enjoyment. I supposed he made a notation of my reaction as well.

* * *

Clean, refreshed, and secure in the knowledge that I had a temporary bubble of safety where the relationship question was concerned, I proposed we head downstairs to check on Cro before going to get food. Miss Delphine left him to his own devices regularly for long periods of time. He had access to water and shade. I knew he was alright, but I felt obliged to make sure.

"I suppose we should bring him into the apartment tonight."

"Does he sleep inside with Miss Delphine?" he asked.

"He does."

I could see the mound of mostly black fur lounging on the back porch. As we rounded the truck, Jack grabbed my hand, which made me tense for some odd reason.

"Jumpy?" he asked.

"I thought you were about to break your promise."

"I never break my promises," he said, with deep sincerity. "I just remembered you didn't get to show me that thing you wanted to show me."

"Oh, yeah," I said slowly. "That thing."

"Can you show me now? We've got time, since I won't be jumping your bones again for at least an hour." He nudged me and laughed.

"Let's feed Cro first."

I unlocked the door using Miss Delphine's keys, and we went inside. I looked in the pantry for a bag of dog food. Jack found it in the laundry room and pulled out a cup of kibble. Cro must have agreed, because he stood there wagging, his tail slapping on the leg of the kitchen table. Jack poured the food into his bowl while I gave him fresh water. Once he was happily chomping away, I beckoned for Jack to follow me.

"I know this seems weird, but just come back here with me."

"It does seem weird, but okay."

I walked him through Miss Delphine's pristine bedroom to the bathroom where I found her nitroglycerin. Dusk was falling outside, and even though the bathroom had a window, I flipped the switch to light the space.

"Yeah?" He asked. "What am I looking at?"

"The floor," I said.

"Okay?"

Realizing he didn't see it, I knelt down and traced my finger along the white V on one of the small, six-sided green tiles. The way they were fitted together, the pattern took on a flower quality.

"This doesn't look familiar to you?" I tapped my finger on the slick surface.

Focusing on my finger, his eyes got big and his mouth fell open, then he shifted his gaze to me. "It's the same tile you found on your mama's grave stone."

I nodded. "The exact same tile." The questions buzzed through my head like bees pouring out of a hive on the first warm day.

CPSIA information can be obtained
at www.ICGtesting.com
Printed in the USA
JSHW031433160422
25001JS00006B/130

9 781950 367191